A GUEST TO DIE FOR

JACK STAINTON

This novel is entirely a work of fiction and any resemblance to actual persons, living or dead, is purely coincidental.

An imprint of Windmill Streams *Publishers*

A Guest to Die For

ISBN: 9781916497849

For Deb

1

THE LAST TWELVE months had been the year from hell. The redundancy, splitting up with my fiancée, the subsequent depression and the accident.

I was about to embark upon the biggest gamble of my existence to date, one I had to take. A last chance in life, maybe. My doctor said I had become clinically depressed. 'Clinically', it sounded so final, no coming back.

Forty-two years old, moving abroad, speaking only a handful of words and taking on a business I had no prior knowledge of handling. It felt so daunting, but I was running, escaping my past.

Deep down, it felt right, the ideal solution. No, the *only* solution.

The queue of cars looked huge. Three lanes of vehicles with the letter 'J', all suspended on paper hangers from our rear-view mirrors. Two children kicked a football between the cars before their dad shouted at them to get back in. A row of vehicles slowly started to peel forward in the distance.

Then, before I realised, I was moving towards the train.

No turning back, this is it, Dan.

An attendant marshalled me down a steep slope towards the large, silver carriages. It amazed me how all those vehicles could cram into the shuttles upstairs and down. My car crept to a halt and another member of staff advised me to take up every single inch of space available.

"Keep it in gear and leave your handbrake off," he instructed. It didn't feel right, but I did as I was told.

As the train pulled off and entered the tunnel bound for France, I reached for my coffee and noticed my hand shaking. A mild panic attack made me open my door and stand outside the vehicle. The enclosed space did nothing to appease my state of mind. I paced up and down the short footpath, families staring at me from their windows.

Forcing positive thoughts and memories into my head, I tried to recall childhood holidays.

The summer holiday was invariably the highlight. All of my friends preferred Christmas, Santa Claus, and presents. But for me it was always travelling. Going somewhere different, the planning, saving my pocket money, exploring new places; the annual escape.

The panic attack abated. A new life was my aspiration, my destiny. A strange tingle of excitement zipped through my body. The feeling I love, at last doing something that made me feel alive. A slight spark of hope.

It's also the ideal opportunity to put the past behind me.

The train slowed to a halt and before I knew it, I drove up a steep slope and into a foreign country. Forty minutes after leaving England, my car wheels touched base in France.

My brain inadvertently forced a small smile to my lips. My satnav informed me I was nine hours and forty-one minutes from my destination. The children who were playing football in the queue earlier pointed and laughed from their rear seats as I overtook them on the dual carriageway. A wave of vulnerability washed over me.

Why are they laughing at me?

I swooped onto the A26; Paris bound. Reaching for my phone, I found my favourite playlist and sound filled the car. Emily used to find my taste in music depressing, melancholy, but I sang along as I settled in for the long journey ahead. The road signs informed me I was abroad. They may be blue or red or round or square, but they still looked different to those back home. This was France, and it already felt as though it was pulling me in, somehow accepting me. I choked back a sob and forced myself to concentrate on the positives.

If only Emily were here. If only it had worked out.

Just after one o'clock in the afternoon, I pulled out of the service station onto the A10 south of Paris. A much-needed break and a stock up of cheese, a French stick – what else? – and a huge packet of crisps to keep me going. Although I craved caffeine, I was unsure of how to order a coffee, so went for the bottled water instead. Learning the language would be of paramount importance.

Sept euros et quarante quatre cents s'il vous plaît is what the attendant said as I bagged my bread and cheese. I had to Google translate the numbers at the bottom of the till receipt back into French to practise what she had asked for but, even on my phone, they spoke far too quickly.

. . .

The rest of the journey dragged slightly, and I realised just how vast a nation France was. The motorways were fantastic for getting from point to point in as little time as possible, but you don't see the full splendour of the country. However, as I left the A20 near Brive-la-Gaillarde and swung onto the A89, I knew I was nearing my target. The familiar countryside of South West France opened up before me. The satnav directed me ever closer to my destination, and the scenery took my breath away, even though I'd visited the area many times before. It had only been the previous weekend that I had flown over to oversee my furniture arriving. But this was now, and it felt so real. My fatigue evaporated as I turned into the small settlement of Monpazier in the heart of the Dordogne. My new home.

Tempted to go into the town centre at the junction, I knew time had drifted by, so I took the left turn following the sign to Cahors. My new house was less than a mile along the main road and, by the time I arrived, I felt a lump in my throat. It almost reduced me to tears. Happy tears, but also full of trepidation and fear of what might lie ahead.

Having unpacked my personal possessions, I ventured inside to assess my new home. Fortunately, the furniture sat just right. The corner sofa fitted perfectly into the lounge, with the back performing a partition to the dining table and kitchen behind. My large television took pride of place in the corner and I had previously arranged for a local expat guy to come and set me up the next day. His business card described him as a 'TV aerial and satellite installer. Also, general handyman'. I already had it pinned to my corkboard in the kitchen.

The kitchen was an average size but more than adequate and had all the essentials. An almost new range cooker had been left by the previous occupants – I still pinched myself they included that in the sale. There was a small downstairs toilet whilst upstairs featured two bedrooms, one en suite, and a large family bathroom with a newly fitted shower in the corner.

I could not believe that it belonged to me. I recalled the day the agent phoned me, explaining that a house had come onto the market suddenly; totally unexpected. They sent me the details, and I instantly knew it was the one, although the agent wouldn't expand on the reasons it had become available at such a reasonable price.

I'd flown over two days later and viewed it. It had looked even better than the online brochure had proclaimed. I'd made an offer there and then, which the owners accepted without a quibble. The agent said they had moved away and were very keen for a quick sale.

Three days later, I received a call that somebody had outbid me, only by two thousand euros, so I immediately counter offered and raised my original price by five thousand. The owners accepted and instructed the agent to sell to me. There had been no more bids as far as I knew.

"It's immaculate," I said aloud, walking from room to room. "There's not a thing I need to do."

It was mid-May and, although it was early evening, the sun still shone, carrying plenty of heat with it. Pouring myself a full glass of red wine, I walked into the garden which surrounded the house on all sides. I passed the terrace containing a large table and comfortable chairs – again left by the vendors. The front of the property contained a midsize pool, which I noticed required a thorough clean as I walked past. Further along, and at the far end of the garden, stood a small, one-bedroom gîte. As I'd left the keys in the house, I peered through the windows. It looked as clean as the house and the previous owners had left everything as they would have wished to find it. There were no gîte bookings on the system, but I had re advertised it with one agent the week before to get the ball rolling again – I couldn't live in France with no income. I was down to my last few thousands in savings which I had taken from the house sale after Emily and I had separated.

Feeling overwhelmed with exhaustion, I took a leisurely stroll back towards the terrace. As I approached the pool on the way back, I noticed a purple car travelling on the main road from town. It appeared to slow a little as it advanced towards the house. Yes, it definitely slowed down. I stood motionless but exposed in the middle of the lawn. The driver accelerated away and disappeared along the D660.

Just a local, being nosey.

Taking my seat on the covered terrace overlooking the pool, I sipped my wine and took in the stunning scenery beyond. Just as I began to relax and let the wine work its magic, I heard another car approaching. This time from the opposite direction. As before, I could hear it slowing down. Feeling a little unnerved, I tilted my chair forward and strained my neck to see around the side of the house.

The dwindling light, coupled with the distance between myself and the vehicle, made it impossible to determine too much. I could make out the whites of the driver's eyes, piercing against the otherwise gloom and staring directly towards me. My heart skipped a beat and my hands began to perspire – something that always happens when I find myself out of my comfort zone.

As before, the car sped away, leaving me feeling unsettled. My newfound enthusiasm evaporated as all kinds of thoughts scampered through my mind.

I couldn't see who, or how many occupants were in the vehicle. One thing I could be sure of though, it was the same car that drove past moments earlier going in the opposite direction.

2

My first Monday morning away and I knew I should have felt alive and rejuvenated.

Back home, normal people are getting ready to go to work.

The car passing by the previous evening still clung to my conscience and had led to a sporadic night's sleep – the first in my new home.

Crawling out of bed and into the shower, I tried to push the negative thoughts to one side. The deluge of water felt good. I loved those 'drench' showerheads which gave the impression of being under a waterfall, gushing with an everlasting stream of piping hot water.

Towelling myself dry, I walked back into my bedroom and rummaged through a suitcase for something to wear for the day.

Normal people will be putting on suits right now. If I was still in England, I'd be putting on a suit now.

I forced a grin and opted for a T-shirt and a pair of knee-length shorts. It looked hot outside, something I needed to get used to.

. . .

Having unpacked and made the house as homely as I could, I drove into town. Monpazier is a beautiful little place. As I walked through its myriad of compact streets, I made a mental note of the small, independent shops; the local Spar and the *pharmacie,* particularly grabbing my attention. Eventually I reached the stunning main square, Monpazier Place des Corniéres.

By now it was late morning, and the temperature already crept towards the mid-twenties. A café bar nestled in one corner. It offered shade, which appeared like an oasis under the beaming sun. As I walked over, fear enveloped me, petrified that my French would make me look foolish on my very first day.

Without warning, the waiter approached, dressed smartly in all white and a blue-striped apron with a white towel folded immaculately over his shoulder.

"Bonjour, monsieur."

"Erm, bonjour," I replied, replicating a child repeating their first foreign words at school.

The waiter smiled and replied in almost perfect English.

"Ah, good morning, a table inside or out, sir?"

Blushing at my pathetic attempt to sound local, I requested a table outside, furthest from the square, hoping thereby that nobody else would talk to me. I'm okay after an alcoholic drink or two, but in the cold light of day I find small talk both infuriating and difficult. It's one of the main reasons I had never held down an office job. All that tittle-tattle and boring work talk. I'm much better off in my own company.

On this occasion, that wasn't to be the case.

Studying the menu, with my translate app open on my phone, I noticed somebody approach me from my right-hand side.

Shit no, don't talk to me, please.

"Good morning."

Looking up, I saw a smartly dressed guy in a denim shirt, white chinos and, I'm guessing, top of the range sunglasses perched on top of his head. He offered me his hand.

Standing up, I scraped my chair on the tiles below. The whole square seemed to fall into silence and stare in my direction.

Feeling myself redden again, I took his hand and introduced myself.

"Hi, I'm Dan. Daniel Kent."

"Great to meet you, Daniel. Brad Jones. I saw you walking across the square. You look new around here. Holiday?"

Brad had an accent from somewhere south of London, Surrey maybe, and spoke somewhat eloquently. He pronounced every syllable with equal merit. At around six foot two, he stood a couple of inches taller than me, had a head of thick brown hair, shaven at the back and sides, longer on top and flicked over in what I believed to be a 'trendy' cut. He was well built and the quintessential good-looking guy who wouldn't look out of place on some reality TV show.

"Er, no. I've just moved into a house, on the outskirts of town," I said, seeming to catch Brad off guard for a split second; he regained his composure quickly.

"Well, that's just great, Daniel. Do people call you Dan?"

He continued before I could answer. This guy reeked

of confidence, the exact opposite of myself. It was difficult to tell if it was natural or staged.

"There's a few of us expats living around here and there's always room for another."

"Thank you, Brad, that's nice to know. Oh, and Dan or Daniel is fine with me."

Still standing, I recalled my manners and asked Brad if he would like to join me. Secretly, I hoped he would be too busy. He said he'd love to.

"Okay, as long as you can translate this for me," I said, pointing at the menu, "and order me one perfect cup of coffee. I'm desperate for caffeine."

Brad laughed, got the attention of the waiter, and ordered what I guessed was what I'd requested.

However, when the waiter returned, he had two large beers on a tray and, although they looked very inviting in the increasing heat, it pissed me off that he had ordered something for me I didn't ask for.

"Hmm, I said coffee, Brad," I said, taking the beer from the waiter.

"Yeah, I know, but this is a special occasion. This is your first day in Monpazier, and that deserves a beer in my eyes."

How did he know it was my first day? I'm sure I'd said I'd just moved into a house nearby, or did I mention last night? Letting it go, I relaxed, thinking I should be grateful that somebody had attempted to speak to me and join me for a drink.

"Okay, cheers Brad."

We clinked glasses, and I took a huge gulp of freezing cold beer. I felt it make its way down to the pit of my stomach.

"However, I'm driving, so we must make it just the one."

Brad laughed and slumped back into his seat.

"Just go with the flow, Dan. This is your new home, your new environment. You're in France now so you need to adapt to the pace."

Brad was right; the environment and pace of life was exactly why I'd moved here.

And to escape your past, Dan.

"Yeah, I know, but I have some jobs to sort out, shopping and stuff. Plus, I'm driving."

"Fair enough, mate, we'll just have the one today."

Brad leant forward, leaving me feeling a little hemmed in. I scraped my chair back again. People turned and looked.

"So, what has brought you here, if you don't mind me asking?"

Depression, losing my job, losing my fiancée, the accident.

I tend to burble when nervous. Words come out in a rush, not always in the right order, which, in return, makes me blush. Taking a deep breath, I tried to compose myself. What I said was in part the truth.

"To put it simply, Brad, I've just had enough of the rat race at home. I've been working in the corporate world for almost twenty years, never enjoyed it and thought, what the hell? If I'm ever going to do something different, then why not now?"

Brad stared at me, as if expecting more. My nerves made me babble on.

"Besides, I recently separated with my fiancée, so have nothing holding me back."

Immediately regretting discussing my personal life

with a total stranger, I tried to steer the conversation into a new direction. I stumbled along.

"What about you? How long have you been here?"

Brad obviously held more interest in my previous comment than talking about himself.

"Single, eh? A good-looking guy like you, you'll have the French ladies queuing up."

I noticed two women look up from their coffees and smile. I'd already overheard their posh southern English accents and assumed they were expats too. This was getting more uncomfortable by the minute. I wanted Brad to shut the fuck up.

"Well, that's not even on the radar at the moment. I just need time to myself and to sort my life out."

Brad allowed the conversation to hang in the air. Once again, the silence broke me.

"I've got a small gîte at the end of my garden that I've just started to advertise online. Hopefully that will pay towards some of my bills whilst I work out what I'm doing long term."

Again, I cursed myself for affording too much information and Brad was quick to pull me up.

"A gîte, eh? I don't want to put a downer on it, but that market is pretty saturated in the Dordogne. Still, if you've put it online, you should get some interest. Take what you can get. Where exactly is your house, Dan?"

Reluctantly, I told him, deciding I had no choice. We chatted more before finishing the cold beers. The alcohol had calmed my nerves, and I regretted driving into town so I couldn't have another. I paid the bill – after Brad had spoken perfect French to instruct the waiter – and stood up to leave.

Shaking Brads hand, I said it had been a pleasure to

meet him. We input each other's numbers into our phones and promised to stay in touch. Despite my nervousness, I felt I'd got along well with him. He seemed very keen to meet up again too.

As we were about to go our separate ways, I realised I knew little about Brad. He had driven the conversation and asked most of the questions. I had just divulged the replies.

"Oh, I almost forgot. You never told me what you do for a living, Brad, or even where you live?"

Smiling, Brad replied, his response leaving me none the wiser.

"I do a bit of this and that, you know? Oh, and I'm never too far away."

3

Cursing myself for not closing the shutters the night before, I awoke to the sun pouring in through the windows. Getting used to not having curtains would be something I'd need to address quickly. However, as I lay in bed, easing myself awake, I watched the perfect blue sky outside, smiled, and realised it wasn't such a big issue. Not in the grand scheme of things at least.

With the stove top coffee maker bubbling away, I picked up my laptop and walked out onto the terrace. Whilst I waited for the coffee to boil, I took in my new surroundings once more. The grass was still lush and green – there had been more rain in the Dordogne that spring – and stretched beyond the pool, down to the gîte and finished at the small perimeter fence. To the right, the fence swooped uphill and separated my garden from a field which then sloped gently upwards towards the horizon. Perched on top of the hill sat a quaint old farmhouse, albeit in need of some repair, with outbuildings extending almost as far as the eye could see. There were numerous pieces of farming equipment nestled between the dilapidated brick-built barns, many of which no longer supported a roof; a tractor, a couple of different-shaped ploughs and various other items that looked as though they'd been part of the farm since it was first built.

After I brought out my coffee and croissants, I opened up my laptop. As soon as it sprang into life, it greeted me with a pop-up confirming that several new emails were being downloaded.

Flicking through them one by one, I could delete most as soon as I recognised spam or subscription newsletters. The final two emails made me pause though. They weren't from addresses I could instantly identify.

The first one was from Andy Jackson, the satellite TV installer and all-round handyman, who'd come as agreed to set up the TV. He had kept his promise and sent me his home address after he had left the previous night. I had found his business card on the kitchen shelf the previous weekend when I'd been across to oversee the delivery of my furniture. It must have been left there by the previous occupants – just as well, as I would have had no idea who else to call. Andy came across as a down-to-earth guy, in his mid to late fifties. He had moved to France a few years ago with his wife and had told me he wanted to ply his trade overseas once the London market had become saturated. I looked up his address on Google Maps; his house sat in a small hamlet a few miles out of town. Andy had suggested I call round whenever I found myself near his home and he said he'd wanted his wife to meet me. It was quite a strange thing to request, but I took it in good faith that they wanted to meet fellow expats.

I made a mental note to write Andy's address onto the back of his business card, and I moved onto the final email sitting in my inbox. It was from an address I didn't recollect, and I opened it with some interest.

Congratulations!

You have a new booking!

Dates: Saturday 25th May to Saturday 8th June inclusive

Contact: Miss Rachel Brookes

Tel Number: Not given

Email: rbrookes121@hotmail.com

Special Requests: None

It had arrived from the online booking company where I had advertised my gîte for rent. Double-checking the calendar on the laptop, I realised that Saturday 25th May was the coming weekend, four days away.

"What the hell?" I said aloud, half in glee and half in trepidation. This was new territory for me, and I did not understand how to run this kind of business. On the other hand, I was charging five hundred euros a week at that time of the year and a thousand euros for two weeks was not to be sniffed at. Could my luck be changing so soon after arriving?

As I entered the details into my online calendar, I heard a faint "Bonjour" from the distance. It was a female's voice. "Bonjour, monsieur, 'ello, monsieur."

Looking up to the hill to the right of my garden, I saw a woman walking alone down the gentle slope. She looked as though she was coming from the direction of the farmhouse.

As I stood and started to walk over, I could see she was smiling and carried a basket with a coloured cloth over the top. I'd never been good with strangers and had always struggled to find the right words. Coupled with being in a foreign country, I met the cheery-looking woman with some nervousness.

We greeted each other across the small wooden fence that separated our properties.

"Er, 'ello, mon ami. Oh, I'm sorry. Hello, my friend."

Without wanting to embarrass myself by attempting French, I replied in English.

"Hello. I'm Daniel, I've just moved in."

Fortunately, her English was almost perfect.

"Hello, Daniel. My name is Laura Allaire. I live on the farm with my husband, Jean-Pascal."

She kissed me on both cheeks.

On first impressions, Laura was not unattractive. It was difficult to gauge her age, but I guessed early fifties. Her complexion appeared blemished, maybe from spending so many hours working outdoors in the searing heat. She had a pretty face and she was wearing a white blouse and a free-flowing skirt to just below her knees. Her top showed off an ample bosom and I had to focus my attention to avert my eyes as we spoke.

"Your English is excellent," I confessed, "but my French is terrible at the moment."

Laura opened her mouth, as if she would reply. She must have thought better of it and instead she looked at the ground between us as if to recompose herself.

There was something about her demeanour that I found intriguing. She fidgeted from foot to foot and seemed to search from afar to find the right words to say. Her shoulder-length, light brown hair flicked across her face and she brushed it aside with her free hand. I noticed several age spots dotted along the backs of her hands. When she looked up, she smiled an unconvincing smile, her lips twitching like an improbable ventriloquist. Her teeth appeared good against her ageing skin. She must have been very attractive during her younger years.

But Laura wasn't comfortable. Was it being in people's company or just mine in particular? Now and then she would turn and look behind her towards the farm before turning her attention back to me.

I filled the awkward silence for us both.

"I fully intend to learn the language as soon as I can find a teacher."

Laura was definitely about to say something, but paused, and again turned to look at the farmhouse. It was as though she sought permission to talk from the old house itself. My eyes followed hers. At last she spoke.

"We own the farm at the top of the hill. We are your closest neighbours."

She seemed as uncomfortable as I did myself in these situations. Eventually she handed me the basket whilst removing the cloth that covered it.

"As a gift to welcome you, I have prepared a little something."

There was a bottle of wine, some cheeses, bread, olives and other items in jars I didn't immediately recognise.

"This is very kind, but there really is no need."

Me and my big mouth again. Laura's smile disappeared, and she looked away, crestfallen.

"Oh no, sorry," I spluttered. "That is just an English

saying. I am honestly very, very grateful. It is one of the kindest things that has happened to me, but it just wouldn't happen in England. I'm not used to it, that's all."

Thankfully, Laura's smile returned, and she reached to hold my hand.

"My pleasure, Daniel."

She held my gaze a little longer than the moment necessitated.

"Thank you very much. You are very kind."

Laura leaned in to kiss both my cheeks again.

Moving backwards, her eyes darted from the farmhouse and then back to me. She took a deep breath, as if summoning up the courage to speak again. I was not expecting her next words.

"If anything, ever happens, remember my door is always open."

Just as I was about to reply, Laura stopped me, holding her finger to her lips to silence me.

"Be careful, Daniel. This may look idyllic, but people are set in their ways around here."

She smiled once more before turning on her heels and disappearing up the hill as fast as she had descended minutes earlier.

4

On the Saturday morning, I'd received an email from Rachel Brookes that her flight would arrive into Bordeaux Airport early that afternoon. Knowing it would take at least two hours to drive to my house, I had five or six hours to get everything ready.

It had been three days since the booking had arrived and I'd spent most of that time cleaning and tidying the gîte. I moved onto the pool area and then the garden which surrounded it. Whilst the new sheets and pillowcases were spinning in the dryer, I went into town to pick up provisions for Rachel's welcome pack.

As I pulled out of the driveway and onto the road into Monpazier, the car passing in the opposite direction looked vaguely familiar. It was travelling slowly for a main road and, looking in my mirror, I'm sure it was the same purple car that passed my house the night I'd moved in. Again, I didn't see the driver but in daylight I could make out it was a Peugeot, and quite old too.

The car had definitely slowed down the night I

arrived, and it ambled along again that day. It was the last thing I needed, something to worry me and occupy my thoughts. It had taken me the remainder of the week to put Laura's comments to the back of my mind.

Be careful, Daniel. This may look idyllic, but people are set in their ways.

Was it a warning? If so, what about? And now the purple car, slowing down outside my house, for the second time since I'd arrived.

Was I becoming over-suspicious?

Turning on my car radio, I tried to blank it all out. Easier said than done.

One of my traits was mild paranoia. I'd often get a sense that people were looking at me. Sometimes I'd convince myself that somebody laughed at me or pointed in my direction. Deep down, I knew there was always a simple explanation, but it could play on my mind for days. It stemmed from being young and moving from town to town and school to school because of my parents' work. As a result, I never really settled and never forged strong friendships. I became a bit of a loner and I'd convinced myself everybody was against me. Although my relationship with Emily had helped – giving me renewed confidence in myself – but when that had come to an abrupt halt, the old anxieties had resurfaced.

An hour before Rachel Brookes was due to arrive, I walked down to the gîte to put the welcome pack on the table. I also wanted to double-check everything looked in order. As soon as I opened the door, something felt different. At first glance, I couldn't see anything out of place, and I couldn't spot anything that may have gone missing.

But, something didn't feel right. The sense of somebody watching me from afar made me feel claustrophobic and trapped.

It wasn't until I had walked throughout the gîte and then back into the living room that I noticed it. On the table in the centre of the room, the new guest book lay open. I knew I had left it closed when I cleaned the gîte earlier. That would be what I'd do, close it, leave it how it should be. The edges perfectly aligned with the sides of the table.

Picking up the book, I quickly thumbed through it, once, twice, not sure what I expected to find. All blank pages, nothing untoward.

Why on earth would it be open?

Replacing the guest book and leaving the welcome pack in the centre of the table, I made my way back to the house. Still feeling as though somebody might be watching, I was caught off guard by the shrill of my mobile phone ringing in the kitchen.

Breaking into a trot, I took the call seconds before the voicemail cut in. I tried to catch my breath before speaking.

"Hello?"

"Hi, Dan."

Instantly, I recognised the voice on the other end.

"Emily! How are you? We haven't spoken for, erm since…"

Emily and I had separated around six months before. She had said she needed to follow her career, although we both knew that was only part of the truth. The company I had worked for made me redundant roughly a year earlier, and I'd fallen into depression as a result. I spent most of the day in bed or messing around on the internet or watching trash TV. Fortunately, we had good neighbours who Emily, behind my back, had asked to keep an eye on me. Sue Wade, the wife, five years my senior, made a special effort in preparing me meals. "You must eat to keep your strength up," she would say with a smile. Her husband Mike tried to get me to play golf or badminton, but mostly he would ask me to go around to their house and watch football on his massive TV, knowing very well that I wanted to stay indoors, alone. He wasn't at all bothered when I predominantly declined. Sue was different though, much keener to see me and she kept my emotions intact.

Emily worked in recruitment and had her own business, which had always been successful. She worked all hours though and our ties suffered.

We argued about anything and everything towards the end and it doomed our relationship to failure. My depression had led to much deeper and more personal arguments and eventually I made the final call. I told her she would be better off concentrating on her business, and I was just bringing her down. That resulted in even more vitriolic outbursts on both sides. It convinced Emily I had other reasons to split but would never say what. I decided it was best to let her scream and shout until she inevitably gave in and agreed to move out. We still held each other in high regard and had vowed to stay in touch. Although I'd started several text messages, I invariably lost my nerve and deleted before pressing 'send'. I guess I'd always wanted Emily to make the initial contact in case she rejected me. I would have done anything for another chance.

"Since we split up. Yes, I know."

I couldn't believe I was talking to her again. She continued while my mind drifted.

"Anyway, I'm good, Dan. How about you?"

"Yeah, I'm good. I'm in Fran–"

"France, yes, I know," Emily interrupted. "I saw Rick's posting on Facebook. I'm so pleased for you, Dan, I genuinely am."

My heart melted for a moment. I still had huge feelings towards Emily and just hearing her voice made me pine for her company. I did my best to keep my tone level and hide any obvious emotion.

"Trust Rick to post it." Rick had always been a very good friend of mine, going all the way back to school. Eventually, we drifted apart, after I met Emily, although she had regular contact with him via social media. In fact, Emily worked as our go-between, relaying everything I was doing to Rick and vice versa, keeping me up to date with his comings and goings. Since Emily and I split, I'd spent more time in his company again and our friendship soon returned to how it always had been. We'd meet for a beer once a week and chat via messaging at least every other day. We had always known each other's business and had a mutual trust. I missed Rick, and I made a mental note to send him a message sometime or even call him.

"Well, if you ever introduced yourself to social media, you might have told me yourself."

"Fair call. So, how's the mad world of recruitment?" Emily hesitated for a moment.

"Well, I could bore you with all the details on the phone, or..." she left it hanging.

"Or what?"

"Or, dumbass, you could invite me over to France and

I'll bore you stupid over one of those bottles of gorgeous French wine. They only cost a couple of quid, don't they?"

Feeling myself flush at the prospect of Emily coming to visit me, I spluttered my response.

"That's great, yeah. When?"

I can be so clumsy with my words once caught off guard.

"Well, don't sound so enthusiastic!" Emily was laughing.

"Sorry, Em." I still loved to call her Em. "Anytime is fine. I'll keep the gîte empty for you, make it feel like a holiday if you like. Did you have a date in mind?"

I hoped she'd tell me to save the gîte for business and she'd stay in my house, but she wasn't forthcoming.

"A few weeks or even sooner. The gîte sounds amazing. Work is kind of, mayhem, and I need a break. So, I thought to myself, do I know any international property tycoons?"

"Perfect. Just let me know. It will be great to catch up. Oh, and I'm very cheap."

"You always were, sweetheart, you always were."

I heard a car pull up onto the gravel outside.

"Hey, Em, I've got to go. My very first guest has just arrived, and I have to show her around."

"Her? You've got a female staying alone with you?"

Was that a hint of jealousy I detected in Emily's voice?

"Hey, I need the business. Males, females, dogs, cats, who cares as long as they're paying?"

"Well, you just behave yourself. I'll be in touch soon. Bye, Dan, love you."

"Bye, Em, take care."

There was a hint of solemnness in Emily's voice. Yes,

she had joked and teased me in her usual way, but there was an inkling that all was not well. Still, just to hear her voice again had made my day.

She'd always had a spark, that's what originally attracted me to her. We had met at a company event in London almost three years earlier. I'd been working for a marketing firm and she was progressing in the recruitment field. I'd hated my job, one in a long line of jobs I disliked immensely. I was thirty-seven at the time and had already had over ten jobs since leaving college. They were mostly in marketing.

Emily had approached me that night. Nothing new there, people always had to approach me. Fortunately, I'd had a few glasses of wine and the conversation flowed. She was different, somehow reading my mind, sensing my nervousness, and putting me at ease. Maybe it was because of her professionalism or, I liked to think, that she saw the vulnerable, down on his luck Daniel and wanted to help.

And she had helped, in bucket loads. We moved in together within months of that initial meeting. She found me a new job – I still didn't like it, but she made sure I wasn't in a direct face-to-face role, which suited me much better. Those were the best two-and-a-half years of my life. I thought it would last forever, but circumstances held all the cards. I'd become a burden, and she needed to escape the shackles.

Lost in thought, a faint "Hello, anybody home?" from outside soon bought me crashing back to reality. Rushing out onto the terrace, a very attractive looking woman greeted me, standing in front of a black BMW. There were two large suitcases by her feet. I took a deep breath.

"Hi, is it Rachel?"

She looked younger than me, maybe mid-thirties, about five foot eight and slim, with medium-length brown hair and dark brown eyes. Wearing a black T-shirt underneath a pink cardigan, tight jeans, and white Converse trainers, she had the appearance of somebody stylish.

She held out her hand.

"Yes. Daniel, I believe?"

Her attractiveness left me speechless and, for the second time in as many minutes, I stuttered my words in the company of a female.

"Yes, Daniel, Dan, whatever. Follow me, your gîte is at the end of the garden."

Rachel turned and let out a faint squeal when she saw the gîte.

"Oh, how quaint. And what a lovely pool. You are so lucky to live here, Dan."

Dan and not Daniel already. Her whole demeanour told me that this woman oozed confidence.

"Is my car okay there?"

"Yeah, sure, anywhere along the driveway, as long as we don't block each other in."

I nodded towards my car at the end of the drive tucked behind the house.

"Here, allow me."

I took one of her suitcases whilst she dragged the other. Mine felt heavy enough to last for weeks.

Following Rachel towards the gîte, I had to stop myself from admiring the view. This time it wasn't the French countryside that held my attention. I had a wry smile on my face thinking of Emily's words on the phone a few minutes earlier.

Well, you just behave yourself.

5

WITH A COUPLE of heated pain au chocolat on a side plate and a full mug of steaming hot coffee, I booted up my laptop on the outside table. Peering up at the deep blue sky, there wasn't a cloud in view, and the sun already a shining yellow beacon, even though it was still relatively early.

It was Monday morning and the beginning of my second full week in southwest France. Although I had to start work on my website, it didn't feel like a job at all. This was a pleasure, not the daily grind I'd left behind. I knew I had to keep reminding myself of this.

I needed to get my personal site onto the worldwide web and then hopefully people would find me and book the gîte direct. Every last penny would subsidise the dream. The escape.

You must leave all that happened behind you, Dan.

Taking a bite of the delicious pastry, I looked up to scan the beautiful garden, the ripples on the crystal-clear swimming pool and up to the open rolling fields surrounding my property.

With the view, the weather, and my newfound contentment, I couldn't concentrate on my website. Whilst staring at an almost blank page on my laptop, a clinking noise and the sound of flip-flops or sandals walking along the side of the pool distracted me. Looking up, I saw Rachel strolling towards me, carrying two tall glasses. They were each filled to the brim with what looked like orange juice and the clinking sound was copious amounts of ice cubes in each.

Although it wasn't permitted to remove glasses from the gîte, certainly not around the pool area, my nerves would not allow me to point out any house rules, especially as it was only the second time we'd met.

"Bonjour, Dan!"

Rachel looked just as nice as she had when she first arrived two days earlier. Her hair was tied up, and she wore skimpy denim shorts and a pale blue vest top. She already had a good tan, and her skin looked immaculate. It intrigued me what she must do for a living. The other thing I noticed as she walked towards me was that she wasn't wearing a bra underneath her vest top. I purposefully shut out the urge to stare as she passed me one of the drinks.

"Bonjour, Rachel. Thank you for the drink."

I felt myself redden at my pathetic attempt compared to Rachel's near perfect French pronunciation. She let out a stifled giggle which only exacerbated my self-consciousness.

"So, how is the gîte?"

"I've been sleeping like a baby. It's just so peaceful here. You are so lucky, Dan."

"That's what I think, just a shame it's taken me so long to pick up the courage to move and start over."

Rachel's brazen self-confidence again became clear, and she pulled out the chair next to where I sat. Placing her drink on the table alongside mine, she sat a lot closer than I'd expected. I took a long swig of the ice-cold drink.

She was obviously intrigued by my background and subsequent move to France.

"Why did it take so long?"

Her abruptness and personal question caught me off guard

"Sorry?"

"Oh, I'm sorry if I'm speaking out of turn. I'm just curious as to why you left it until now, if it's something you have wanted for quite some time. Please, forgive me."

"No, I mean, it's fine," I spluttered. "I've just never really spoken about it with anyone before."

She looked directly into my eyes knowing full well that I was putty in her hands. She had no intention to speak, leaving me no choice but to carry on.

"Well, I've had a few jobs, but nothing to keep me anywhere. My friends have all been married, a couple are divorced, but we have all spread our wings, mostly around Britain, though some have ventured abroad."

"Including you now." She was smiling. Sitting so close, I couldn't help but admire how beautiful she looked.

"Yes, including me now."

"And no wife, girlfriend, boyfriend, for you, Dan?"

Although good looking, the directness of her questions were irritating me slightly. However, she was a paying guest, and it was only polite to engage in conversation. I tried to stay calm and in control.

"Oh, a couple of ex-girlfriends, the last one a year or so ago."

"I see. And male friends?"

"Yes, actually, I've got a close friend. His name is Rick Morley. We tell each other everything."

A few moments of awkward silence followed. I didn't want to pry into her background. In all honesty, I just wanted her to pick up the glasses and go back to the gîte. I was out of my comfort zone.

Rachel still smiled, and she looked directly into my eyes. She looked so damn attractive, so I forcefully turned aside and back towards my laptop.

She followed my gaze.

"Are you working on something?"

Again, straight to the point.

"Well, yes, actually. I need to get a website up and running for the gîte. The agency I've got it advertised with take a small fortune in booking fees. I thought direct bookings would mean more euros in my pocket and not theirs."

I knew I was babbling, and it took all my efforts to keep my responses in check. Rachel edged even closer, and I felt the skin of her arm rest on mine.

Her face was only inches from me now and she lowered her voice to a whisper.

"Great idea, Dan. Have you done any web design before?"

Convinced my voice would go up several octaves, I took a deep breath before I replied.

"Not much. I kind of did some at one of my jobs, so I know the basics. Why, have you?"

I didn't have the courage to twist my head to face her. I could feel her breath on my neck.

"Yeah, I've done quite a few as it happens. Mind if I take a look?"

Before I could reply, she reached across and slid the laptop towards her. As she studied how little I'd done, I instead became drawn to her legs under the table. They were crossed, and the toes from her swaying foot kept tapping my leg. It was impossible to say if this was intentional. I watched her hands move over the keyboard.

"You've not got far, Dan!"

She nudged me so I had no choice but to look up and face her. We were so close.

"I could build this for you. With your help, of course?"

Subconsciously, my voice dropped to a mere whisper too. She had drawn me into the situation like I'd been hypnotised. I spoke whatever words entered my head.

"You don't need to do that, Rachel, honestly. Besides, I need to teach myself, you know, for the future."

"I'll show you all that. I'll do the basic site, get it up and running, add a contact form, stuff like that, just to get you started."

I held her gaze, talking to myself to keep calm.

"You're on holiday. You don't want to be writing websites."

"Nonsense, Dan. It would be my pleasure. Web design is one thing I do. It will only take a few hours and I can dabble in and out when I'm on my own in the gîte or around the pool. I have my laptop I can use too. My gift for being your first guest. I insist."

With that, she stood up, leant towards me, and kissed me on the cheek.

"Deal?"

Her vest top dropped low enough for me to see down. She looked at me watching, making no attempt to move.

I didn't even hear myself speak.

"Deal, but only if you insist."

She broke my stare by standing and collecting the two glasses. My eyes looked her up and down as if she'd cast a spell on me.

"Good. Oh, and I know I'm not supposed to take glasses from the gîte or around the pool. I did read your information pack as soon as I arrived. May I suggest you supply plastic tumblers for guests?"

Rachel walked away, smiling, knowing she had me exactly where she wanted.

Turning and walking backwards across the lawn, she spoke one last time.

"Oh, Dan. I'll need your hosting company address, so I can work on the website. And your username and password of course."

6

A SHORT WHILE LATER, as I contemplated going for a swim before lunch, I saw Rachel emerge from the gîte. She'd changed into tight jeans and a loose-fitting T-shirt.

She smiled when she noticed me sitting on my terrace and gave me a little wave as she passed on the way to her car.

I'd been waiting for an opportunity to speak again. This time I fully intended to be in control.

"Oh, Rachel, one minute. I've got the website address and my login details here."

I waved my notebook above my head.

She couldn't resist another excuse to take a swipe at my ineptitude.

"Very technological, Dan. You know they have invented email, now don't you?"

Feeling myself blushing slightly, I closed the notepad and put it back down and tried to recompose myself.

"Yeah, of course. I just didn't think, sorry. I'll send them over to you now."

"That would be best."

She grinned as I fumbled to open my laptop.

"Do you need anything from the supermarket? I'm just going there now to get some essentials."

"Nah, I'm fine thanks."

Feeling as though I should thank her for all she was doing, an idea entered my head and escaped my mouth before I could think it through.

"By the way, I'm going into Monpazier later this week, maybe Wednesday. Would you like to join me?"

"Sounds great. You can be my tour guide. What kind of time?"

"Oh, late afternoon. We can walk from here, probably grab something to eat? My treat," I added.

"Perfect. I'll be ready at four?"

I tried to tone my enthusiasm although I'm not convinced I did.

"Excellent! There's a large hypermarket over at Siorac, a Carrefour. They are open this afternoon if you need a bigger shop?"

"Yes, I know. I've got Google, a satnav, all the mod cons, Dan. Unless you want to draw me a map?"

"Bugger off!" I shouted, smiling back as she climbed into her car. She blew me a kiss as she drove past, the radio blasting some pop song over the speakers. I'd only known her a couple of days, but it pleased me we were getting on. One of my fears had been how I would connect with the guests.

Secretly, I was quite relieved Rachel had gone out. It gave me some space to think. The teasing was fun, but I couldn't allow it to get out of hand. She was far too good looking for me and I began to wonder what she could possibly see in me.

Is it flirting or is she after something else?

I also recalled the phone call with Emily over the weekend. I was already looking forward to her visit whenever she could make it with her busy schedule. Rachel was fun, but Emily had been my one true love. I wondered if there would be any chance of a reconciliation but with all the history, I very much doubted it.

With the place to myself, I decided to take a swim. I thought it would look bad if I used the pool whilst any guests were around. After all, they had paid for exclusive use.

As I enjoyed the cool, clear water, I looked around and had to pinch myself to believe where I was and the cards that life had finally dealt me. I'd had a particularly hard time of things back in England and, even before I'd met Emily, life had never been a bed of roses. I'd never settled, either professionally or domestically. However, as I lazed around in the pool, I thought things were finally getting better. Maybe this was my life calling?

The distinctive melody of the cicadas filled the air. A buzzard, or maybe a red kite, soared and swooped overhead as I lay on my back and slowly swam up and down the pool.

Whilst towelling myself dry, I heard my phone ringing on the terrace table. Walking over, I picked it up, without hesitating to read the caller ID.

Slightly out of breath, I made a mental note to do more to get myself fit.

"Hi."

"Hey, Dan. It's Brad, Brad Jones."

I was having one of my senior moments as I just couldn't place the name.

My silence prompted him to speak again.

"Brad, from the café. We met last Monday. In town?"

"Hey, Brad. So sorry. You sound different on the phone."

He didn't sound different at all, but I wanted to cover my incompetence.

"How's things?" I asked.

"Great, just great. How about you?"

"Yeah, good thanks. I'm settling in, loving the pace of life."

"That's the beauty of France, and especially the Dordogne. Do things at your leisure and let the rest take care of itself."

Brad paused, obviously wanting to ask me something.

"Any luck with the gîte yet, Dan?"

The question caught me off guard.

"Oh, well, yeah, actually. Somebody checked in on Saturday. It was quite a surprise to get a booking so quickly. Is that why you called?" I added, with a hint of sarcasm in my voice.

"Hell no, chill out. I'm just asking. Is it a family, a couple?"

Unsure of why Brad pressed the matter, I gave him the benefit of the doubt that he was just being friendly and lightened my response.

"A single female actually. Fit too, if that's not too sexist."

"Well, look at you. A week in France and you've already got yourself a catch."

I immediately went on the defensive, recalling my thoughts about Emily from earlier.

"It's nothing like that, Brad. She's here for two weeks and every penny counts. It's purely business."

"If you say so! Anyway, Dan, the real reason I called is to remind you that if you require any help to settle in, I'm always at the end of the phone. I know it can be daunting moving abroad, so if you need anything, just ask."

"That's kind, Brad, cheers. I'll give you a ring soon and we can meet for a beer and a chat. I need to find my way around the area, so maybe we could even take a drive and you can show me where everything is. You know, all the essentials?"

"Be my pleasure, Dan. Look forward to it. You take care now."

"You too. Bye."

Brad could be brash, and he certainly wasn't an introvert, but he seemed okay and could be just the friend I needed.

Later that afternoon, whilst watching a movie on satellite TV, I heard a car pull up onto the drive outside. Craning my neck to peer over the back of the sofa, I saw Rachel walking towards the gîte. She was carrying at least three supermarket bags in each hand. I stopped myself from conducting my gentleman host duties, not wishing to looking too keen. I wasn't there to get into some kind of relationship, especially with guests.

. . .

With the movie still playing in the background, a knock on the door prevented me from falling into a deep sleep on the sofa.

My immediate thought was that Rachel had dropped by again. I was reluctant to let her in but had to remain friendly.

"It's open."

"Bonjour, Daniel. Are you home?"

Springing to my feet, I saw Laura at the open door. She was peering inside and having a good look around. I walked outside, pulling the door behind me.

"Laura! How are you?"

We kissed each other on each cheek.

Laura's hair hung loose, making her look less stern than at our initial meeting. Her green eyes were unusual and somehow mesmerising. She was wearing a different knee-length skirt from when we first met and a pale yellow blouse.

"I am well thank you, Daniel. And how are you settling in?"

"Good. Everything is fine so far."

"And you have a guest?"

So much attention around Rachel.

"Yes. She arrived on Saturday. All very sudden."

It was difficult to gauge if Laura accepted that somebody was staying in the gîte or not.

"Well, you've done very well. We noticed two cars on your drive and then I saw her this morning, carrying drinks."

Have they been watching me?

Laura spotted the concern on my face.

"Please don't misunderstand me, Daniel, we are

thrilled for you. It's just everybody knows everybody around here and we, how do you say it, we notice things."

Laura smiled again, which put me back at ease. She changed tack.

"Now, why did I call? Ah, oui. Jean-Pascal and I would like to invite you round for a barbecue on Saturday evening. Just to say welcome to our new neighbour."

As before, she then looked over her shoulder, back towards the farmhouse.

What was she looking at?

"That's very kind of you, Laura. I would love to. What should I bring?"

"Bring? Bring? What do you mean? You are our guest and we don't expect you to 'bring' anything."

Laura moved to leave and kissed me on both cheeks again. She then gave me a hug, pressing herself against me a little longer than I expected. I felt myself hug her back. I was genuinely being friendly, nothing else.

As she turned to walk back towards the field to home, we were both stopped in our tracks. A movement had alerted us to the end of the garden.

In unison, we looked up. Simultaneously, we saw Rachel watching us from the gîte window.

7

On Wednesday afternoon, I heard a knock on my door. It was exactly four o'clock.

Rachel looked as radiant as ever. She had scraped her hair back off her face and tied it up in a neat ponytail, finished with a small yellow ribbon. The ribbon matched her bright yellow top, which was tight fitting and showed off every curve imaginable. She was complete with knee-length, tight denim jeans and the same Converse trainers I had noticed the day she arrived.

Ever since I'd invited her into town with me, I had regretted it. It wasn't my style; this was out of my comfort zone. What would we talk about and how would I react to her obvious flirting?

I cursed myself again under my breath as I greeted her. Outwardly I knew I had to make an effort.

"You look great. Ready to go?"

"You look good too, Dan. Ready when you are."

We walked in silence towards town, both enjoying the scenery and seemingly at ease in each other's company. I particularly enjoyed the peace and quiet. The sound of the cicadas were louder than ever as the sun began to lose some of its intense heat. The occasional car passed by; each time the occupants nodded or waved a cheery hello in our direction. We both reciprocated.

As we approached the centre of Monpazier, we first turned right and then immediately left onto Rue de l'Ormeau du Pont. The shade of the houses on both sides of the narrow street felt most welcoming. Two cats lay contented on adjoining windowsills, their little faces looking up at us as we walked by. We strolled on towards the central square, Monpazier Place des Corniéres.

As we reached the centre, Rachel spotted some outdoor seating at a bar. It looked as though it doubled as a small restaurant too. It was at the opposite end of the square from where I'd met Brad the previous week, so I was glad to explore and try somewhere different.

We sat at a table, basking in the late afternoon sun, and ordered a bottle of white wine. I don't normally drink white, but Rachel insisted and when it arrived in an ice bucket, I was pleased I had gone with her instincts.

The waiter poured us both a glass and returned the bottle to the cooler.

"Salute!" she exclaimed, and we chinked our glasses together. The ice-cold wine slid down my throat and I could feel its onwards journey to the pit of my stomach.

Sitting back and finally attempting to relax, I became taken aback when Rachel leant forward, her elbows propped on the table. She looked straight into my eyes and asked me directly what was on her mind. Her voice was even and serious.

"So, tell me, Dan. Do you fancy that farmer woman?"

"Sorry? Who?"

"That farmer's wife, the one you were hugging and kissing and hugging some more on your doorstep on Monday night. Frankly, I thought you had more taste than that, Dan."

Her mouth sat in a hard-straight line and she turned her head towards the sky. She looked ridiculous, like a child sulking after she'd been told off for being naughty.

Her incredulous accusation was not something I found at all palatable. It suddenly clicked with me, she must have been speaking about when she had watched me and Laura from the gîte window on Monday afternoon.

"What on earth are you talking about? We were just being friendly. She's married, and I'm sure they're both very nice people. I'm not going to ignore my new neighbours, am I?" My words blurted out without me taking a breath.

She opened her mouth to reply, but I didn't allow her to talk.

"And unless you don't realise, it's the French way, hugging, kissing…"

"She has got huge breasts, though hasn't she? Is that why you kept her in that embrace so long?"

"This is ridiculous. Are you being serious, or is this some kind of wind-up, Rachel?"

I stood and fumbled for my wallet in my pocket.

Rachel immediately retracted and sat back in her chair, showing a much less aggressive demeanour. She attempted to level her voice too.

"Where are you going?"

"I don't need to sit here and listen to this, Rachel. I live here now; I want to settle here and that means getting on well with people. You," I said, looking directly into her eyes, "you are my guest, at my house and if you don't like it…"

"Sorry, I'm so sorry. Daniel, please sit down."

She surveyed the people at the only other occupied table, smiling at them. Remarkably, I don't think they'd heard much as they just smiled back.

Rachel took my hand and pulled me down.

"Please stay, please. I obviously got completely the wrong end of the stick."

Sitting down, I allowed her to finish what she wanted to say. Unselfconsciously, she still held my hand across the table.

"I like you, Dan. You are a good friend. You can do much better than that farmer's wife…"

I tried to stand again, but she pulled tight on my hand.

"Sorry, I'm sure she's very nice but I don't want you coming over to France and just jumping into something you will regret later on. You seem, how can I put it, a little insecure. Maybe it's because you've only just arrived here but don't go befriending every person you meet. At least don't get over familiar with everyone."

"What, such as coming out to dinner with someone I only met four or five days ago?"

"Don't be silly, we just get along. Some people just kind of click, and we are two of those people."

She leaned over and kissed me directly on my lips. Rachel was obviously a girl who was used to getting her own way. Looking at her then, I couldn't believe she was the same person who had asked me such belittling questions only two minutes earlier.

What the hell was that all about?

I unlocked my hand from Rachel's and took a huge

gulp of my wine, draining what was left. I then picked up the bottle and refilled my glass. My hands were shaking, and I was doing my level best to remain outwardly calm. I should have trusted my instincts and cancelled the evening.

"What about mine?" Rachel enquired, pushing her glass towards me.

Looking at her then, butter wouldn't melt in her mouth. I had to admit to myself that the kiss, albeit very brief, had felt very sensual. She had an aura of self-belief about her. What did she want from me?

Refilling her glass, I returned her smile. Although I still wasn't happy with her questions, I didn't want a misunderstanding, if that's all it was, to come between us that evening.

She's only here two weeks, Dan. That's nothing.

I then decided not to mention that I would be going over to the Allaires' house for a barbecue on Saturday night. I needed to keep that to myself.

Fortunately, Rachel relaxed and soon fell back into her ways of making fun of me and flirting at the same time. We finished the bottle and then ordered another. As always, with alcohol, my confidence grew. Trying to steer clear of any confrontational subjects, I thought I'd ask a little more about her background.

"So, you live near Dorking, in Surrey?"

She was immediately back on the defensive. Her whole manner could change with the click of a finger.

"How do you know that?"

I smiled, hoping to get back at her little digs from

when she teased me about emailing rather than writing passwords in my notebook.

"Your booking, online. It had your address on it. You know, Rachel, technology?"

To my relief, she grinned and gave me a pretend punch on the arm.

"Yeah, you got me. Okay, yes, I live in a small village in Surrey."

Although she relaxed, she wasn't at all forthcoming. I pushed for more.

"Do you work? Married, partner?"

"Wow, so many questions, Dan."

"Hey, sorry if it's too much. I…"

"It's fine. I don't mind. Okay, I'm thirty-nine, single, never married, had a few flings but nothing serious. I'm self-employed and I also run a few websites. That's how I know about setting them up."

She leant forward.

"Oh, and I'm 36-26-34. Anything else?"

Fortunately, I'd had enough to drink to not feel or look embarrassed by her reply.

"No, that will do fine."

By now, Rachel was loving the attention I bestowed upon her. She watched my drunken eyes work their way up and down her body.

"Well, just let me know if I need to prove anything to you. You know, in case you don't believe me."

8

THE REST of the evening had passed with no repeat of Rachel's earlier personality shift. We had ordered food and chatted about what I needed on my new website. She told me how she had taught herself to build sites from scratch. As a result, she said, she made a comfortable living working with clients and having a couple of other interests – she never expanded upon this. Exactly how profitable it all was, I had no idea, although she gave an outward impression that she wasn't short of money.

Rachel's early perception of me had been accurate too. A little insecure, I think she said. She was right. It had upset me she'd been so insightful. My shyness had always left me vulnerable. I could be susceptible to allowing people into my life, without having the nerve to push them away. I'd never been the guy who would approach a woman in a pub or club if I found them attractive. It always had to be the woman who approached me. If I'd had enough to drink, we would get along fine, and chat and laugh.

Although the accusation that I hugged Laura too enthusiastically had left a sour taste in my mouth, I was doubting myself – Rachel may have been right. Had I been over familiar in our embrace? Surely not, I'd just been reciprocating what the French do naturally, on a day-to-day basis. You see it in the street, in restaurants all the time.

'Women, eh?' I voiced my thought, subconsciously reminding myself that I was still single and, mostly, happier as a result.

After arriving home from our meal the previous night, I'd called Brad and asked if he wanted to meet for lunch sometime. I needed some male company. Fortunately, he said he'd be available to meet the next day and suggested we went to a village called Beynac-et-Cazenac. He told me of a bar and restaurant overlooking the Dordogne River which sounded perfect.

The following day I woke early and, deciding it would be nice to take a stroll along the river before meeting him, I got myself ready and set off for the aforementioned village.

Brad knew his way around. The village location on the river was picture-postcard quaint and had the most dramatic back drop. I'd noticed many signs for campsites in the area and knew it was a hotbed for tourists. I needed to add places to visit in the information pack for guests in the gîte. This place would certainly get a mention.

Finding a parking spot in the communal car park, I checked my phone and realised I had about forty minutes before meeting Brad. Having found the restaurant, I noticed the path continued along the wide expanse of the river, which curved majestically into the distance. With the footpath safely walled from the road, I observed just how clean everything was. No litter, no graffiti and, unlike walking back home in England, no dog shit to look out for. It was a pleasure to look around and take in the scenery.

"Hey, Dan!"

This time I had no issue recognising the southern English accent of Brad. Turning, I saw him jogging slowly to catch me up. We shook hands and even had a quick embrace, again reiterating my thoughts that this *is* what they do in France.

Although disappointed not to walk for a while, it felt comforting to see a familiar face.

"Great to see you again, Brad. You sure know some of the best spots."

"Yeah, it's cool here. Good for walking, you can hire canoes, and the river is great for swimming in too. You can bring a picnic, find your own spot and spend all day here."

"Well, it certainly is an excellent place. Shall we lunch?" I said, turning back towards the restaurant.

"Yes please, I'm starving."

We found a table overlooking the river and ordered two beers. For food we had a sandwich each and a side of fries. Brad did all the ordering in French, even though the waiter spoke perfect English.

"So, tell me, Dan, how is your guest? Erm, what did you say her name was again?"

Not believing I'd ever given Brad her name, as far as I recalled anyway, I replied, thinking this might be a good opportunity to discuss her reaction last night.

"Her name is Rachel. We went for a meal last night, actually, and–"

"Hey, you did, did you?" Brad butted in, playfully punching my arm. "Tell me more."

His light-hearted behaviour towards myself and Rachel was beginning to grind me down.

"Look, I said, it's nothing like that, Brad, honestly. I'll treat any guests I have to a meal or a drink, if they're okay with it."

Brad was about to interrupt again, but I wished to do the talking for a change, so I raised my hand to cut him off.

"There's something I wanted to ask you anyway, if you don't mind?"

"Fire away."

"Well, I have neighbours, they're farmers. They, well she, has been genuinely kind to me the couple of times we've met since I arrived. She even brought me a welcome basket, which I thought was nice. She didn't have to, after all, and you sure as shit wouldn't get that back at home."

"Fair call."

"So, yesterday, the wife, erm Laura, came down to my house and invited me to theirs to have a barbecue or something on Saturday evening. Thinking nothing of it, I gratefully accepted. Laura then gave me the obligatory kiss on each cheek, and then…"

Brad leaned forward, suddenly showing some interest.

"And then?"

"Nothing, she just gave me a hug, for, maybe a few seconds, no more."

"So?"

"Well, I thought nothing of it but as Laura turned to leave, we saw Rachel staring at us through the gîte window."

Again, the same reply from Brad.

"So?"

"So, is exactly what I thought. Until that is, when Rachel and I went for the meal last night, she kind of accused me of fancying this Laura woman. Said she saw us hugging and asked if I found her attractive. It was so weird."

Brad's response wasn't what I'd been expecting.

"And do you fancy this Laura woman, Dan?"

"What? Not you as well, Brad. No, I don't fancy her. As I said, they're just kind people, and I thought that's what French people did, hugged and kissed a lot. Isn't it?"

"Yeah, sure they do in comparison to us Brits, but did Rachel see something more in it? I don't know, man, I wasn't there."

Getting a little annoyed at the lack of support from Brad, I ground my teeth before replying.

"No! She did not, unless…"

"Unless what, Dan?"

"Well, unless she's a bit, you know?"

I tapped my temple with my finger to suggest Rachel might have a screw loose. Brad was not letting up in his defence of her.

"You can't go around accusing people of being unstable, Dan."

Before I could reply, he continued.

"Look, this is evidently a misunderstanding. You're a good-looking guy and, from what you say, this Rachel is a good-looking girl. You're both single," he halted, "aren't you?"

"She said she is, and I am, yes."

"So then, Rachel obviously thinks you're more suited to her than a French farmer's wife and she probably doesn't understand the local culture of kissing and hugging. You're too uptight, Dan. Like I said on the phone, this is a completely new way of life. Just relax and go with the flow. If Rachel reacts like that again, make sure she knows you don't 'fancy' the farmer, eh?"

He laughed and took a large swig of his beer. Brad wasn't even trying to conceal his favouritism towards Rachel over Laura. I couldn't quite understand the preferential treatment even though I knew Rachel would be more his type. But that made little sense either, he didn't know either of them. As far as I was concerned, he'd never even seen them. I let it go; it wasn't worth falling out over.

"Guess you're right. I put it down to a misunderstanding myself, and now you've said that, it makes more sense. Another beer?"

"Thought you'd never ask."

Nothing else was mentioned of the Rachel, Laura incident, and we enjoyed a good hour in each other's company.

When we reached the car park in the village, it surprised me Brad hadn't left his car there too. There had been several free spaces when I'd arrived and there were still quite a few when we returned.

He noticed the quizzical look on my face as I scanned the car park.

"Mine's along the road, near the river."

"Oh, okay."

I knew I hadn't sounded convincing, but Brad

brushed it aside and shook my hand before making his way back along the river.

The day out had been just what I'd needed. I'd found a great place to visit, a lovely place to eat and a good friend in Brad.

9

I'D ALLOWED a few jobs to creep up on me since I'd arrived in France. One of them was mowing the vast expanse of lawn. Fortunately, the previous occupants had left their ride-on mower in their haste to move on.

The midday sun already beat down, so I grabbed my large floppy hat and made my way to the shed. I silently prayed the mower would behave itself and start first time.

Having never driven one of those things before, I felt a tingle of excitement as I wheeled it out of the shed. I was like a child at Christmas.

Turning the key, it fired up first time, leaving a large plume of blue smoke escaping from the exhaust. The piece of machinery was nearly new and must have cost several hundred euros to buy – I felt so grateful I hadn't had to pay for a new one myself. Such a strange gift to leave behind.

It was light and easy to manoeuvre, and I soon fell into my stride. It didn't take long for a warning light to appear on the dashboard. After an initial panic, I soon realised it was informing me the grass catcher was already full. As I emptied the cuttings behind the shed and walked back to the mower, I noticed Rachel positioning a sun lounger next to the pool. I'd been hoping to avoid her for a few more days. I'd wanted the whole situation to calm down and return to normal. I figured the longer I stayed out of her way, the better. My heart beat a little faster as I realised, I still had to mow the lawn at the far end of the garden near the gîte and around the pool.

Restarting the engine, I continued where I'd left off and carried on mowing. Hopefully, I would get away with a courtesy nod or wave. It was one of those many occasions when I wasn't in the mood for polite conversation.

As I drove toward Rachel, I noticed she was wearing one of those sarong things, multi-coloured and covering her body, her face shielded from the strong rays by sunglasses and a large straw hat.

Rachel lowered her sunglasses as I rode past and mouthed "Good morning." I turned the corner and, bobbing up and down towards her, I tipped my hat and smiled. As I carried on, I hoped that would be the pleasantries out of the way for the day. My hopes would soon be dashed.

A good thirty minutes later, the lawn was almost complete. I had to ride past Rachel one more time, swoop around the gîte, and then head back to the shed to dispose of the final grass cuttings.

As I rounded the final corner, Rachel stood from the sun lounger and waved her arm, as if flagging down a taxi.

Shit.

Taking my foot off the accelerator, I came to a halt just yards from where she stood. I cut the engine.

"Hi, Dan."

"Hi. Enjoying the sun?" I replied, nodding towards the sun lounger and trying to keep everything light-hearted.

"Yes. It's gorgeous isn't it?"

Putting my hand back down on the key to start the motor, Rachel interrupted my movement by stepping forward a pace.

"Dan, I know it's a strange request, but would you mind applying sun cream to my back?"

It was exactly the scenario that I desperately wanted to avoid. She continued, spotting my reluctance to help.

"I can't reach, and with this sun," she looked skywards. "I really don't want to burn myself."

She smiled that 'innocent little child' smile which could turn the most blood sucking meat eater into a vegetarian.

Most single men would have leapt at the opportunity to rub suntan lotion onto a beautiful woman like Rachel, but I wasn't most men, and I knew the situation could soon drift into dangerous territory. She wasn't letting up in her pursuit of my attention. The flirting was becoming dominant in our every meeting. I wasn't comfortable with either her actions or what may lie behind them. Reluctantly, I gave in to her demands.

"Well, okay Rachel, but I have a lot to do today."

Whilst I climbed down from the mower, she stood a few feet in front of me, undid her sarong and let it fall to the floor. She was wearing the skimpiest lime green bikini, which showed off her already tanned body in all its glory. She knew exactly what she was doing, playing on my timidity. She walked back to the sun lounger, lay down on her front and looked over her shoulder, her eyes innocently beckoning me forward.

I could feel my hands clamming up. I wished she had wine with her so I could take a drink, something to calm my nerves. I needed to get it over and done with promptly, so I grabbed the sun lotion and applied a good covering all over her back.

As I started to rub the cream in, Rachel lifted herself onto her elbows.

"One moment, Dan."

Her hands moved behind her back and she slowly undid her bikini top. It was held together with two ties that met in the middle. Letting the straps fall either side of her body, she slowly lay back down.

Tilting her head and looking up, she teased me with a sexy whispered voice.

"Okay, carry on, Dan."

Rubbing the lotion in circular movements, I couldn't help but feel turned on. This was not familiar territory for me. It had also been a long time since I'd had any intimacy with a female. Emily had been the last woman I'd slept with, several months previously.

"That feels good, Dan, you're a natural. You have covered *everywhere*, haven't you?"

"Yes, everywhere. All done."

Standing, I tried to hide the obvious sign that I had enjoyed the experience as much as Rachel seemed to. Unfortunately, she noticed.

"Hmm, I must call you back later when I want my front doing, Dan." A little schoolgirl giggle escaped her mouth.

Blushing lightly, I started to walk away.

"Well, I'm sure you can manage that yourself, Rachel."

As I climbed back onto the mower, I attempted to show I was in control of the situation.

"Anything else you need before I carry on?"

"That's your choice, Dan. I'm here all afternoon."

A movement caught the corner of my eye, somewhere beyond the gîte. Was it somebody walking along the road beyond? No, it seemed closer than that. Then I heard a clicking noise, it had come from further along the road, closer to my driveway but behind the hedge which separated my plot from the D660.

Just as I contemplated further investigation, my phone started to ring. It was outside on my terrace. With my mind all over the place, that would be the last time I remembered the footsteps and clicking noises – until much later.

Jogging back, the phone cut off when I was within seconds of retrieving it. Looking at the missed calls, I was pleased I hadn't made it. It was Emily, and before I called her back, I needed a glass of cold water to regain my composure.

A few minutes later, I sat on one of the terrace chairs and dialled Emily's number. As the call connected, I noticed Rachel sat up in her lounger, looking over at me. The moment had gone, and I found myself annoyed for letting her lead me on like that. Why was she still looking at me, watching everything I did?

"Hi, Dan."

The voice on the phone snapped me back to the present.

"Oh, hi, Em. Sorry I missed your call. I've been mowing the lawn," my voice still sounded wobbly.

"Yes, you sound out of breath."

Emily chuckled, and when she realised I would not reply, she continued with what she was calling about.

"Good news, Dan. Well, at least I think it's good news."

"Go on," I replied, non-committal.

She let out a nervous laugh, so unlike her. It immediately made me think of her manner on our previous phone call.

"I can come out three weeks on Sunday, the twenty-third of June. Is that okay with you?"

"Sounds great, Em. Which airport are you flying into? I can pick you up."

"I haven't booked the flight yet, just checking it's okay. I'll message you as soon as I've paid for it. That okay?"

"Perfect. Looking forward to seeing you again. It's been too long."

"Yes, should be good. Listen, I have to go, I'm on my lunch break. Love you, bye, Dan."

"Love you too…" but Emily had already hung up.

Although it was good news that Emily wanted to visit, her confirmation somehow made me feel uneasy. I was angry that it had taken until now for her to contact me again. I didn't do social media, but she could always have sent the odd text message. I'd always thought it should have been down to her to approach me first and I felt used that now I was in France, Emily was taking advantage of me to get a free holiday.

Don't be so negative, Dan.

I cursed myself. It was just my suspicious mind rejecting any positive news. My feelings towards Emily had never diminished, and I knew that was the overriding reason for my nervousness at her upcoming visit.

As I stared at my phone trying to calm myself down by taking deep breaths, I detected somebody very close to me. I spun around and my heart momentarily missed a beat. Rachel was standing feet away from me.

She wore a smile on her face, but her personality had changed noticeably from the sun cream incident minutes earlier.

"Who was that?" She looked at the phone in my hand. I couldn't believe what she'd just asked me.

"Hey, sorry? That's kind of personal, Rachel, don't you think?"

"Love you too," she mimicked. "Who do you love, Dan?"

Once again, I found myself astounded at Rachel's overreaction and prying into my private life. I didn't feel the need to hide anything from her.

"If you must know, Rachel, it was my ex-fiancée. She is coming over to stay soon."

She looked surprised, a little hurt even. I continued, purposefully making a point.

"But don't worry, it's well after you've leave."

She opened her mouth as if to reply but couldn't formulate the right words. She just smiled at me, turned on her heels and mumbled something beneath her breath as she walked away.

Although difficult to hear exactly what she said, it sounded unnervingly similar to "We'll see about that."

10

THE FOLLOWING EVENING, I was due at the Allaires for the barbecue. I couldn't remember if Laura had said a time or not. If she had, I'd forgotten. So, I decided about seven o'clock and started to walk around to their farm.

I was feeling a little apprehensive. I hadn't met Laura's husband yet – Jean-Pascal – and I worried what we would talk about all night. On top of that, my French was abysmal. Would they judge me? Question why I moved to a country where I couldn't even speak the language?

Thinking it would be rude to walk over their field, I strolled along the road and then took the long driveway up to the house. It was a fine evening, with a light breeze, giving momentary respite from the heat of the sun.

As I walked up the final ascent to their home, I noticed how run down it was. I hadn't been this close to their property before and had only viewed it from the bottom of the hill. There were sizeable cracks in the facade and the wooden windows were rotting away. I glanced around for a car, but there were only two tractors parked in the field beyond. Even they looked dilapidated, the paintwork a thing of the past. I was taking it all in when I heard Laura calling me from the side of the house.

Walking round, she was already standing, waiting to greet me. I noticed her prod her husband on his upper arm, prompting him to stand too. I'm not convinced he would have stood at all if it wasn't for Laura.

Already feeling uncomfortable, I painted on a smile and walked towards them. Jean-Pascal looked tired, almost worn out. He was of broad frame, muscular more than heavy. His full head of hair was greying at the temples but was otherwise dark brown and stuck up in all directions. He was wearing a mustard colour thick jumper, not at all suitable for the balmy evening. As he reached out his hand to shake mine, I noticed holes under the armpits and at the elbows.

Jean-Pascal's handshake was harsh and firm, squeezing the blood down to my fingertips. His palm felt hard, full of calluses. Real workman's hands. His dark brown eyes stared directly into mine. He gave nothing away.

Although under strict orders not to take anything, my English politeness would not allow me to go empty-handed. I removed a fine bottle of red wine from my bag and passed it to Jean-Pascal. Again, Laura nudged him, and he spoke for the first time.

"Too much, too much," is all he could muster. Laura sounded a faint tut of her tongue.

I retrieved a fresh bunch of flowers from my bag and passed them to Laura.

"Oh, my goodness, Daniel, they are beautiful! Aren't they beautiful, Jean?" Jean just nodded.

Thinking he wasn't much in the mood for chatting, I focused my attention on Laura.

"Nothing is too much for you. You have been so welcoming."

I followed them over to their extensive patio where the barbecue was already alight. This area matched what I had seen of the rest of their house, at least from the outside. There were huge cracks in the paving stones, and several weeds had poked their way through and spread their leaves to make the best of the weather.

Jean-Pascal averted my attention and pulled out a chair for me to sit down. He spoke for the second time.

"I know this wine and it is very expensive. You must have a lot of money, Daniel?"

Before I could reply, Laura let out a false laugh.

"Don't embarrass our guest, Jean, and fetch three glasses."

He looked as welcome of the reprieve as me and for a moment I wondered if it would be the last I'd see of him that night.

The wine tasted delicious, and the atmosphere became more amiable after Jean-Pascal and I polished it off. Laura said she didn't drink and kept to a glass of tap water. Jean-Pascal volunteered to open another bottle and, although it tasted more like vinegar than wine, it pleased me he appeared to be coming around to my company.

Via Laura's prompts, he steered the conversation onto his farm and the hardships they were facing. They seemed adamant to get the point across. My mind returned to his comment about me being wealthy. He kept goading me with remarks about my swimming pool, the gîte and me not having a 'proper' job. Now and then he would laugh, just about keeping it friendly banter. Although Jean-Pascal relaxed with the wine, there was still an edge to his manner. I wasn't feeling relaxed, but the last thing I wanted was to fall out with my new neighbours.

As if sensing my false laughs at Jean-Pascal's little digs, Laura changed tack.

"Well, I would like to know more about you, Daniel."

Before I could reply, an all too familiar voice interrupted our discussion.

"Wouldn't we all!"

Oh, shit!

We had been so deep in conversation, none of us had heard, or even noticed, Rachel walking up the driveway towards us. She looked so brash, giving the impression of an invited guest. She too carried a bottle of red wine.

Laura shot me a look. I shrugged my shoulders in return.

"Is anybody welcome?" Rachel continued, "or is it a closed party?" She smiled at each of us.

Jean-Pascal stared at his wife who, in response, stared at me. It soon became apparent that I had to talk next. I felt so awkward.

"I, erm, I'm not sure, Rachel, how did you know…?" I looked at Rachel, then at my hosts.

The last thing I expected was for Jean-Pascal to pull out a chair.

"Rachel, sit down please."

Laura looked at him aghast. This wasn't going to plan. Again, I tried to temper the situation.

"Everybody, this is Rachel. Rachel, Jean-Pascal, Laura."

They all nodded at each other. Even Rachel's initial enthusiasm wavered as the tension heightened.

"Rachel is staying in my gîte for two weeks. She goes home next weekend."

The last sentence was deliberate. One, so my hosts knew that she would soon be leaving and two, to gauge Rachel's reaction. She stared at me, cocked her head to one side, and gave me a sarcastic smile.

This time, Laura attempted to diffuse the atmosphere.

"Yes, we knew you had a guest, Daniel."

The comment didn't go unnoticed by me. She then forced a smirk and turned to Rachel.

"Rachel, you are welcome to stay. We are just about to eat."

"Only if you're sure," Rachel replied, a cute little smile appearing on her face, looking directly at me. She could be so cunning.

We ate, at first in silence, all glancing at one another between mouthfuls. The chat from earlier had ceased between the three of us and now the conversation became more stilted.

Typically, Laura tried to lighten the mood.

"So, how do you like Monpazier, Rachel?"

"It's lovely, Lauren," she replied.

"It's Laura, not Lauren," I said, staring directly at Rachel.

"Oh, sorry…" she said, before Laura took over.

"No problem. I know French can be a little difficult for the English sometimes."

Fuck, one-nil to Laura.

Rachel, for the first time I'd noticed, blushed ever so slightly. She saw me smiling.

"Well, your French is much worse than mine, Dan. I can speak the language very well, actually."

Suppressing the urge to tell her to grow up, I remembered where we were and tried to keep it neutral.

"Fair enough, but I'm looking out for lessons. I want to learn the language."

Laura gave Jean-Pascal a look. He didn't look too happy but nodded an approval before staring at the food in front of him.

"Erm, Daniel," Laura looked at me and she reached out and held my arm. I couldn't help but notice Rachel staring at her. Jean-Pascal continued to look at his plate of food.

I shifted in my seat and an embarrassed cough escaped my mouth.

"Yes, Laura?"

"I have, well, I did, in the past, taught French to an English person who moved into the area. It was a few years ago, but because I lived in London…"

Rachel couldn't help herself.

"What? You lived in London? When?"

Laura looked taken aback. Jean-Pascal looked up from his food.

"If it's any of your business, Rachel, when I was twenty, I moved to London to look for work. I stayed maybe four or five years, and my language improved. I taught French privately to wealthy people, so I learned English fairly quickly."

I glared at Rachel and then turned my attention back to Laura.

"So that's why you speak English so well?"

"Yes, well, quite well. I taught Jean-Pascal too, but he could be a rotten student," she replied, looking over at her husband.

Fortunately, he saw the funny side, and he sarcastically grinned in return.

"You are a rotten teacher you mean." He reached out and squeezed Laura's hand.

We all laughed, apart from Rachel. I watched her out of the corner of my eye, dreading what she might do or say if things continued to transpire against her.

Turning back to Laura, I wanted to keep the mood light and Rachel quiet.

"I'll be happy to pay you, Laura. You tell me how much. I would be so grateful."

Laura opened her mouth to reply when Rachel spoke up.

"I could have taught you French. Anybody can teach it, can't they, Laura?"

The atmosphere changed immediately. Jean-Pascal let go of Laura's hand. I knew I had to speak before he did.

"Sorry?" I said, looking directly at her.

"You only had to ask, Dan; I could have taught you. The basics, anyway. I could easily teach you as much as her."

She glanced at Laura and then back at me. My anger began to boil over.

"You go home next week, Rachel. I couldn't learn French in a week. What a stupid thing to suggest."

Jean-Pascal let out a little laugh.

"Yeah, stupid," he added.

Rachel's chair scraped backwards on the patio.

"I'm tired now," she announced, "and I wish to go back to my gîte."

She held out her arm in my direction.

"Dan, will you please escort me?"

For the first time in years, I raised my voice. It caught everybody off guard, including myself.

"No, I won't, Rachel! I'm with my neighbours…"

Without as much as a thank you to her hosts, Rachel turned and stormed off down the drive.

The three of us stared after her, watching her stride back towards the gîte.

The last thing we heard was the slamming of the door.

11

It had been three days since Rachel stormed away from the Allaires' barbecue, and only five days until she went home. Laura and I had decided we would wait until Rachel left before starting with our French lessons. She suggested it would be quieter at my house. Jean-Pascal had looked at her when she proposed that, but she ignored his silent protest. We agreed to start with a one hour lesson and see how it went from there. Laura put all my details into an address book. I hadn't seen anybody use one of those for years. It was black and had those little tabs for each page of the alphabet. I had smiled to myself as she entered my address and phone number.

Since then, I'd kept myself indoors or waited until Rachel's car pulled away before I ventured outdoors. I had been avoiding her at all costs. She could be so highly strung, bordering schizophrenic in her behaviour.

So, on that Tuesday morning I watched until her car was out of sight before I made a move.

I didn't know where she had gone, but I'd seen her

from my kitchen window as she walked to her car and then drove off. It felt safe to walk into town, where I wanted to find my bearings and wander around alone.

I felt slightly better for the fresh air and I headed directly to the Office de Tourisme. My thought process was to pick up some leaflets and add them to the information folder in the gîte. I hoped it would be straightforward.

The tourist office was located in the corner of the main square, the place I'd socialised with both Brad and Rachel. It was the busiest part of town – if I could ever describe it as busy – and centred around four walkways, all contained under medieval archways. It's a stunning piece of architecture and easy to see why it draws in tourists from all around the world.

The office was quiet, just an older couple looking through some books on the far shelf. I gathered my confidence to approach the older woman behind the counter.

"Er, bonjour, madame."

The lady serving looked to be in her late fifties, early sixties even. She was small, tiny. I imagined a large gust of wind sweeping her off her feet. She had grey hair, tied into a bun, sharp features and a pointed nose.

She spoke in broken English.

"'Ello, monsieur. 'Ow can I 'elp you?"

Is it so fucking obvious that I'm in no part French?

The conversation continued in English. Although it pissed me off that she didn't entertain me with one word of French, she came across as most helpful and agreed to get somebody to drop off a load of leaflets directly to my house. It had been exactly what I'd hoped for as I would be able to replenish stock once the guests had used the flyers in the gîte.

Leaving the office, I checked my phone and saw the time had just past twelve o'clock. The temperature was already rising into the high twenties and I noticed a few people were sitting on seats in the bar at the far corner of the square. I ventured across and took the same table I'd met Brad at a couple of weeks before. It faced the open space of the square and looked like the perfect spot for people watching.

"Une bier, s'il vous plaît," I said as the waiter approached. I felt myself redden as a couple of locals looked in my direction.

"Tres bien," replied the waiter.

Got it! He understood me.

"Et allez-vous manger avec nous aujourd'hui?"

What the fuck?

"Do you, I mean, parlez vous anglais?"

"Ah, oui, monsieur. Will you be eating today?"

"Non, merci. Just a bier."

With that, the waiter walked away, smiling to himself. My lessons with Laura couldn't start soon enough.

The beer arrived, and just as before, it hit all the right spots as I took the first gulp.

As I put my drink down on the table, something caught my eye. At the far end of the square, I could swear somebody was looking in my direction. It was difficult to see because they were in the shade, underneath one of the many arches. Sliding my sunglasses onto the top of my head, the person slid further back into the shadows. They must have known I was watching them.

Three or four cyclists rode into the square, past the arch the person was in. By the time they had passed, I couldn't see anybody there anymore. Then, in the opposite corner, somebody dashed out of sight, away from the square. The only thing I could see from such a distance was their shoes. White trainers.

White Converse trainers?

Feeling unnerved, I finished my beer faster than I had initially intended. Again, my moment of peace had gone. I paid the waiter, without attempting French, and started to walk back to my house.

Thoughts echoed around my head. Would Rachel follow me into town? And if so, why?

As I neared home, I could see the gîte in the distance. Shortly after, the pool came into view. Once adjacent, my eyes scanned everywhere for any sign of life.

That's when I spotted her. Lying on a sun lounger, reading a book. If it had been Rachel in town, how could she have possibly got back so fast? Even if she had beat me back, she still had to change or get undressed to lie by the pool? Then I realised, she'd been in her car. Yes, that would have been easy. It would have taken me at least thirty minutes walking back, more than enough time for her to drive back and change.

Fortunately, I had picked up three or four leaflets in the tourist office for my benefit. It would be a perfect excuse to go down to the gîte and place them inside the information folder.

With a momentary glance in her direction, I didn't slow down as I passed her, instead walking straight on towards the gîte.

"Hi, Rachel. I'm going to put these leaflets in the information folder. I just picked them up in town."

"Sure, go ahead. It's unlocked," she replied, somewhat cheerily given our last encounter.

Walking in, I noticed the place was immaculate. Everything packed away in the kitchen, the cushions plumped up on the sofa and there were even fresh flowers in a vase on the table. Putting the leaflets inside the folder, I took one last look round. I didn't know what I was looking for, but curiosity made me continue. As I was leaving and about to close the door, I saw her pair of white Converse trainers. They were just inside the entrance.

My mind raced. Would it be weird to pick them up and feel if they were warm or sweaty? I needed to know if it had been her.

As I started to bend down to inspect the shoes, a shadow formed on the floor, quickly filling the space up to the training shoes. I stood quickly and spun around. Rachel stood inches in front of me.

"Hey, you made me jump," I said, holding my heart as if to exemplify my point.

Fortunately, she didn't seem to have guessed my intentions and her mind was elsewhere. She struggled to find her words.

"Sorry, Dan. Look…"

She looked behind her, as if she'd heard someone approaching. I followed her gaze and, when we were both satisfied nobody was there, she continued.

"Look, I'm so sorry about the other night. I've no idea what came over me. I felt tired, grumpy, women's problems, you know?" She then peered up at me, gooey eyed and innocent.

I remained determined not to give into her.

"It's not me you need to apologise to Rachel, it's the Allaires. You turned up uninvited and then acted incredibly rude. You don't have to live here, I do. What the hell will they think if all my guests act like that?"

"You're right, Dan."

Rachel smiled and took me by surprise by taking my hand in hers. She looked down at them interlocked as she spoke. I've no idea why I didn't immediately force her to let go.

"I will go into town tomorrow, buy some flowers and wine and apologise personally. Is that okay with you?"

"That would be nice, Rachel, and also take a weight off my mind. The last thing I need is to fall out with them."

"Okay, consider it done. I will read my book now. Oh, and I've spent the last couple of days working on your new website. It's looking good but I won't show you until I've done the basic layout, okay?"

Still she held onto my hand. I resisted letting go.

"Thanks, Rachel."

She pulled her hand away, stepped closer, and kissed me on the cheek.

"Friends?" she asked.

"Friends," I said, smiling. I just wished she could have always been that normal and pleasant. I reminded myself that she would be leaving at the end of the week.

As I walked back to my house, I noticed a cat asleep on Rachel's car. I'd seen it roaming around the field belonging to Jean-Pascal. Without thinking, I sauntered over. The cat pushed its head up towards me with a cry for affection. When I stroked the cat, it started purring and pushed towards me for even greater attention. I rested my other hand on the car bonnet to keep my balance.

That's when I noticed why the cat was sleeping on Rachel's car. I'd no idea how long she had been back, but the engine gave off enough heat to send any feline into a mid-afternoon catnap.

12

The days were drifting by, each one enveloped by the next. I had so many plans for the house and garden and didn't really know where to start. Maybe Emily could help me once she arrived. She'd always been good at that kind of thing. I secretly couldn't wait to see her again.

As I walked outside onto my terrace that morning, armed with my already traditional coffee and pain au chocolat, I noticed the drop in temperature. For the first time since I'd arrived, some dark clouds lingered overhead. I decided it would be the perfect day to make a start on my new vegetable patch.

The new life had been a dream of mine for the past few years. As an introvert I'd become accustomed to loving my own company. It's nice to have friends, acquaintances even, but I have always been more than happy tootling around, minding my business and keeping myself to myself. My thoughts often wander from the exotic to the inane. France was allowing me the perfect opportunity to refocus and find myself again.

Since losing my last job, Emily, everything, I'd spent my days watching daytime television. So many programmes about giving up on the rat race and doing something different with your life. Every time, it struck a chord and made me realise they were talking directly to me. Now here I was, and I cursed myself for not doing it years before. Could it be my destiny calling?

Rachel snapped me out of my daydream. I muttered obscenities beneath my breath. It was one of those times I craved to be alone.

"Morning, Dan," she said, walking towards me with her laptop already open in her hand. "May I?"

She pointed to the seat next to me.

Reluctantly I agreed. What choice did I have?

"Please, sit down. Can I get you a coffee?"

"No, I'm good thanks. I'm going for a drive around to explore whilst the weather is cooler. Can I just show you the website, you know, what I've done so far? If you like it, I can have it in place by the time I'm due to go on Saturday."

Due to go?

"Sure, let's have a look."

She pulled her chair uncomfortably close again and pushed her laptop in front of me. I had to admit the website looked great. It comprised of just four or five pages, 'home', 'about us', 'contact us', that kind of thing, but she'd done an amazing job in such a short space of time. I couldn't control my enthusiasm.

"Hey, it looks fantastic. So professional. I take it there will be a facility to book direct from the site?"

She nudged me playfully on my arm.

"There will be, Dan. Do you think I'm some kind of amateur?"

Subconsciously, I wilted into my chair.

"Sorry, of course not. Will it be finished by Saturday?"

"I'll try for Saturday, but the booking page will be the most in depth. The site isn't live yet, this is all just in the program where I'm building it. You will need to fill up some pages and add photographs, but I can show you how to do that. I think you should do some Google Ads too, Dan. The site won't feature on page one of search engines for ages, so you need to increase traffic by paying for it."

She knew what she was talking about and I was grateful for the help.

"Good idea, Rachel. Now, don't take offence, but I really want to pay for this."

"Nonsense, I won't have a word of it. Can I just ask that I can use it on my website? It's good to have a portfolio of work."

"Sure you can."

An idea flashed into my head. I knew very little about her work and thought this would be a good opportunity to find out more about Rachel and what she did.

"What's the name of your website?" She noticeably faltered at my question.

"It's erm, down at the moment. I'm doing some maintenance on it."

Rachel looked away, embarrassed by her own response. She'd come across totally unconvincing, an almost childlike reply. What was she hiding?

The silence was broken when Rachel turned back towards me. She spoke as if her previous statement had been something I'd imagined in my head.

"I've had a lovely two weeks, and as tomorrow is my last night, I'd love to cook you a meal in the gîte."

"Thanks, but that won't–"

"Nonsense, Dan. I won't have you saying no."

She stood, closed her laptop, and continued to give me instructions.

"Seven o'clock sharp. Dinner will be served either indoors or on the patio, weather dependant."

What harm can it do?

"And if I say no?"

"Well, you wouldn't want to upset me, would you, Dan?"

With that, she turned, walked down the garden and disappeared into the gîte. I sat staring at the closed door long after she'd gone inside.

It's a good job it was cooler that day because preparing the vegetable bed proved to be a much harder task than I'd initially thought. I'd decided to create it at the far side of the garage, out of sight of any guests in the gîte and the pool. It was a decent size, and I'd marked it out to be within touching distance of the perimeter fence. The border which backs onto the Allaires' sloping field down from their house.

Even though I had the best intentions to provide some of my own food, I had no idea what would grow successfully in the French climate.

As I dug into the earth, I dreamt of buying a small orchard of walnut trees, or olives to produce my own oil. Even a modest vineyard to make my own vintage wine. My thoughts ran away with themselves.

I'd need string, maybe some netting to protect the

young plants from snails and slugs. And then I'd need the plants, of course. I made a mental note that I'd have to find a garden centre. Do they have garden centres? Maybe Brad would know of one nearby. Perhaps I could take Emily to one when she comes over. She would love that, helping me choose plants.

My mind drifted onto Emily.

Why has it taken her so long to get in touch?

Deep down, I knew she wouldn't have wanted this lifestyle. It would have been so slow. Emily liked the city breaks, the twenty-four seven mentality where nothing ever sleeps.

Car tyres on the gravel broke my thoughts. Looking up, I saw Rachel pulling out of the driveway in her hired BMW. She waved her arm out of the window as she pulled off, heading away from town toward Cahors.

Her last words before she left my table this morning burrowed back into my mind.

'You wouldn't want to upset me, would you?'

What on earth had she meant by that? Had she been joking, just teasing me as she already had done frequently?

Or was it some kind of veiled threat?

13

THE NEXT MORNING my back was killing me. I had aches in muscles I didn't even know existed. The vegetable patch had been dug, raked and prepared but I knew I had overdone the exertion.

Why did I do so much yesterday?

The idea of moving here was to take it easy, take my time. There is no rush. Now I was paying for it, and I gingerly climbed out of bed to make my way to luxuriate in the heat of the shower.

I'd also had no luck trying to find a local garden centre online. I promised myself to ask Brad. I couldn't ask the Allaires in case they took offence that I hadn't asked for their help in the first place.

As I dried myself off, I heard my phone ringing. I'd left it on the end of the bed and as I picked it up; I noticed Brad's name on the Caller Id.

"Hi, Brad, how's it going?"

"Good, mate, good. Just a call to see if you fancied

going kayaking during the week. Thought it would be cool. Maybe drive back into town after and grab a beer."

My relationship with Brad was growing stronger, and I had been glad of his call.

"That sounds great. Give me a day or two because I did some gardening yesterday and, quite frankly, I can barely pick up my toothbrush, never mind a paddle."

"You idiot," replied Brad, laughing.

"I know, I know."

A thought entered my mind.

"Brad, why don't you come around here after we've been kayaking? I'd like you to see the place."

Brad seemed reluctant; I didn't understand why.

"Yes, I guess I could. Don't want to put you to any trouble though."

"No trouble at all. There's plenty of beer and wine in, and I'll just stick a couple of pizza's in the oven."

"Okay, fair enough."

He still didn't warm to the plan, but I let it pass. I asked him if he knew of any local garden centres. He recalled seeing one in a nearby town and I wrote down the directions before we said our goodbyes. I promised to call him over the weekend once my back felt better.

I'd rested most of the day. I'd planned on having a swim to help ease my muscles, but unfortunately, I hadn't seen Rachel leave the property all day and her car hadn't moved. I nodded off late afternoon and woke with quite a start just after six o'clock. Feeling very unenthusiastic about my meal with Rachel, I dragged myself upstairs, showered quickly, changed into a blue linen shirt and jeans. Grabbing a bottle of red wine from the rack, I made my way down the garden. Sometimes I'd agree to do things that seemed a good idea at the time, only for the eagerness to evaporate as the actual event approached. This was certainly one of those occasions.

The weather had broken again since I'd had my afternoon nap, and a thick layer of cloud covered the sky. The temperature had also dropped several degrees.

I noticed the table outside the gîte wasn't set up, so I assumed we'd be eating indoors. I involuntarily shivered and suddenly felt very claustrophobic. I took a deep breath and tried to calm my breathing.

Knocking on the door, I was greeted by a stunning looking Rachel, and the aroma from the kitchen smelt simply divine. I'm not sure which one made me want to drool the most.

Rachel had her hair down and curled at the ends. She wore some make-up, but to be honest, she was one of those women who didn't need much at all. She was wearing a white blouse, teasingly undone to show some cleavage, but not at all tarty. Her jeans were tight, showing off her shapely legs and her white sandals completed the sexy, yet elegant look. Rachel was naturally pretty, but even she had exceeded herself that night.

"Come in, Dan, you look great," she said, kissing me on each cheek. I passed her the bottle.

"You too, Rachel. Something smells fantastic," I replied. I attempted to keep the conversation neutral and my testosterone levels under control.

"It's just fresh pasta, some pesto sauce and garlic bread. Nothing too fancy, but all homemade, I might add."

"You didn't have to go to all this trouble."

Stepping inside, I noticed the dining table complete

with new a tablecloth. The place mats looked brand new too. Two scented candles flickered in the centre, completing the scene.

A romantic dinner for two?

A flash of panic crawled under my skin. I couldn't let this get out of hand.

"Where did you get the tablecloth and mats, Rachel?"

"In town. Don't worry, you're not keeping them. I'm taking them home," she giggled.

I wondered if Rachel had had a glass or two of something before I'd arrived. She was in a very chirpy mood.

"Glass of red, or would you prefer a beer, Dan?"

"Red sounds great."

The meal was delicious, and the conversation flowed just as well as the wine. The alcohol allowed me to relax. My best intentions were already under threat and I made a conscious effort to slow down my drinking.

We chatted, we laughed, and we almost cried when she told me more about her past. Her mother had died when Rachel was only seven years old. She'd had a rough upbringing after that. Her dad had taken to drink and eventually she and her older brother, Nathan, had to move out of their family home on recommendations of social care. They moved in with her strict aunt and uncle, with great reluctance from both parties. Her relatives hadn't wanted kids of their own, and it soon became apparent that they didn't want anybody else's kids either. One night, Nathan climbed out of the bedroom window to meet a girl in town. Rachel said he would have been about fifteen at the time. After he had left, her uncle discovered his bedroom window ajar and waited patiently for him to return. Rachel had pleaded with him not to hurt her brother. When Nathan arrived home, he climbed into bed, thinking he'd gotten away with his escapade. However, his uncle switched on the bedroom light and beat him several times with a thick leather belt. He vowed to never let him leave the house again. The next day, her uncle nailed down the sash windows in both Nathan's, and Rachel's bedrooms. Had it not been for school, they wouldn't have left the house again until they were both old enough to go to college or find a job.

Nathan finished school at sixteen and immediately left home, telling his aunt and uncle that he'd secured an apprenticeship down in Dorset. Three weeks later, when Rachel was leaving school, Nathan waited at the gates. He told her to come with him to the train station. She had been scared but followed his lead, completely trusting him and thinking anything would be better than going back home. Once they arrived, he took her down to a small, one bedroom flat in Dorset that he had secured with his first pay packet. She registered at a new, local school. Rachel added something about their landlady knowing somebody who could make it all possible, but I didn't quite understand how. She stayed there until she quit school at sixteen, went to college in Dorchester to do a computer course, and then at eighteen, she had her first job at a local IT consultancy.

"Wow, you've been through so much," I said, inadvertently holding her hand across the table. Rachel wiped away a tear that had escaped and rolled slowly down her cheek.

"Yeah, well, I don't like to talk about it much," she replied, sniffing.

She looked at my hand on hers.

"Thank you, Dan, for being such a great listener. You're such a kind person. Bring the wine over, let's sit on the sofa."

Rachel was already walking over to the lounge area. She moved the cushions from the two-seater sofa and threw them onto the spare chair. It left me no choice of where to sit. After the story of her upbringing, and the amount of wine we'd both drunk, I felt pleased I had to sit next to her anyway. Rachel was obviously very vulnerable. We had that much in common at least.

As I sat, I groaned as my back creaked into a new position.

Rachel looked concerned.

"What's wrong?"

"Oh, it's my back, my shoulders, my arms, my legs," I laughed. "I think I kind of overdid it in the garden yesterday."

"Come here," she said.

I sat on the edge of the sofa as instructed. She sat cross-legged behind me and began to massage my shoulders. Her fingers and thumbs worked in a circular motion. It felt so good, and I let out a slight moan.

"If you want me to do this properly," she whispered, "you'll have to take your shirt off."

With the combination of the drink, the conversation, and the feeling of Rachel's hands working their magic, I didn't hesitate to undo my buttons. As I went to pull my arms through, Rachel stopped me.

"Allow me," she whispered in my ear, and she slowly slid my arms out of the shirt, lifted it off my back and dropped it to the floor.

"Hmmm," I heard her say beneath her breath.

She massaged my back all over, then my shoulders again before standing and walking in front of me.

Undoing her blouse, she let it drop to the floor.

I knew I should have stopped her, but I was caught in the moment. It had been a long time since I'd been with a woman and her story had resonated with me. We had both been through so much.

Rachel unhooked her bra, sliding the straps down her arms and, again, dropped it to the floor. She took my hand, lifted me off the sofa, put my hand on her breast and kissed me. It was a breathtaking, deep, sensual kiss.

What was I doing? Knowing it was wrong, I still couldn't stop myself. Rachel was good, way out of my league and it had been so long since I had felt this way. Her body looked amazing, and that kiss.

Her hand reached down, undid my jeans and slid inside. She smiled and whispered in my ear.

"Fuck me, Daniel."

As she led me to the bedroom, I put up no resistance. Convincing myself that it was the right thing to do, I obliged and followed her upstairs.

14

"Hi, honey."

What? Oh no… where the hell am I… who's that talking to me?

"Guess what?"

Rolling over in a bed with an unfamiliar smell, I attempted to adjust my eyes to the surroundings.

"I've decided to stay."

My head throbbed, and my mouth felt parched. The space I'd rolled onto felt warm, but nobody was there.

What on earth is going on?

My eyes gradually focused, and I saw an outline of somebody standing next to the bed. I smelt coffee; the aroma pouring up my nostrils, feeling sweeter with every inhalation. Adjusting my eyes until they were almost fully open, I made out the figure of Rachel. She stood only feet away. I forced myself to focus. My mind worked overtime, trying to recall what the hell happened here last night.

"What did you say?"

I groaned as I sat up and took the steaming coffee from her hand.

She put her coffee down on the bedside table, undid her dressing gown and revealed her nakedness.

Fuck. Oh no, Dan, you didn't.

I looked underneath the cover. Naked too.

Fuck again.

Rachel climbed into bed and took my coffee from me, leaving me craving for the taste of caffeine. Next, she moved closer and kissed me on my mouth. At first, I began to reciprocate, then common sense kicked in and I pulled myself away. Her hand was already under the cover, touching, feeling.

"No!" I exclaimed, pushing her aside.

She looked alarmed at first, before a smile returned to her face.

I desperately tried to recall everything that happened last night. Then I suddenly remembered what she'd just said as I awoke.

"What did you say, Rachel, you know, just now?"

"I said I've decided to stay."

She still tried to kiss me.

"Last night was amazing, Dan. We are meant for each other."

"Whoa, hang on, Rachel."

I pulled the cover up over my chest. Stupid given the circumstances; we'd spent the last few hours in naked bliss next to each other.

"What do you mean? You're due to leave today. I need to clean the gîte, get it ready for the next guests."

"You don't have any 'next guests', Dan. Remember, I've been working on your website."

Her fingers tried to pull the cover down my chest as she spoke. I gripped even tighter.

"As part of the booking page you asked me to complete, I needed to cross reference to the sites you have the gîte up for rent."

This was getting out of hand. I was in a state of shock trying to take it all in.

She hadn't finished and added, rather ominously, "You have *no* other bookings at all."

"How did you get into those other websites? I've never given you my usernames or passwords."

I became more anxious and irritated in equal measure. I pulled the covers tight to my chin.

"Oh, come, Dan. It didn't take much to work out you're not very computer savvy. You're a prime candidate for using the same username and password for every website you visit."

"That's out-of-order, Rachel. You have no right–" but Rachel put her fingers to my lips.

"Shh, Dan. Don't ruin a great night. This is supposed to be good news. You now have extra money coming in and we can see each other for a while longer."

She may well have been right about the money, but she was definitely wrong about 'us' becoming any kind of item. I tried to control my emotions.

Think, Dan, think.

There was no way I could tell her I'd made a massive mistake, not within minutes of waking up next to her, but I also knew I had to put a stop to this immediately.

"We need to talk, Rachel, but not now. Let's both calm down and reflect on this later. We both had a lot to drink last night."

Her face dropped, and she climbed out of bed. I'm sure I heard a snuffle as she walked to the bathroom.

"We'll talk, soon, okay?" I said.

No reply.

You fucking idiot, Dan.

I lay in bed, cursing myself over and over.

It was now three weeks since I'd moved in. What happened the night before had left my plans in disarray. Back in my house, sitting in my lounge, I felt almost too afraid to leave my own front door. It had been difficult saying goodbye to Rachel earlier that morning. The atmosphere had been fraught with emotion and she seemed genuinely shocked that I wasn't pleased with her staying. What on earth had I done? However attractive she was, there was something about her that scared me. She could go from being the nicest person you'd ever wish to meet to a conniving little shit at the snap of a finger. On top of that, Rachel had said she'd booked herself in, using the fucking online system I had asked her to develop for me.

I remained on my sofa for what felt like hours. I periodically made myself a fresh coffee, but otherwise I just sat there, staring into space. My mind drifted to my ex-fiancée. Emily was due over in a couple of weeks, and it still intrigued me; why her sudden interest to contact me again? She had been my best friend and there were still days when I missed her terribly. Could she be looking for reconciliation? I was sure it was what I wanted but one thing was for certain, if Rachel didn't leave before Emily arrived, then any reunion would be very difficult. I cursed myself again.

The two-and-a-half years I'd spent with Emily had been magical – well, the first two were magical until I lost my job. I never really knew what 'falling in love' felt like until we started going out. We grew up in the same town, went to the same schools, and would even attend many of the same house parties together in our late teens. However, it would be almost two decades later when we got together. We were both approaching forty at the time and both had been in relationships before, but nothing like this.

Emily said the same, that she'd never known a feeling like it. 'Like butterflies dancing in her belly' she had put it. Kissing her felt like all my fantasies coming together at once. Her lips so soft it made me melt into submission within seconds every time. We also got on so well, had so much in common. From politics to travel. The only thing we differed on was our taste in music.

We bought a house together, well, Emily bought a house, and I contributed as much as I could towards my half of the mortgage and bills. She always said it didn't matter, she was career focused, and I wasn't. As long as we were together, who was counting the pennies? But it made me feel uncomfortable. Coming from a background where 'the man earns the money, the woman raises the kids', it was difficult to accept.

As time moved on, it became increasingly obvious that Emily's career was taking over her life. She left the house soon after six o'clock most mornings and returned home around twelve hours later. We would have a meal together – mostly me talking, her looking at her phone – and then, inevitably, she went to her study for a couple more hours on her computer.

Then my company made me redundant. I couldn't

contribute anything, and the final year together became much more of a strain. Sue Wade, the next-door neighbour, would pop round and see if I was okay. She and her husband Mike had a dog which Sue and I would take for long walks. She was a good listener and helped me through the darkest times. One night Emily said that I needed to get out in the real world rather than keep taking a canine out for walks. Fortunately for Emily, we didn't take the dog out anymore after that.

We both knew that our relationship was falling apart. I'd slipped into a deeper depression and rarely stirred from my bed before lunchtime. Emily's work had taken over her life completely and when we spent time together, she seemed preoccupied with what I'd been doing all day. With the neighbours no longer calling round either, it was time for us to separate and see what paths life had in store for us. The saddest thing of all was that deep down we still loved each other.

Deciding that it would be best to never mention the previous night to Emily, I needed to see Rachel to arrange how long she could stay. She hadn't said and, as far as I knew, she hadn't booked an extension to her holiday. It was imperative in my mind that she went before Emily arrived. Nobody else needed to know what happened. Nobody.

Despite my reservations towards her, I had to admit that she'd worked very hard on the new website. I needed to check something.

Picking up my laptop, I typed the website direct into the address bar. The day before I had received the message, 'this website is currently down for maintenance'.

However, this time it loaded up, it was live and working. I started to navigate around, my hands shaking. At the top of the page, next to 'Home' and 'About Us', was 'Book Here'. I clicked on the link, and sure enough, the booking form displayed, along with a live calendar highlighted on the current date.

The next four weeks were shaded grey.

The key, underneath the calendar, said, 'white = available, grey = unavailable'.

15

NEXT MORNING, as I sat on my terrace contemplating how to discuss things with Rachel, I noticed Laura strolling down the hill from her farm. She was walking directly towards my house. Fortunately, Rachel's car wasn't on the driveway, so she must have gone off exploring for the day. At least she wouldn't be watching me and Laura this time.

As she approached, I took in Laura's infectious smile. She almost bounced on her feet, sending ripples throughout her body. But her smile didn't hide the sad look about her. That was maybe in her eyes. I asked myself if life fulfilled her with Jean-Pascal and the farm way of living? I wondered if she'd lived there all her life, apart from the few years she'd spent in London. I doubted she would ever travel again; they seemed so set in their ways. Laura carried a look as though the weight of the world was on her shoulders. Whenever she spoke to me it felt as if there was always something else she wanted to say, but somehow couldn't – or, more to the point, wouldn't.

"Hi, Laura, so nice to see you," I said, pushing my chair back and standing to greet her.

We kissed, but no hug this time.

"Bonjour. You need to speak in French, Daniel, else you'll never learn."

"Yes, you are right."

The smile soon left her face and became replaced with a somewhat serious undertone.

"Erm, Daniel."

"Yes, Laura?"

I looked directly at her, not knowing where this would lead, but having a horrible feeling, nonetheless. Had she seen me leave the gîte early the day before? Did she know I'd stayed over all night?

Oh shit.

"We, you know, myself and Jean-Pascal, we noticed that Rachel's car was still here all day yesterday. We thought she was going home on Saturday?"

Sighing with relief that she hadn't asked what I'd been dreading, I still had to tell her the truth about Rachel wanting to stay. Laura made no secret of not liking Rachel. Even the mention of her name came out as a snarl.

"She told me yesterday that she wanted to stay, maybe for a few more days."

I had no intention of mentioning the month blocked off on my website. I also realised the Allaires were not the people to find out that information for themselves. I began to relax a little. This was none of her business, but I still couldn't take the chance that anybody else knew what had happened.

"I've agreed to her staying a little while longer," I added, a little more confidently.

"I see."

Laura was obviously not happy with the arrangement.

"It is your business, Daniel, but please don't get too close with her. I can smell trouble."

"Hmm, okay, Laura."

Did she know? I felt myself blush.

"Please be careful, Daniel. Look after yourself. And if that girl knows what's good for her, she needs to be careful too."

What on earth does she mean?

That had been the second warning Laura had given me.

She must have noticed me going a deeper shade of red and fortunately she changed the subject.

"Anyway, what I really came to see you about this morning was your French lessons. If Rachel is staying, do you want to start your French lessons, or do you want to put them off indefinitely?"

The emphasis had been on 'indefinitely' – I wasn't comfortable with Laura's insinuations but, then again, I wanted to keep her sweet. I could understand why she'd asked, after all, we had decided to start once Rachel left. But why should Rachel being around stop what I wanted? It would also take my mind off things, get my life back on track. We agreed to go ahead with the lessons.

I also made a conscious decision that I would see Rachel later, tell her she could only stay for a week. I went through what had happened and tried to convince myself I had done nothing wrong. A single female rented my gîte. She had asked me to put sun lotion on her back; a reasonable thing to ask if you're on your own sat around a swimming pool. She then turned up uninvited at my neighbours' barbecue but left soon after not feeling very well. Then she cooked me a meal on her last night, well, supposedly last night. We'd had too much to drink and slept together. Were we the only couple in the world who had ever done that? No way, I'd even done it myself in the past. Somebody, somewhere on the planet was doing exactly the same thing right then. It's normal, heterosexual behaviour. Get a grip, Dan. Congratulate yourself on pulling a very good-looking woman. Now, take her money and let it be one of life's experiences.

After satisfying myself that I could handle the situation, a surge of anxiety hit me as I knocked on Rachel's door. My newfound confidence from earlier began to evaporate like water.

Do I have feelings for this woman? Do I really want her to leave?

I was trying to be strong, although not assuaging my inner doubts. The door sprang open, making me jump.

"Hi, Dan, come in," greeted Rachel.

She was wearing a baggy T-shirt; it was far too big and looked like a man's. She still looked stunning though.

"No, it's okay, really. Just need to clear up how long you're staying."

Rachel appeared taken aback, like a soft punch had landed in her stomach.

"Oh, right? Do we really need to discuss this now?"

"Yes, we do. It's my business, Rachel, not a charity."

The words came out a little stronger than I'd intended. Standing there, I knew I had feelings for Rachel. If it wasn't for the fact that Emily was due to visit, I wondered if I would have acted differently. I found myself saying one thing whilst thinking something different. I tried to keep the conversation friendly and neutral.

"Well, do you have a date in mind, Dan?"

Rachel had already composed herself; she could change like a light switch.

"How about one week, until Saturday?"

"Can I make it two weeks, please, Dan? Pretty please?"

She stroked my arm with her fingertips, sending a shiver down my spine.

"Two, maximum." I realised I'd given in far too quickly, but she was too strong willed for me. I was a fucking walkover for her and we both knew it.

Then I saw my opportunity to gauge her reaction. I knew she would have no idea if I'd visited the new website or not.

"Once the website is complete, you can probably add that to the new booking page? It would be great to put a calendar up, so punters can see when the gîte is available."

For the second time, Rachel had taken another blow, this time a little harder. It immediately put her on the ropes. I could see she was struggling to think on her feet.

"Well, yeah, a good idea."

It had flummoxed her, albeit momentarily. But again, like any good boxer worth their weight, she sprang back up and delivered a punch straight back between my eyes.

"In fact, I've finished the booking page, Dan. I noticed it had two new views from an IP address I didn't recognise last night. I'd been secretly hoping that people who neither of us knew were finding it already."

Shit, she was good.

"And I booked out a month when I tested it. Take a

look when you get back. If you like it, I can just complete the contact page and it's ready to go live."

She smiled, a look of defiance in her eyes, as if to say, 'You'll never beat me, mister.'

"That's great, thanks," I spluttered, but I wasn't done yet. Surprising myself, I composed myself once more. I went for the jugular.

"Two weeks is great, just perfect actually. My ex is coming out to stay two weeks today, on the Sunday. Can I just remind you of the policy that you need to vacate the gîte by ten o'clock on the Saturday morning? That will give me enough time to clean–"

"Your ex?"

Rachel interrupted, again knocked sideways. Regaining her composure, she continued.

"Why is your ex coming? I thought you said this is a business, Dan, not a home for family and friends."

"Actually, that's none of your business, Rachel. Just make sure you vacate on time on the Saturday."

I turned to leave, but I wasn't finished yet. Looking back, I felt a small grin creep up. I wasn't sure where I was finding this confidence from, but I was on a roll.

"Oh, and I'll send an invoice via the agency for the two-week stay. The balance is due immediately."

Maybe my shy and gauche demeanour were evaporating at last. As I started to walk towards my house, I hadn't anticipated that Rachel would deliver the final knockout punch.

"Dan?"

"Yes, Rachel?"

"Does she know you fucked me?"

16

THE NEXT DAY had been a washout. For the first time since I'd arrived the rain was relentless. It hadn't stopped until early evening. I'd spent the morning painting the spare bedroom. It had been my intention to ignore all thoughts of Rachel, but my mind kept doing cartwheels wondering if she would somehow carry out her threat and tell Emily. In the afternoon, I unpacked and put away the rest of my possessions, and had a general tidy up. Brad had phoned later, and we had organised kayaking for the coming Saturday. It was still undecided if he would come back to mine afterwards or if we'd end up in town for food and beers.

I'd arranged my first French lesson with Laura for the Wednesday evening and would subsequently try to keep to one night every week. We decided an hour would be sufficient to begin with. She'd give me some other learning material to do in my own time in between lessons. We had agreed to do them at my house because it was quieter there.

"Jean-Pascal has the TV on loud because he's going deaf after riding around on a tractor all his life," she had laughed. Something didn't sit comfortable though, and her reason hadn't convinced me.

The following day was much brighter. Whilst I stood in the shower, I watched the sun creeping in and out of the clouds through the skylight above.

'What should I do today?' I thought to myself as I dressed and made my way downstairs for my petit déjeuner – I'd spent a couple of hours the night before trying to learn basic French words. One of my favourite sayings, for no clear reason, was petit déjeuner.

Looking at my map, spread out across the outside table, I decided to drive to a village called Villaréal. It was the place Brad had told me had a garden centre. My exertions in digging the vegetable patch could not go to waste, so I needed to buy some plants to get started.

As I took the first left after leaving my house, onto the D2, the sun crept out from behind a cloud. It lit up the hills and trees which spread out as far as the eye could see. I passed Monpazier on my right and soon found myself out in the open countryside.

Cranking up one of my favourite albums on the car audio system, I couldn't help but smile to myself. This was where I lived now, for real. Passing signs for chateaus, campsites and other areas of local interest, the road wound and meandered through woodland and acres of fields filled with different crops. It was one of the prettiest drives I'd ever been on, so much to see. I wished I was in the passenger seat so I could take it all in and I made a mental note to take Emily along the same road when she visited.

My mind drifted to the inane jobs I'd done back in England. Telephone sales, marketing, data entry, driving for a skip hire company and driving a furniture removal van. And now this, taking in some of the most unspoilt countryside I'd ever witnessed. The lack of other cars on the road was another thing I couldn't get used to. I'd been traveling about six or seven miles before I saw any other vehicle at all. I glanced in my rear-view mirror again and spotted a white van approaching, gradually gaining on me.

Keeping my eye on the road ahead and singing along with the music, I hadn't realised the van was right behind me until he sounded his horn. Slowing to let him pass, I became both irritated and eager as to why he refused my offer. The road was straight enough and there wasn't another vehicle in sight.

Slowing down further still, to make my intentions obvious, the van braked sharply behind. The tyres screeched as they gripped the half-baked tarmac. The driver sounded his horn again, this time in a continual blast for several seconds.

What the fuck does he want?

I increased my speed once more. Soon, the van was right on my tail again. Glancing in the rear-view mirror, I could have sworn the driver was smiling but I couldn't make out any other features. He kept faking to overtake me but as soon as I slowed to let him; he braked hard and swung back in behind me. By now, I was driving far too quickly given the fact that I didn't know the road at all. Fortunately, it was a mostly straight thoroughfare, but I had no intention of slowing for the bends either. The van kept up whatever I tried.

The sign for Villaréal was just ahead. The van inched ever closer to my rear. With the slightest touch on my brakes, I could easily have sent him careering into the back of me. For a second I was tempted to do just that, but I soon realised I did not know who I was dealing with here. I also had no idea what their intentions were.

After entering the outskirts of the village, I saw a sign for a roundabout ahead. From memory, this was my turning off to the garden centre. I could feel myself sweating profusely.

Faking to take the second exit, I veered left at the last second and carried on taking the third exit, leading directly to my destination. The van's tyres screeched again as they gripped the surface, and to my amazement, they swerved and switched direction and followed me.

The garden centre was just ahead on the right. I could see the sign and there were rows of compost bags at the gateway. Slowing down, I signalled, giving the van as much notice as possible so he didn't career into the back of me.

What the hell do I do?

I had a split second to decide.

Braking sharply, I yanked the wheel and turned into the centre entrance fearing for anybody in my way. This time, he couldn't react quickly enough and instead, he swerved to miss me and sped on by. His horn blasted in anger until he was out of sight and sound.

Pulling to a halt in the car park, I leant forward on my steering wheel, panting heavily, constantly checking my rear-view mirror for any sign of the van returning. A bead of sweat trickled down my forehead and dripped onto my lap. What on earth was that all about? And, more to the point, who the hell had been driving?

Looking around, I noticed several plants for sale. There were a number of different compost bags, ceramic pots and even some gas cylinders. There were only a couple of other cars, but I couldn't see any actual people. I desperately wanted to see some other form of life, just for reassurance. Still trying to get my breathing back to normal, I turned off my ignition and climbed out of the car. I needed the fresh air, even though it was very warm.

Leaning on the car, filling my lungs with oxygen, I attempted to steady my heartbeat. Then I heard a vehicle approaching. I said a mental prayer, pleading that it wasn't the same white van. I spun to look at the car park entrance.

Shit!

A van signalled to turn into the garden centre. I turned my back on whoever it was and leant on the driver's side door of my car. My hand gripped the handle, ready to get in. The van pulled up right beside me. I could feel the heat from the engine on my back and the smell of burning rubber drifted up my nose.

I stood motionless waiting until the driver got out of the van before making my move.

I pulled on my door handle and slowly opened it. If I acted fast, I could squeeze in, start my ignition, and pull away.

My heart missed a beat when I instantly recognised the driver's voice. He recognised me too.

"Dan!"

Slowly, I turned around. My heart was doing somersaults. Walking around the front of his van was Andy Jackson, the guy who had set up my satellite TV.

"Andy," I replied, hardly audible as I exhaled the full capacity of my lungs in sheer relief.

He stared at me, a genuine expression of concern spreading over his face.

"You okay Dan? You look like you've seen a ghost."

Keeping my car door open, I tried to look casual and leant my elbow on the roof. I glanced at his van, trying to check if it was him who had just chased me. I couldn't be sure and I needed to see the front, the one that had just driven inches from my car boot.

"Well, yeah, I think so. Listen, have you just driven from Monpazier direction?"

I stared directly at him.

"You what, mate?" he replied.

Andy looked genuine. Either I'd got the wrong person or Andy was winding me up.

"Did you just follow me from Monpazier?" I asked, pointing down the road, like it would somehow spark a memory.

"No, not me. I've just come from a job. I've just called here to grab some terracotta pots for a woman who I'm landscaping a garden for. Gotta take the money where you can, eh, Dan?"

I tried to remember exactly what make of van it had been that followed me. It was no use. In my panic to escape, I couldn't recall. They looked the same height and shape, but there were loads of vans like that on the road. They are also mostly the same colour too – white.

It felt good to be out of my car and back on firm ground in my garden. After chatting to Andy in the car park, I had convinced myself that it couldn't have been him.

He'd even agreed to come around and fix some kitchen shelves for me. However, after buying several plants and returning to my car, I could swear I could still smell burning rubber from Andy's tyres. I desperately wanted to look at the front of his van, but he had followed me back to my car, even opening the driver's door for me to get in.

As I lined up my newly bought vegetable plants into rows, I heard the familiar sound of car tyres crunching on the gravel behind me. Standing up to see who it was, my back creaked and I winced in pain. Rachel must have seen and got out of her car and came rushing over.

"Are you okay Dan?" she asked, with a genuine look of concern on her face.

"Yeah, yeah, I'm fine," I replied, placing both hands on the middle of my back and forcing my pelvic region forwards.

"That looks familiar," Rachel smiled, looking directly towards the front of my jeans. I blushed.

"Let me give you a hand, Dan. You will do yourself an injury if you're not careful."

Containing myself, I kept Rachel at bay and said I'd be okay once I started planting and moving my joints. Although she looked genuinely concerned, I was grateful she didn't move any closer and offer further help.

Wishing I could turn back time, I just wanted the days until she left to pass without further drama. A pang of guilt washed over me as she watched me aligning the plants in my newly dug plot. She had paid me for the gîte within an hour of asking on Sunday night. The money would be handy, even if the situation wasn't. However, what she had said about if Emily knew we had slept together was like a dagger through my heart. I hadn't stopped worrying about the implications since.

My back twinged again, and the pain shot through my muscles. Reluctantly, I accepted her offer to help plant up the stock. Lettuce, tomatoes, peppers, courgettes and green beans. By the time we had finished, I'd been grateful for her support. I wanted her to leave as soon as the job was complete, but she sat down at my outside table. It left me no choice.

Grabbing two beers out of the fridge, I joined Rachel on my terrace. She looked delighted, even though she tried to play it down.

"Just this one, Dan. I'm walking into town later to get something to eat. Be great if you'd join me?"

I hesitated.

"Not this time, eh? My back's playing up. Think I'll just crash out on the couch and watch some TV tonight."

Although she looked hurt, she still forced that all engaging smile across her face.

"Sure, Dan," she said, standing to leave and taking a gulp of beer from her bottle.

She licked the beer from her lips, in a slow circular motion. With her free hand, she pulled her T-shirt from behind tight across her chest. She knew she was turning me on.

I sat down quickly, trying to keep my emotions under control and look as uninterested as I could manage. She looked directly into my eyes knowing full well that I wasn't fooling anyone.

"Well, if you change your mind, you know where to find me."

17

"HELLO," she said, waiting patiently for my replies.

"Bonjour."

"Goodbye."

"Au revoir."

"How are you?"

"Wait, hang on–"

"In French, Daniel, en Français, s'il vous plaît."

We both laughed. My first French lesson was hard going, but at least it had been light-hearted on the whole.

I'd also noticed that Laura had made more of an effort with her appearance that night. When I'd opened my door to let her in, she lit up the otherwise gloomy skyline. A steady drizzle had fallen most of the day and I'd been cooped up inside – it was actually nice to see someone. After I took her coat, I noted she looked much younger than the other occasions we had met. Wearing tight jeans, red sandals and a light pink blouse, she had surprised me. Previously she had dressed conservatively and somewhat old-fashioned. That day, she wore make-up. Not gaudy, but subtle, just the right amount for a woman of her age. Somebody who still tried with their appearance. She still had that air of sadness or concern written across her face, though when she smiled, the weight of any burden lifted from her features. However, I noticed that Laura didn't smile that much.

We sat at my dining table, opposite one another. She had prepared some notes and also had cue cards with single words or phrases. One side written in French, and English on the reverse. Whether Laura already had this information from previous teaching exploits, I didn't know. I hoped she hadn't gone to so much trouble just for me. She refused my offer of money, even though she hinted Jean-Pascal wasn't happy about the arrangement at all. She wouldn't expand when I asked what the problem was, but she looked at the door every time she spoke of her husband.

The hour went quickly. We spent more time speaking in English than French, but it had been a good start for me. She was a good teacher, a natural, and I had already gained so much confidence in at least attempting the words and speaking as a French person would.

"Just practise, Daniel. Keep saying the words and phrases out loud, when you're driving, when you're gardening, when you're in the shower…"

Laura blushed and busied herself picking up the cue cards. I suddenly felt uncomfortable too. To ease the situation, I stood and walked into the kitchen. After a few seconds for us both to compose ourselves, I returned with a bottle of wine and two glasses.

"Please join me, just to say thank you?"

Again, she looked at the door as if expecting her husband to have his ear pushed against the other side.

"Just some water for me, Daniel. I don't drink alcohol. Besides, Jean-Pascal will wonder where I am."

Was Laura scared of Jean-Pascal? She seemed afraid to even mention his name, yet on other issues she had a rebellious side which occasionally rose to the surface. Recalling the way they looked at each other when she first suggested teaching me, it came as no surprise that Jean-Pascal wasn't happy with this arrangement.

"Does he not trust you, Laura?" I asked, purposefully turning my back to her to stop her from clamming up. I busied myself uncorking the bottle of red.

She scrambled for words and appeared taken aback by my suggestion.

"Why, of course, silly? We, well, we spend all our time together when he's not out in the fields. It's kind of got to be a, how should I put it…?"

"Routine?" I completed her sentence, turning and offering her a glass of water.

"That's not fair, Daniel. Understand, this is our way of life. We're farmers, not rich farmers and we rely on each other for company. Anything out of the ordinary, like me teaching you French, is just different for us, that's all."

"Yeah, I understand."

I changed tack and steered the conversation away from Jean-Pascal.

"Well, you're a very good teacher, cheers, Laura."

The wine was to die for in France. At home, I drank whatever was on offer in the supermarket. I never paid attention to where it came from or what particular grapes were involved. I'm no connoisseur, I just know what I like and don't like, but almost every bottle I'd had in France had been delicious. "No preservatives," Brad had explained to me when we were last out, "that's why you don't get a hangover." He'd been right, I didn't get a hangover, well, not the 'can't lift my head off the pillow' hangover I'd get at home if I drank more than one bottle. Just another reason for me to pat myself on the back for making the move across the Channel.

"And you're a good student," replied Laura, dabbing the corners of her mouth to remove any residue of the water she'd just sipped.

We finished our drinks, chatting about my new veg patch. Laura said Jean-Pascal would love to help. All I needed to do was ask. She didn't even sound as though she had convinced herself and I knew I wouldn't be bothering her husband with mundane tasks such as weeding my vegetables.

Laura stood to leave. I could see she wanted to say something, but her conscience was telling her otherwise. I couldn't let it go.

"What is it, Laura?"

"It might be nothing, and I don't want you thinking I'm some gossip, Daniel, but…"

"But?"

"Well, yesterday, while you were out."

While you were out? Shit, doesn't anybody miss anything around here?

"Rachel called at our house."

Laura now had my full attention. *What the fuck has she said?* My heartrate increased dramatically.

"She bought me a lovely bouquet, tulips, lupins–"

I interrupted, impatient for the punch line, which was the inevitable conclusion.

"Yes, and?"

Laura glared at me.

"Well, if you'll let me finish, Daniel. She brought Jean-Pascal a bottle of wine, you know, that expensive stuff you brought round to our barbecue?"

I just nodded, needing to know, yet dreading where the conversation was going.

"She apologised for her behaviour, said she had been exhausted and knew she had been out of order."

Praying that Laura had finished, I allowed myself to breathe again.

"Well, that's good, isn't it? I thought she–"

She held up her hand to stop me.

"After I'd accepted her apology and thought she might not be so bad, she said she wanted to ask me something."

Oh fuck, what did she want to ask you?

"She asked how much I know about teaching."

I stared, open-mouthed, as Laura continued.

"I wasn't very pleased with her question or what she might be implying. So, I told her I had over five years' experience in London and another year in France. Do you know what she said, Daniel?"

"I've no idea, Laura."

But please just fucking tell me.

"She said she doesn't want me ripping you off and wasting your time. If I can't teach you any better than a five-year-old, then I shouldn't be doing it at all. She said you had become very good friends and she was only asking because she has your best interests at heart."

Oh fuck, why, Rachel, why?
"Daniel, may I ask you something?"
Oh shit, no.
"Are you sleeping with Rachel?"

18

It had been two days since my first French lesson with Laura, and I was still reeling from her parting question. I'd denied everything. Even though I felt it was nothing to do with her, I nevertheless attempted to worm my way out of it. However, my real anger was directed towards Rachel. Why would she say something like that to Laura? Asking what her teaching skills are like and not wanting me to get ripped off. Just as my personal affairs had nothing to do with Laura, the way I conducted my business had equally nothing to do with Rachel.

The day after my lesson, I had been momentarily distracted when Emily sent me an email. She confirmed her flight into Bordeaux Airport was going ahead on Sunday twenty-third June. She hadn't booked a return flight yet. She also mentioned something along the lines of, 'if she could do some work from here, she might stop a few extra days.' I thought Emily staying in the gîte would be a good idea. It had been a long time since we'd had any kind of contact and I wasn't sure how comfortable we'd be with each other, especially living in each other's pockets. Though secretly, I hoped she would ask to stay in the house with me.

I hadn't seen Rachel for three days. I didn't know where she went off to on the days she wasn't around. Although I was mildly curious where she went, it pleased me in not having to confront her for a while.

By this stage, the whole situation bothered me. I'd hardly slept the previous night, wondering why Rachel was acting as she did. On one hand, she could be very helpful and friendly, albeit a little too friendly. On the other hand, she showed signs of extreme jealousy, like she somehow owned me. Snapping when I told her Emily was coming to stay, storming away from the Allaires barbecue because Laura had offered to teach me French. And then there was the time I could have sworn I saw her watching me in town and when she sarcastically said 'you wouldn't want to upset me' – well, I believed it to be sarcasm. Booking an extra two-week stay without my consent was the icing on the cake, or so I thought. I was just happy she would have left before Emily arrived. Otherwise, I'd be treading on eggshells every time both were in hearing distance of each other. Emily had a feisty side to her too and that would be one confrontation I was pleased would never happen.

That day, Rachel's car was in the driveway and I could see her, sat outside the gîte drinking coffee and reading a book. I still felt angry enough to confront her and ask why she would speak to Laura like she had a few days earlier.

Finishing my coffee, I summoned up enough courage

to get it over and done with. I was still unsure exactly what I would achieve, but it pleased me that I was taking things into my own hands. Getting over that first self-conscious hurdle would be a result.

She turned as I walked past the pool, approaching her.

"Hi, Dan." She noticed that I wasn't in a jovial mood. "Something wrong?"

"Can we talk, Rachel, just for a few minutes?"

"Sure, it's not the website is it? Is it still okay?"

Rachel pulled out a chair for me next to her. I purposefully avoided it and sat down opposite, as far away as possible.

"Laura tells me you went round a few days ago."

She immediately went onto the front foot with her response, confidence dripping from every pore.

"Yes, as you suggested, Dan, if you recall?"

Shit, she is good at this.

My confidence evaporated as her self-assurance came across in waves. I attempted to keep my voice level and firm.

"And if you recall, I suggested taking some flowers round and apologising."

"You mean *exactly* what I did?"

"Oh, I grant you did that much. The idea then was to walk away, say no more. But you couldn't manage that, could you, Rachel?"

I sat back in my chair, relaxing ever so slightly, feeling rather smug. Conversely, Rachel sat forwards in her seat and stared directly at me. She raised her voice, catching me off guard.

"I DID walk away, Dan!"

She looked deadly serious. I began to lose my nerve

and started scratching an imaginary itch on the side of my face.

"What about asking her about her teaching qualifications, or not wanting to rip me off?"

I struggled to recall exactly what Laura had said. As per usual, as soon as I strayed from the script, I became a bumbling wreck. Hopefully, my exterior gave none of this away to Rachel.

"What?!"

She stood up, hands on her hips. Her chair clattered to the ground behind her.

Then she played her ace card.

"Let's ask her, shall we?"

Shit, shit, shit. This wasn't how I'd just played it out in my kitchen only five minutes earlier.

"No. We can't just go marching up there, Rachel."

I turned to look at the farmhouse, as if to remind Rachel where I meant. Something caught my eye. Was there somebody in the Allaires' garden right next to the front door? It was hard to distinguish at the top of the hill. Rachel grabbed my attention.

"Well, who do you believe Dan, me, or her?"

Good point. At that moment in time, I didn't know who or what to believe. The only thing I knew for certain was that the Allaires would be my neighbours for the foreseeable future. They were the people I needed to stay friends with, keep in their good books. This would all blow over once Rachel went home. It was obvious that Laura and Rachel didn't like each other, and it could have been playground tactics, trying to outscore each other. I should have let it go, but something nagged at me and I didn't know what.

My tone became somewhat more neutral for the first time since the conversation began.

"Let's just leave it, Rachel, eh?"

"Ignore her, Dan, she's just jealous of us."

Rachel pulled up her chair and sat back down. She smiled but did not take her glaring eyes off mine. I became more curious.

"Have you told her anything, you know, about us?"

"No, don't worry. Then again, maybe I don't have to."

"What do you mean?" I asked, already dreading the reply.

"Did you just see someone watching us from up there?"

She nodded her head in the exact path to where I thought I had seen someone, just a few moments ago.

"She probably watches all the time," Rachel continued in a mocking tone. She was loving every single minute of the conversation and the direction it had taken.

"Surely not," I replied, turning my head to look up towards the farmhouse. Was Rachel right? Did Laura watch from her house? Did she watch Rachel sit with me on my terrace the day we talked about my website? Did she see me put the suntan lotion on Rachel the day I mowed the lawn? Did she watch us walk towards town that night? Did she, *oh God no*, did she watch us go into the gîte that night and me not appear again until the next morning? Or was this Rachel preying on my insecurity? Teasing me. Suggesting that Laura is the unstable one and Rachel is just a perfectly normal human being who just liked me enough to have a holiday fling?

"You tell me, Dan." I turned back to face her and her friendly, smiling face had returned. She stood to go inside.

"Want to come inside and help me make some lunch?"

At that precise moment, I asked myself why hadn't she got a boyfriend, a husband? She was so bloody good at manipulating me. Surely, she could manipulate any man, at the very least, the gullible men. I was so tempted by her offer.

"Not now, Rachel," I stammered, "I have work to do. Shopping, all the usual stuff."

I was rambling; she knew it.

"Well, once you're finished with your errands, maybe I can tempt you with a drink, or something. I'll be in all night tonight."

Of course I would not go round for a drink, or 'something'. Instead, that evening, I cooked myself a meal. It's something I rarely did, but that night, I just wanted to be alone. I can spend hours, days even, by myself. It's the introvert in me and I'd never seen it as a negative, quite the opposite. I've seen TV programmes of these hermits living up on mountainsides, in small caves, never meeting or speaking to anyone. "That could well be me," I used to say to Emily. She never laughed, just groaned.

My mind drifted back to Laura. Had she made it up as Rachel had implied? Surely not, why would she? Then again, had it been her watching from the farmhouse earlier and, if so, why, what was she looking for? I really didn't want to fall out with Laura. Her teaching was good and the notes and cue cards she'd left after Wednesday's lesson were helpful. They were still scattered all over my coffee table as I ate my meal. I'd already taught myself about ten new words and I was determined to speak as much of the local language as I could. Laura was my best hope for that.

My phone rang, it sounded faint; I must have left it outside on the terrace table. As I opened the door, it was twilight, with the moon illuminating the terrace from up above the Allaires' farmhouse. The phone still rang, but it wasn't where I'd left it. I'm sure it had been where I was sitting earlier, in my usual chair, overlooking the pool and garden. However, it now lay at the far end of the table, somewhere out of reach from my seat. It stopped ringing, a number I didn't recognise. Pressing the button to spring the phone back into life, something else was amiss. The screen lit up on my contacts app, and it was scrolled roughly halfway through the list. I hadn't used my contacts page for ages.

Somebody else must have been outside on my terrace and, whoever it was, they'd been looking through my phone.

19

BRAD HAD PICKED the perfect spot to go kayaking. A small place called Montayral on the River Lot. It was approximately thirty minutes south of where I lived. When we arrived, the instructor gave us our lifejackets and a white plastic barrel, complete with a lid. Apparently, it was to keep our possessions, such as phones and wallets, dry whilst out on the river. After he gave us a smattering of safety advice, a small minibus took me and Brad a few miles upriver. We could then paddle our way back to where we had left the car.

That had been the first thing that struck me. That morning, Brad had phoned, asking me to drive. He also didn't give his address but opted for me to pick him up outside the *mairie*, town hall, in Monpazier centre. He took it for granted that I wouldn't object to driving and that I wouldn't ask questions. He was right on both counts, but it still made me wonder about all the secrecy. As soon as I could pick up the courage, I promised myself to ask him where he lived once and for all. I also found it strange that I'd never seen his car, even though we'd met up a few times by then.

Once our instructor had given us our final directions – there wasn't much to it to be fair; point your canoe in the right direction, paddle when you need to, although the river will carry you along anyway, count the bridges because, after the third one, you will see your mooring on the left which is where your trip will end – we were on our way.

As soon as I'd worked out how to paddle, stay straight, turn to the right or left, I began to relax and take in our surroundings. We were deep in a valley, with both banks covered in trees, stretching up for what seemed an eternity on either side. The sun shone alone in a cloudless, azure blue sky, and beat down relentlessly on the river below. Fortunately, I'd remembered my wide brimmed hat which protected my neck as well as my head and face. Brad's long thick hair acted as good as any deterrent against the strong midday rays.

It was just what I'd needed, a day away from everything. My mobile phone being scrolled through had played on my mind all night. The combination of somebody looking at my contacts and having the audacity to do it on my doorstep had made my hair stand on end. The van chase, Laura's questions, Brad's obscurity and Rachel's jealous interludes all added to my woes. France was supposed to be stress free, yet incidents were transpiring against me. I tried to push all negative thoughts to the back of my mind.

We paddled side by side, acknowledging families on the riverbanks, picnic blankets unfurled as the children splashed in the water of the small naturally made inlets. It felt idyllic, at one with nature. Brad broke the silence, as we passed two younger women swimming and laughing as they fought over a huge inflatable tyre.

"Wouldn't mind either of them trying to mount me," Brad laughed, unable to take his eyes off them.

"Like you would stand a chance," I replied.

"Hark at Casanova here." And with that, he brought his paddle flat down in the water right next to my canoe, drenching my T-shirt.

"Fuck off!" I shouted, immediately apologising silently to any families who might have been within earshot. Fortunately, nobody heard, as far as I could tell.

Brad contained his laughter and soon paddled up alongside me again.

"Talking of Casanova," he continued, "how are you getting on with that Rachel bird?"

Something inside me wanted to tell Brad everything, but then something else niggled away at me. I felt unsure if I could trust him. He seemed a good guy, a bloke's bloke is the way I'd describe him. Liked his women, liked his beer. However, a tiny shred of aggravation burrowed into my brain with Brad. He was forever talking about Rachel and asking how I was 'getting on' with her. I wasn't sure he would accept the truth, anyway. He definitely seemed keen on her. I also had no idea what he did for a living, where he lived or how long he'd been in France. So many unknown quantities, yet he would chat to me about anything else. Deciding not to tell him anything about our night together, or her jealous mood swings, I still wanted to ask somebody about her staying an extra two weeks.

"There is something, Brad–"

"You're shagging her," he interrupted.

Did he know something? It was almost as if he knew

yet wanted me to let the secret escape rather than admit anything himself. It annoyed me.

As I was about to reply, something caught my eye in the trees, high on the riverbank. It was difficult to make out as the woods were dense, but I'm sure somebody was there, watching. Yes! Somebody was there, and they started to walk parallel with our canoes, zigzagging between the trees. Suddenly, they stopped, possibly unable to walk any further in the undergrowth; a motionless figure left behind in the shadows. I turned my head as we continued downstream but soon the silhouette disappeared altogether. Brad snapped me out of my trance, unaware of what I'd been staring at.

"Well? Are you shagging her?"

He was laughing. I put whoever had been watching to the back of my mind and concentrated on getting Brad off my back with his endless teasing.

"Just listen, will you? She is going home a week today…" suddenly something hit me.

"How do you know she is still here, Brad? She was due to go home last weekend and we haven't spoken since, well, since we arranged this day out."

Brad's smile immediately dropped. He looked down at his right paddle drifting on top of the water, away from my eyes. It appeared as though his mouth was moving, as if thinking aloud to himself, running an excuse through his mind to check its plausibility. After a few moments he turned back to me, determination and a hint of anger written across his face.

"You never told me she was due to go home, Dan. How the hell should I know what dates she's booked with you?"

Was he right? Had I not mentioned to him when she

would be leaving or that she'd decided to stay on an extra fortnight? Feeling foolish, I tried to steer the conversation back onto my original track.

"Sorry, mate, I was sure I'd told you."

Fortunately, Brad relented.

"You're losing the plot, Dan," he quipped. "Anyway, what were you going to say about her going home next Saturday?"

"I think I am losing the plot. I'd better fill you in…" and I told Brad about Rachel deciding to book an extra fortnight on the day she was supposed to leave.

"So now you think she might book another two weeks next Saturday, then another two, then…"

"I've no idea, Brad," I interrupted him, dreading the thought he might be right. I hadn't even considered that.

"What I do know is that my ex-girlfriend is due out a week tomorrow, the day after Rachel's booking ends. I'm just worried that Rachel might do exactly as you suggest, Brad."

"Look, mate, and tell me if it's none of my business, but Rachel is a paying guest. I'm assuming you'll let your ex stay for nothing?" I nodded. "Well then, it's a business you're supposed to be running, not a home for family and friends."

Wait! Have I heard that before? 'Not a home for family and friends.' Isn't that exactly what Rachel had said when I told her Emily was coming over?

My response came out a little more aggressive than I'd intended, but my mind was all over the place.

"It's my business though, Brad, and I'll run it how I want to."

Brad's previous comment still played havoc with my thoughts. *Does he* know *Rachel?*

"Hey, sure. It's your business. However, you said the first time we met, you remember, in the café in Monpazier? You said you needed to let the gîte out to pay towards your bills, pretty sharpish if I recall correctly. If you run a holiday let, I don't think you can pick and choose who you allow to stay. You'll be making potential punters fill in an online questionnaire next, asking if they're likely to extend their stay because you like people to stick to their original plans."

Although I would not admit it, Brad was correct. I had told him I needed paying guests when we'd first met. I also couldn't run a holiday letting business and vet every guest who enquired or booked a visit. Rachel staying would be two more weeks pay. It was just the thought of her being around whilst Emily was here that kept nagging at me. Emily could easily stay in the house, in fact, she should anyway. The gîte was for renting and Emily would be staying for nothing.

"Fair point, Brad but, between you and me, there's something about Rachel that I don't like, and I don't want her staying any longer than necessary. It's my choice and if she doesn't leave by this time next week, then I'll bloody well make her."

I caught a look on Brad's face. He suddenly paddled faster, visibly not impressed with my reply. He kept himself a good few lengths in front of me.

I couldn't quite decipher if it had been a look of anger or a look of disappointment? Maybe both.

20

THE NIGHT BEFORE, I had dropped Brad off outside the *mairie*, after we'd finished kayaking. We'd had a couple of beers at a small bar we noticed on the way home. Despite the earlier conversation surrounding Rachel, the rest of the day had gone off really well, and I felt I was forming a strong friendship with Brad. Although he wouldn't let me drop him off at home, he agreed to come around to my house on the following Tuesday afternoon. He even suggested going for a swim in my pool. I needed to find out more about his background, especially if we were to become good friends going forward. His insistence around Rachel was something I only had to put up with for a few more days. I didn't mention the person in the woods watching us – watching me – as I knew he would only have taken the piss. Who could it have been? It was maybe somebody out walking, and they just happened to be watching the river and not me at all. I brushed it aside thinking Brad would have been right if he had indeed taken the piss out of me.

After dropping Brad off, I'd decided it would be best to book at least a week in the gîte for Emily's stay. Not only would it give me the opportunity to test my website but also to warn Rachel off that she couldn't block book any further weeks beyond that Saturday.

Just as I began to settle down outside with my laptop, Jean-Pascal waved to get my attention. He was on a quad bike and had stopped next to our perimeter fence. The quad bike had a small trailer attached, full of cut wood. No doubt for storage before winter for use throughout the cold months. Despite always looking haggard, he managed to muster a modest grin. It exaggerated the deep lines around his eyes following years of working outside in the relentless sun.

As he strolled over, I noticed a slight limp in his right leg and a grimace every time he set his foot down. Despite the fine weather – it must have been approaching the mid-twenties – Jean-Pascal was wearing a thick dark green jumper, heavyset jeans and big brown boots. Both boots were sporting a small hole in the big toe area.

"'Ello, Daniel," he said, with no enthusiasm. He'd almost reached the table. I offered my hand which he declined.

"No, my hands are too dirty for your office work," he smiled, glancing down at my laptop.

"Can I get you a drink, Jean-Pascal?"

"Ah, non merci. I came to offer my 'elp."

He was already looking over to where my new vegetable patch was.

"Laura thought it would be a good idea if I offered to spread some of my, what is the word, *natural* fertiliser over your new vegetables?"

"Do you mean 'organic'?" I replied. "What's in it?"

"It's my compost. I 'ave so much. It's just broken down from grass and leaves and anything else I throw in. Makes our vegetables and flowers grow quick."

It sounded ideal although it disappointed me, he had said it had been Laura's idea and not his own.

"That would be great, but only if you have enough?"

"Ah, we 'ave enough."

With that, he turned to walk back to his quad bike. It hadn't been the friendliest of visits and I couldn't help but think he'd come under sufferance.

"Thank you, Jean-Pascal," I shouted after him. He waved his hand disconsolately over his shoulder.

"Let me take my logs up to the storage. I'll load my trailer and come back down."

As he drove away, I lifted my laptop lid to bring it to life. Thinking back to my conversation outside the gîte with Rachel, I tried to recall the outline or stature of whoever had been watching us from the farmhouse. Jean-Pascal was a heavy-framed, huge, broad-shouldered guy. It didn't seem likely that it could have been him. That only left Laura, but why?

The sound of new emails arriving turned my attention back to my original task. The usual mix of spam and newsletters I'd subscribed to over the years started to fill my inbox. Then one from an address I now recognised, the booking agency I had the gîte online with.

Congratulations!

You have a new booking!

Dates: Saturday 5th July to Saturday 12th July inclusive

Contact: Mr Eric Fleetwood

Tel Number:
Email: eric_fleetwood47@freewave.com
Special Requests: None

Quelling the desire to stand up and do a little dance, I double-checked the dates. Launching the calendar app on my phone, I checked to see exactly when the booking was for. Only three weeks away, great news. It was just under two weeks after Emily was arriving, but I guessed she would have left by then because of her business commitments.

In my excitement, I almost missed the final email. This time addressed personally to me and not via the agency. It took a couple of read throughs, but I soon realised it was another booking. It had come directly from my new website. Dated next year, April time, so I assumed around Easter. Immediately I checked my website, scrolled through the months until next April, and sure enough, there it was, seven days greyed out. I tried to book the same week myself, but it presented me with a very courteous message informing me 'my chosen dates were not available, please check again'. I then needed to update the site to include the first booking next month so nobody else could double up.

My enthusiasm was short lived. As soon as I launched my website in administrator mode, I realised I did not understand how to block pre-booked dates to make them unavailable.

Shit, I must ask Rachel.

. . .

Jean-Pascal arrived about twenty minutes later. I was just about to set off towards the gîte. He had driven around the road and come in via my main driveway to get the quad bike and trailer up to my veg patch.

"Do you need my help?" I enquired, stopping in my stride.

"Non, non, you go, Daniel. This will take me ten minutes."

Leaving him to it, I walked on towards the gîte. Jean-Pascal would be my excuse not to stay and talk to Rachel.

As I approached, the door swung open and Rachel stood waiting. She must have seen me through the side window. She had a robe on, and her hair was tied in a towel.

"Oh, sorry, Rachel, bad timing" I said, already turning on my heels. I kicked myself as I knew what would follow.

"Nonsense, Dan, come in. I'm just out of the shower."

She gave me that all too familiar smile as she untied the towel and let her hair escape. Instantly, she tilted her head to one side and scrubbed her head to dry it quickly and stop any water dripping. I had to admit to myself, even straight out of a shower, Rachel looked fantastic.

"Why the laptop, Dan?"

She had already dragged out a chair at the table, beckoning me to take a seat.

Reluctantly I sat down. Rachel pulled up a chair right next to me. Her dressing gown left open far enough for me to see inside, leaving very little to the imagination. She noticed me looking and hunched herself a little closer. She smiled as she spoke. I tried my best to compose myself and to get the conversation over and done with as soon as possible.

"Well, good news and bad news."

"Go on, Dan," she teased.

I purposefully trained my eyes directly onto the laptop screen.

"Well, the good news..."

Something stopped me in my tracks. My subconscious fear immediately drew my attention back to Rachel. She was looking directly into my eyes, showing no interest in what was on my screen, or what I was talking about. Her hand touched my knee.

"...the good news is..." I was floundering for words.

Just fucking concentrate and get out of here, Dan.

"...the good news is, I've had a booking on my new website and–"

She interrupted.

"Do you mean *our* new website, Dan?"

There was another one of her small connotations which planted a little seed in my mind. Deciding not to quibble, I carried on babbling.

"Yes, well, there's another new booking via the agency too, it's, erm, for August."

I tried to think on my feet. I didn't want Rachel to know the booking was in three weeks' time and I also didn't want her to know that I would add Emily's stay. All I wanted was for Rachel to show me how to bloody do it and I could get out of there.

"And the bad news is that I don't know how to show a booking as taken on my, sorry, *our* website..." I smiled, trying to keep it as sociable as I could.

"That's easy, Dan."

She took control of the laptop and showed me how to

bring up a calendar plugin which she had installed during developing the site. She selected some random dates, highlighted them and marked as 'unavailable'. She then removed the dates, and they immediately changed back to 'available'.

Shit, that really is easy, I thought, now planning my escape.

"Thanks, Rachel, can't believe I didn't work that out for myself."

I was already closing the laptop lid.

"That's why I'm here, Dan, always willing to help you."

I noticed her hand perched on the belt of her robe. I felt myself blush, and I quickly stood to leave. Fortunately, I saw Jean-Pascal's quad bike in view outside the window. He must be round the back dealing with the vegetables. It was the perfect excuse to get out of there.

"I know, and I'm very grateful, Rachel." I nodded out of the window in the quad bike's direction, "and I'd love to stay but I have Jean-Pascal round helping me with my garden. I promised I would be straight back to show him what I need doing."

Rachel followed my line of vision out of the window and her expression immediately changed from flirting fun to an exasperated disappointment. It was becoming obvious by now that Rachel could well be falling for me. I didn't understand why, though. She was far too good looking. Could she be after something else?

"Okay, go, Dan. It's important you stay good friends."

The sarcasm in her voice rose to the surface. It annoyed me.

"Yes, it is *very* important, Rachel," I replied. "Now, I must go and help."

Kissing her on the cheek as I left – I really wanted to keep her sweet for the last few days of her stay – she returned it with a peck on my lips.

"You go and help, Dan, it's great you have nice neighbours."

She smiled, but again, it reeked with derision.

"Thanks," I replied, trying to keep it impartial, and I left the gîte.

As I walked back towards my house and Jean-Pascal, I felt her eyes burning into the back of my head. I had no intention of giving Rachel the satisfaction of turning around to look.

21

THE NEXT MORNING, I awoke with new vigour. The news of my new bookings for the gîte buoyed me. I was determined to focus on the positives of my new life in France. I couldn't allow the actions of an infatuated woman, staying for a few weeks in my gîte, to temper my ambitions.

After breakfast, I inspected the work Jean-Pascal had done on my vegetable patch. To be honest, he'd made a fine job of it, distributing the mulch type fertiliser, filling areas around all the plants. Even if it didn't work, it looked good. I felt fortunate to have neighbours willing to help, even if Laura had been behind the latest offer. I'd half expected the compost to be thrown all over the place in defiance, but no, Jean-Pascal had carried out the job as though it were his own plot.

Walking back to my house, I started doing mental calculations in my head. The gîte would give me sufficient income to live off if occupied forty or fifty percent of the year. Would that be enough, or did I need more? I didn't move to France for the money. It was the freedom, the escape of the nine to five routine plus the memories I needed to leave behind. However, a project would be nice, something I could dip in and out of whenever the urge took me. Something that one day might earn me more money. I locked up the house and made my way to the car.

Taking a left out of my driveway, I plugged my phone into the USB port and cranked up the music. Looking in my rear-view mirror, I noticed I was smiling from ear to ear. It had been a long time since I'd felt that way. Was I finally living the dream?

I had no idea where I was or where I was heading. Deep wooded territory replaced the open fields. Trees engulfed both sides of the road, casting giant shadows across the surface. Small clearings in the woods often caught my eye. What could they possibly be for?

Approaching another lovely looking village by the name of Frayssinet-le-Gélat, there was a little church on my right, and I noticed a small bar across the road as I took the next turning. I guessed I must have been driving on some kind of huge loop, which would eventually take me back home. My satnav was in the glove compartment if I needed help, but I was just enjoying the freedom and watching the countryside whizz by. Passing a small cemetery on the left, I found myself back out on the open road admiring the stunning scenery which greeted me at every turn. The twists and turns of the D673 kept my speed down. It was because I was driving so conservatively that I noticed a sign on my right. It pointed down a narrow lane, barely wide enough for two cars. The sign said 'À vendre' – for sale – and it fuelled my imagination.

Finding a safe place to turn around, I made my way

back and turned left into the lane. Roughly two hundred yards along the lane, I saw exactly what I'd been looking for. A cute little house, complete in the buff colour brickwork which attracted me to so many properties in the area. It looked empty, so I pulled my car to a halt outside. Turning off the engine, I got out for a closer inspection. As I stepped onto the tarmac, I heard another vehicle, not too far away, maybe passing on the main road.

The house was just like the ones you drew as a child. Door in the middle, two windows either side downstairs and two identical windows above. There were blue shutters on each one, all of which had seen much better days. Both downstairs were hanging from their hinges whilst upstairs they were still intact yet in a state of ill repair. All four would need stripping back, repainting, and attaching back to new brackets.

A job even you could do, Dan. My mind began to run away with me.

Peering through the front windows, one at a time, I could see a living room on one side and the kitchen on the other. It looked as though it just needed cosmetic touches. Paint, maybe some new kitchen units, new floorboards, unless the existing ones could be sanded and saved. Stepping back, I heard another car on the main road. Glancing up, I couldn't see anything. Ignoring it, I walked to the rear of the property for further inspection.

The back of the house was even more impressive than the front. A good-sized garden – it would be described as 'huge' back in England – laid mainly to lawn but with fruit trees surrounding the borders. A thick forest encroached almost to the end of the plot and provided a natural border on two sides. A small greenhouse sat at the far end next to a large garden shed. Both looked as though a good storm would be the final day of reckoning.

As I peered through one of the back windows, I heard a car approaching. It sounded as though it had just turned down the lane and was driving towards me. I would tell them I was just having a look around if they stopped to ask.

My mind was going crazy with excitement and ideas. Could this be a property that I could refurbish over time and then rent out? It was the perfect holiday escape, no neighbours, pure tranquillity. Walking towards the centre of the garden I imagined a pool, surrounded by decking, sun loungers, and maybe a covered pergola attached to the back of the house. Walking further, I inspected the fruit trees. What were they? I'm not any kind of expert. They could even be walnut trees for all I knew, as I understood there were a lot in the Dordogne. I took some photographs on my phone so I could check online later.

As I turned back round to inspect the roof, I could hear the car outside the front – it was stationary. The engine carried on ticking over as I heard a door open, then quietly close. Slowly, I walked sideways to see who it was. I noticed somebody strain their neck to peer around the property. Somebody wearing a hat, maybe a baseball cap. They were some distance away from me, and it was impossible to make out any features. I cautiously took another step forward when my visitor suddenly sprang back out of sight. They must have seen me. Whoever it was, they immediately started running. The next thing I heard was the car door opening, slamming shut, the car tyres squealing and the vehicle speeding off.

Jumping to life, I sprinted up the garden, safe knowing that whoever it was had fled and was no longer a danger to me. Just as I turned the corner and reached the front of the property, I saw the car. It was turning right, at the end of the lane, back onto the D673. Although it was almost out of view, I instantly recognised the purple Peugeot – the same vehicle that I'd seen driving slowly past my house the day I arrived in France and again a week later. I decided to give chase.

I pushed my accelerator as hard to the floor as I could. I needed to know who it was. I also needed to know why they were spending so much of their time concerned with my business.

I soon spotted it in the distance. It was only a small Peugeot, but the driver must have been pushing it to the limit. As I turned the next bend, I lost them again, but by the next corner, it came back into view. They must have spotted me as they were slowly eluding me, the distance between us growing by the second. I continued to chase, just hoping to get close enough to read the number plate. It was futile. The purple car was now a small dot, pulling further and further away.

My heart was still racing when I arrived back home. Without thinking, I drove straight round to my neighbours and up their driveway. Fortunately, both Jean-Pascal and Laura sat at the outside table.

The Allaires stood up as I got out of my car and jogged over to them. Laura looked at her husband and then back towards me. Jean-Pascal didn't move. He also didn't look very pleased that I'd taken it upon myself to drive directly to their house. Laura spoke before I could say anything.

"What on earth is the matter, Daniel?"

I spoke whilst trying to catch my breath. I noticed I was shaking slightly too.

"Sorry to impose on you, but I've just had an encounter whilst out driving."

Laura pointed to the seat next to her.

"Sit down, keep calm, Daniel. You look very pale, doesn't he, Jean?"

Jean-Pascal ignored his wife's question.

"What is this 'encounter'?" Jean-Pascal enquired.

I couldn't be certain, but for a fleeting moment I'm sure there was a slight grin on his face.

"Do you know the owner of a Peugeot car, a small one. It's purple?" I blurted out.

"Purple? What is 'purple'?"

"Violet, colour." Laura answered Jean-Pascal's question with a tut.

"Well, let me see." He considered his reply.

"No, I don't think so." He looked at his wife. "Do you?"

Laura responded almost instantaneously. A little too quick maybe.

"No, not at all. Why?"

I began to feel ill at ease. I didn't sense they were taking me seriously. I couldn't leave it there, so I told them the rest.

"Well, I've seen it a few times, driving past my house. The night I first arrived, another time and then again now. I was out for a drive and stopped to look at something…"

I told them I'd spotted a house for sale and was inquisitive about what it was. I didn't want to let on that I might be considering acquiring another house; I thought it would come across as bragging. Jean-Pascal had never been overly impressed with me buying one house in France, let alone another. I informed them exactly where it was in case that may help them recall who was the owner of the car. Laura nodded that she knew which house I was talking about.

"I erm, I have a friend back in England who might be interested in buying a holiday home. So, I stopped my car along the lane to have a closer look. Then, this Peugeot slowed right down, stopped even. The driver looked at me, then when I looked back, he sped off. I chased him but soon lost him."

It wasn't the whole truth, and I knew it had sounded like a pack of lies as soon as the words left my lips.

Jean-Pascal was quick to ask.

"Did you recognise him, the driver?"

"No, he was too far away. He had a baseball cap on or something similar. I didn't see his face at all."

"How do you know it was a 'he' then?"

Laura took me by surprise. All these questions made me doubt my story.

"I'm sure it was."

They looked at each other and then back at me. Neither would say anything, so I spoke again, this time a little more brash.

"I just hoped one of you knew the car. You know most things going on around here."

"Sorry, Daniel," replied Jean-Pascal. He looked at his wife again. I'm certain he winked at her. What was going on?

Before I could say anything, Jean-Pascal completely changed the subject.

"Anyway, how did you like the vegetable patch? You

had better be quick. I'll be having them for myself once they're ready to eat."

It was difficult to decipher if he was being serious or not. Laura tried to lighten the mood.

"Ignore him, Daniel." She shot her husband a look.

"Ah, oui, only joking." But still no smile.

Laura went off at a tangent again. My head bounced between them akin to watching a tennis match.

"Are you enjoying life here, Daniel?"

What a strange question.

"Yes, it's great thanks. Why do you ask?"

"Oh, nothing, you just seem down, you know, a bit worried, preoccupied with everything."

This wasn't how I'd planned for the conversation to go once I'd reached the Allaires. I'd expected help or at least sympathy. Instead, I was getting the third degree. I felt guilt shifting onto my own shoulders.

This is crazy, Dan. Make your excuses and get away.

I started walking backwards towards my car, making it quite clear that the conversation had gone as far as I'd wanted it to.

"I'm okay, honestly. Just a bit shook up, that's all."

She wasn't about to let it go.

"What, with that Rachel girl in your gîte and now this car episode. Are you sure everything is okay?"

22

It had played on my mind all night. Why would the Allaires be so elusive and dismissing of my encounter with whoever was driving the Peugeot? I could understand Jean-Pascal not taking me seriously. He probably enjoyed the fact that somebody was stalking me, but Laura had caught me off guard. Until that point, she had seemed to have my best interests at heart, even including giving me a couple of warnings. Did they know the driver? That was the only thing that made sense if they were trying to avoid the issue. If they didn't know him – or her, as Laura had pointed out – then why wouldn't they help me, or even take me seriously? I needed to get Laura on her own to ask.

The next day, Brad had agreed to come around for a couple of beers during the afternoon. I'd called him beforehand to see if he had anything on. At first, he had sounded reluctant but eventually he said he'd arrive around two o'clock. It seemed strange, because he appeared to change his mind after I told him Rachel had gone out early.

It was another very warm day, and I had given my vegetable plot a good soaking that morning with the hosepipe. Unless I'd been mistaken, some of the crop had grown more rapidly since Jean-Pascal had worked his magic compost into the bed. I was already impatient to eat my first ever home-produced food.

The rest of the morning, I pottered around. My mind drifted back to the house I'd seen for sale the previous day. I'd already decided I would show Emily when she came over. She was very good at making business decisions and would no doubt point out all the pitfalls that my current mood of euphoria could not imagine.

Brad arrived at two o'clock, almost on the dot. I was sat on my terrace overlooking the pool, the gîte below, and then the road beyond that. I'd noticed Brad walking from the direction of town, up towards my house. He kept looking around, from side to side, as if nervous or as though he expected someone to be following him. As soon as he saw me, he waved, and his demeanour shifted back to the outgoing, confident person who I'd met a few weeks previously.

"Hey, Brad." I stood, acknowledging him as he approached the outside table. "No car?"

He passed me a carrier bag containing a few bottles of beer.

"Hi, Dan, erm no, I thought we were having a drink. Don't need a car if I'm drinking, do I?"

His smile remained, but I could sense a hint of sarcasm and maybe a little annoyance in his voice.

"Fair point," I replied, "and there was no need to bring beer. I've got plenty. Talking of which, want a cold one out of the fridge?"

"Thought you'd never ask," he responded, taking a seat with his back to the house and overlooking the pool area.

Brad certainly seemed a good guy, although a little hard to unravel. He had an air of exuberance and was outwardly confident, but there was something else about him I couldn't put my finger on. One minute he'd be full of life and bullshit – in a fun way – and the next he'd be looking over his shoulder, petrified of someone walking out of the shadows. That day I wanted to find out a little more about the real Brad Jones.

We sat and chatted over a couple of beers, talking football, the weather, the state of the political scene back home in Britain and other day-to-day stuff. As I stood to fetch us another drink, Brad asked if he could have a tour of the garden, saying, "let's see what you've bought yourself then, Dan. After all, you've been dying to tell me," he said, punching my arm in jest.

Secretly, it pleased me he'd asked as I hadn't shown off my new property to anybody yet. Emily was the one whose opinion I wanted, but Brad would do for now.

We started by the pool and down to the gîte. I could see Brad wanting a closer look as we approached.

"Go on, look through the window. She's not in."

Sheepishly, Brad stepped closer, although still keeping a safe distance.

"Go on," I encouraged him, nodding towards the window.

He obliged and looked inside, first through the side window facing my house and then around to the front and the window next to the door.

Nodding his head in approval, he swiftly returned to walk next to me.

"Nice," he said, "very nice. Is the bedroom upstairs then?"

What a strange question.

"Yes, it is, why?"

I tried to catch his expression, but he turned his head away from me. His ears had gone pink, and I knew he was blushing.

"Oh, I'm just getting the layout in my mind, you know, trying to picture the whole place."

Something was amiss. Brad's behaviour wherever Rachel was concerned bordered on bizarre. Deciding to let it go, we continued our stroll, along the perimeter fence separating my land from the Allaires'.

We continued past my garage and my new vegetable plot. Brad nodded his approval but showed no more interest than that. I felt a little disappointed, and we carried on towards the field behind.

"This is a big plot you've got yourself here, Dan," he said, scanning the large open expanse.

"Yeah, I'm not sure what to do with it all yet–"

Brad interrupted me, his eyes focused beyond the line of trees forming a natural boundary between my land and the Allaire's farm.

"What's that?"

I tried to follow his eyes, but he was already walking towards whatever he had spotted. I trotted after him.

"What's what?" I asked, catching him up, but as we

made our way between the trees, I could see what Brad had noticed.

"Well I never," I said. "I've never seen that before. Then again, I haven't ventured this far up the garden. I just thought it backed straight onto the neighbours' field."

In front of us stood a water well, the type you would see in a children's fairy tale book. The base was formed of bricks in a circular formation, with a wooden structure atop it, leading to a tiled roof above sheltering any debris from dropping below. It even had a small handle on one side to lift the bucket in and out of the water below. However, it wasn't in very good condition. There were bricks on the floor that had fallen from the circle and several tiles were missing from the roof; most scattered on the ground so at least it looked as though I could repair it. The centre piece, along with the bucket, were missing completely.

"Wow, it looks like it's been here since the house was first built," exclaimed Brad. He then looked up at the Allaires farmhouse and then back towards my house.

"In fact," he continued, "I bet it belonged to that farmhouse originally. Look…" he said, pointing at the Allaires' building, "… it's the same stone that's in most of their house."

He was right; the brickwork was darker, more reddish than the buff colour of my house.

Brad began searching along the ground for something.

"Found one!"

He walked over to the well and he dropped a large rock directly into the centre. We both stood in silence, waiting for a splosh as it hit the water. It was pitch black inside but there was no 'splosh', just a dull 'thud', followed by the echo as the stone hit solid ground. I found it rather creepy. Brad smiled like a child who had discovered a secret den or an underground passage. He dropped another massive stone into the well.

Thud.

"That needs covering up really," I suggested, beginning to walk away.

"Just don't fall down it one night when you're pissed," Brad laughed out loud and dropped another rock.

Thud.

He was still laughing when he caught me up as I made my way back to the house. His enthusiasm was short lived.

Just as we passed the veg patch, Rachels car turned into the driveway. Brad immediately checked his stride.

Noticing him holding back, I couldn't resist a little joke in return.

"Come on," I beckoned. "She won't bite."

That's when I caught the unusual expression on his face. The all too familiar confidence visibly drained from him. He stood motionless, looking petrified.

Rachel climbed out of the car before I could say anything else to him.

"Hi, Dan!" she almost squealed. Then she spotted Brad. "Who's your friend?"

"Oh, this is Brad."

I turned to face Brad to introduce him. It was like looking at a different person. He stared blankly at Rachel.

"Brad, mate, you okay? This is Rachel."

Rachel walked over and kissed him on both cheeks. He still didn't speak.

"Lovely to meet you, Brad. Do you live locally?"

Good question, Rachel, that's exactly what I want to know.

"I, yes, I live in town."

Brad nervously pointed beyond my property as though we did not understand where 'town' was.

Rachel teased him, looking toward Monpazier. She really took no prisoners.

"Oh, that 'town'."

"Yes, sorry, I mean, you know, in town."

"And what do you do, in 'town'?" enquired Rachel. She was like a wasp attacking a caterpillar, almost for fun.

"I, kind of do what I can, you know. I have some business interests and stuff."

So bloody secretive, why won't he share anything?

"Sounds fun."

Rachel turned to me, getting bored with her new game.

"Oh, Daniel, I forgot to kiss you too."

She leant towards me, but instead of kissing each cheek, she kissed me directly on the lips, a little longer than necessary.

"It was, how shall I put it, nice meeting you, Brad," she giggled, turning on her heels and walking off towards the gîte. We both stood admiring the view until she was out of sight. Instantly Brad's confidence returned.

"Wow, she's fit, mate."

Hold on, did I just imagine you squirm and stammer your way through your introduction to Rachel?

"Yeah, she's okay," I replied.

"Okay? Are you fucking kidding? Come on, own up. Have you shagged her?"

"No!"

I was getting annoyed with him. Just seconds earlier he'd been a nervous wreck, almost too scared to talk to Rachel and now he probed me with personal questions. I didn't want to fall out with Brad, so I tactfully changed the subject.

"Come on, let me show you inside my house."

Leading Brad back towards the terrace, I turned around and caught him smiling. He paid no attention to me or where we were walking. Instead, he stared directly at the gîte.

23

THE KNOCK on my door at seven o'clock signalled the start of my second French lesson with Laura. I had become more and more apprehensive as Wednesday approached, especially given our last encounter when I'd called about the purple car following me.

"Bonsoir." I greeted Laura in my best French to lighten the atmosphere. I needn't have worried. Laura had returned to her familiar self, although I caught her taking a glimpse over her shoulder towards the farmhouse when I opened the door.

"Bonsoir, Daniel," she responded, carrying her folder full of notes under her arm. It was the first time I'd seen her in shorts. She also wore a sleeveless shirt. It was like addressing a different person once she got away from her husband and on neutral territory.

We sat down at the table as usual and, after pleasantries, I practiced what she had previously taught me. We then went onto some new words and phrases. She was trying to introduce the concept of masculine and feminine noun gender. It sounded all so confusing to me, but at least Laura made it entertaining and we spent more time laughing than we did learning.

When Laura opened up, she could be great fun. She had a terrific sense of humour. It's as though she let her guard down when we were alone but remained loyal towards Jean-Pascal when we were in his company. I wondered how she acted when those two were alone. She also bordered on flirting with me, pushing boundaries on how far she dare take it. Even that night, as we laughed when I got my le's and la's mixed up, she reached out and grabbed my hand, almost involuntarily.

"You're not even trying, Daniel," she giggled, then realised she was holding my hand, looked up and whispered, "Sorry," before removing it.

What is it she wants? She doesn't fancy me, it's not that kind of affection. It's flirting fun but only that. It's as though she's trying to get close enough to tell me something but can never bring herself to talk.

My mind drifted back to when we first met.

'If anything ever happens, remember my door is always open'.

Another thought entered my head.

Does Jean-Pascal bully her? No, surely not. He's more of a gentle giant than any tyrant.

We finished the lesson as I couldn't take in any more in than the hour's tuition allowed. I left Laura to pack away and went into the kitchen to fetch us both a drink.

As I returned, I noticed Laura leaning on my chest of drawers with her hands placed on top. I couldn't see what she was doing. When she heard me approaching, she stared upwards, looking at the photographs I had framed and tacked to the wall. There were a couple of my parents, a few of myself and friends on previous holidays, plus another of me and Emily sitting on a beach on some Greek island. Laura jumped as I clinked the glasses together to get her attention and I spotted her left hand was now in her pocket.

"Oh, sorry, Daniel. You must think I'm awfully nosey." She was blushing.

"Not at all, they are mounted on the wall after all. If I'd caught you going through my cupboards, I'd be alarmed," I joked. But Laura didn't see the funny side and immediately went on the defensive.

"What makes you think I'd do a thing like that? I've never done that."

"Whoa, hang on, it's only a joke." I held out her glass of water whilst I took a sip of my wine.

She backed down.

"Okay, sorry, Daniel." She looked flustered and kept one hand in her pocket whilst taking the water in her free hand. "Who are the people in the photographs, anyway?"

I went through them one by one, introducing her to the closest people in my life. Once I'd finished, I remembered what I'd wanted to ask her.

"Laura, do you know anything about that old well in my field behind the house? I saw it for the first time yesterday, in amongst the trees."

"Oh, that ancient thing?" she replied. "Well, I'm not sure if it's in your field or ours…"

"It's inside the fence, on my side," I interrupted.

"Is it?" she asked. "Oh, I hadn't noticed. It's ages since I've been down there. I should think the water is dried up by now. I can't even remember when it last had water in it. Why do you want to know?"

There it was again. I thought it obvious she knew

more about the well but had no intention of sharing it with me.

She carried on pretending to look at my photographs with her back to me. I decided it would be for the best not to press the issue.

"No reason, just curious why it's there and hasn't been blocked off or something. If I ever have children to stay in the gîte, I must cover it somehow."

Laura turned to face me.

"You can't have children stay, Daniel, can you?"

It came out much stronger than she had intended. She must have noticed the look on my face and immediately tried to level her voice.

"The gîte is one bedroom, isn't it? That's only enough for one or two adults. No children could ever fit in there at the same time."

She had a point, but it had been the abrupt manner of her tone that had caught me off guard. I was also annoyed that she was telling me who could stay in my gîte. My property.

I would not be outdone, but I also didn't want to fall out.

"Well, a dog maybe, or even a single parent with a child."

She just looked at me. I sipped my wine before continuing. I had to ask.

"Can I ask why you and Jean-Pascal didn't want to help the other day? I thought you would be the ideal people to ask who owns that purple car."

My question seemed to upset Laura even further. It was her turn to take a sip of water before replying. She spoke evenly and without emotion.

"As I told you when we first met, Daniel, people around here are set in their ways..."

"But..."

Laura removed her hand from her pocket for the first time and held it in the air to stop me.

"We don't know who owns that vehicle, Daniel, nor do we care. If we could help, we would. There is nothing more to say on the subject."

She passed me her glass and put her hand back into her pocket. I wanted to press her on why Jean-Pascal had apparently found it amusing that someone had followed me, but I knew it would get me nowhere.

Once she'd left, and I'd closed the door, I leant my back against the wall, deep in thought. There was something she wasn't telling me, something that had happened here. I looked around the living room, hoping whatever it was would leap out and reveal its secret.

24

MAKING COFFEE NEXT MORNING, I jumped when I heard tyres crunch on the gravel outside. I was becoming more and more on edge by the day. Looking at my phone, I noticed it was only eight o'clock. Who could it be? I wasn't even dressed.

"Morning, anyone about?"

It was Andy Jackson. I'd completely forgotten he was coming around to fix my kitchen shelves. Opening the door wearing only my shorts, I found Andy holding a toolkit and taking a good look around my garden and down to the gîte. He had a grimace on his face when he turned to meet me.

"Shit, sorry, Andy, I forgot all about it."

"Nice to be wanted."

"Let me get dressed. I'll be right with you."

Andy had unloaded the rest of his tools from his van and began to help me clear the kitchen area before he could start work. I'd asked him to move some cupboards around, so they were all together – I've no idea why the previous owners had sporadically placed them around the walls – and I needed three new shelves putting up. I still had possessions packed away in boxes and wanted them out where I could use them.

"Strange, the way they had put these units up, you know, the people who used to live here."

I was thinking aloud rather than directing my observations towards Andy.

"Each to their own, I guess. They were a nice couple."

Andy's response caught me off guard.

"You knew them?"

"Yeah, did quite a bit of work here, especially on the gîte. They were decent people."

It intrigued me. The previous couple had lowered the house price below the market value – considerably so, according to the agency. I'd never met them. The agent showed me around on both of my viewings. There was no forwarding address, and I knew nothing about them.

Andy continued to chat as he started work.

"Yeah, come to think of it. They left rather suddenly after I thought they were doing all right for themselves."

The way the house had come on the market late last year had surprised the local estate agent too. I had registered with them as soon as Emily and myself had split. They'd sent me through various details, but none were suitable as I'd wanted a separate gîte or annex that was already up and running. The agent then called me and said they had just taken on the ideal property, close to town. The owners had requested a quick sale.

"Hmm, I think the agent said something about an

illness in their family. It surprised me how cheap it had been."

Andy carried on busying himself. His tone dropped slightly, losing the chirpiness of his London accent.

"Hmm, not sure about the illness story. Not what I heard."

Before I could ask what he'd heard, he spoke over me, this time with a little more irritation in his voice.

"Actually, I thought about buying it myself."

I wasn't sure if he was being serious or not. He must have sensed my hesitation, and he stopped what he was doing to address me direct.

"Not much money in the satellite and odd job market, you know." He looked around the kitchen as he spoke. "Ready-made business this one."

I knew there had been some other interest, but the agent had told me very little.

"Well, I think somebody else bid for it, but the agent told me it would be mine if I could go to a certain price."

Andy stopped what he was doing and turned to face me.

"Even if you got it for full asking price, you got yourself a bargain. It's a gem, plenty of land too if I remember correctly."

Andy picked up his cordless screwdriver to remove the first cupboard.

"But still a surprise they upped and left so quickly. The family illness story never convinced me," he added before the noise from his work drowned out anything else I could say.

Andy seemed like a good bloke, although it was clear he wasn't happy that I now owned the house. There was a definite hint of envy in his voice and mannerisms. Did he actually put a bid in himself? He'd just said there wasn't much money in what he did for a living. I also still had a nagging feeling at the back of my mind that it had been Andy who had chased me on the way to the garden centre. It would make sense if it pissed him off about the house, but then why do any jobs for me at all when I'd asked for his help?

Between drilling and banging, he told me about the gîte and how he'd totally refurbished it. He'd also done some work on the house, electrical stuff, and rewiring the garage.

Andy began packing his tools into the van just before lunchtime. He'd done a good job with the kitchen and everything was laid out exactly how I'd wanted it. All I needed to do was to refill the cupboards and put the items I needed readily on the shelves. It would become a more functional kitchen and I intended to tip Andy well for his efforts. I knew I'd be calling him again.

"Who's that?" Andy asked, loading the last item into his van.

I followed his gaze. Rachel was walking up the garden towards her car.

"That's my first guest in the gîte. Her name's Rachel, from Surrey. She's been here a while now. Goes home in a couple of days, actually."

"Think I've seen her round town." He leaned in close to me and lowered his voice. "She's well fit, mate. You should get in there."

Fortunately, Rachel arrived before I went into full-blown blushing mode.

"Morning, Rachel, this is Andy, he's just been refitting my kitchen."

"Nice to meet you, Andy."

"You too, love. If I'd have known you were here, I'd have come and asked for a cup of sugar."

Flirting was one of Andy's tricks of the trade. He'd met his match with Rachel though. It came as second nature to her.

"Well, I would never say no." She turned to face me directly. "Would I, Dan?"

I was so pleased Andy had been in a hurry. Without even looking at my reaction, he climbed into the driver's seat of his van.

"I'm going to go home and pour all my sugar away, then I'll be back." He winked at Rachel. "Keep in touch, Dan, you know, if you need anything else doing."

"Definitely. Oh, hang on, Andy. I haven't paid you yet." I patted my pocket, feeling for my wallet. "Shit! I've got no cash. Can I drop it off at yours?"

"Whenever, mate. I'll call by when I'm passing. I know you wouldn't dare short-change me."

I felt uncomfortable with his response. It came out both harsh in tone and content. I found his unpleasant streak disconcerting.

Andy started the engine and reversed out of my drive. He waved his hand out of the window as he drove away towards town. I turned to Rachel, wanting to keep everything pleasant before she left in a couple of days.

"Going anywhere nice?"

"Just to the shop. I want to buy Nathan, my brother, a little present to take back."

I attempted to give the impression I had forgotten she was leaving.

"Oh, yes, you leave Saturday, don't you?"

Because of my buoyant mood, an idea entered my head. I spoke before I thought it through.

"Listen, to say thank you for being my first guest and for all your help with the website, I'd love to take you for a meal tomorrow night. What do you say?"

Her response shouldn't have surprised me.

"Dan, that would be amazing. You don't have to buy as I know you're still finding your feet in France, but I'd love to go to dinner with you. Go halves on the bill?"

I felt a little offended about the money. It wasn't as if I was destitute. Her offer could well have been genuine though, and I would not let any ill feeling come between us at that late stage.

"It's my treat, take it or leave it."

"In that case, I take it." Her mood suddenly became more cordial. "Thank you, Dan, for *everything*."

As I walked back into my kitchen, I wondered what Rachel had meant by her last remark. With my mind wandering, I began to put some crockery into a cupboard Andy had just moved. As I left the kitchen to fetch another box of belongings, an almighty crash sounded from behind me. I rushed back into the room. The cupboard I'd just filled lay smashed on the floor. It looked beyond repair and the contents in an even worse state. Every item seemed to be in a thousand pieces.

I moved closer to the wall to inspect where the cupboard had fallen from. The strangest thing struck me. Tipping the cupboard over on its side, I searched frantically for what I was looking for. Nothing; I couldn't find any more anywhere. I went back to the wall in case I'd missed them.

But no, there were only two screws holding the whole cupboard up. The two at the bottom were still in the wall, but now bent down, staring directly at the floor. There were no others. The top two were missing completely.

25

IT HAD BOTHERED me all night and most of the following day. Every time I attempted to erase it from my mind, the sound of the cupboard crashing to the floor came rushing into my thoughts. The obvious question that just wouldn't elude me was whether Andy did it on purpose. If he didn't, it had to be shoddy workmanship – not something I would expect from somebody with his experience. If it had been done purposefully, then why? The answer became self-evident – because I bought the house from under his nose. It was all I needed on top of everything else that was going on around me.

That evening, as I started to get ready for my meal with Rachel, I cursed myself for ever suggesting it. I needed Rachel gone to give me one less thing to worry about.

As I dressed, Emily sent a text confirming her flight. She was due to arrive at Bergerac Airport at three o'clock on Sunday – only two days away. It's only a forty-minute drive, so that would leave me more time than I'd thought to get the gîte cleaned and changed round after Rachel left the day before. I was getting butterflies in anticipation of Emily's arrival. Would she have changed? Would she be pleased to see me? Subconsciously, I had been singing, with thoughts of Emily tumbling through my mind.

"Someone's in a good mood."

Shit, that's Rachel, in my house. I turned away from the mirror to face the bedroom door.

Sure enough, she had walked nonchalantly into my room, as if she owned the place. She caught me just as I buttoned my jeans. It was all I had on.

"Oh, my timing's a little out," she said, walking over and kissing me on the lips.

What the hell is happening here?

"Hey, it's polite to knock you know," I said, fumbling for my shirt which was lying on the bed.

"I did knock, three times, but you didn't answer. The door was open, so I peered in. That's when I heard your awful singing," Rachel laughed. I hadn't realised I had been singing. I had no choice but to let it go. It wasn't worth getting angry with Rachel at this point of her stay. I returned her smile. I was intent on the night going off without incident, yet something in the pit of my stomach told me otherwise.

She watched me get dressed, clearly with no intention of leaving. It felt very awkward, especially as Rachel once again looked amazing. With her hair tied up at the back, she wore a tight, lime green top, showing off every curve imaginable. She had three quarter length jeans on, which must have taken some squeezing into, and yellow boat shoes. Rachel didn't need make-up, but the little she had applied brought out her cheekbones and pouting lips to perfection. She really knew how to dress to impress and I realised I wouldn't be the only male looking in her direction that evening.

We arrived at the same restaurant we had used three weeks previously. It immediately jogged my memory of that night when Rachel had first shown signs of jealousy, the time she asked if I fancied Laura. It put me slightly on edge. A hell of a lot – too much – had happened since then. I just needed to get through the meal. I looked at Rachel as the waiter showed us to our table. She looked content and free from confrontation. I began to relax a little. She had been cheerful enough walking into town, talking about how much she'd enjoyed her stay and how it had recharged her batteries. Maybe I would get away with a pleasant last night in Rachel's company.

How wrong could I be?

After we'd ordered food and the first glass of wine had been poured, Rachel raised her glass and chinked mine.

"Cheers, Daniel, and many thanks for four super weeks in your gîte."

"Thank you, Rachel, the pleasure has been all mine, honestly."

The conversation flowed easily; from the website she had designed to small improvements she suggested for the gîte. Maybe some beach towels when using the pool and a few more plates and dishes in the cupboards, she proposed. It was all useful feedback, just what I needed as a novice.

As I suspected, almost every male in the restaurant gave Rachel some attention. Others looked at me, then back at Rachel, then back at me. I could practically read their minds. *What the hell is she doing with him? They have to be related. The lucky bastard!* Ignoring their jealous observations, I turned back to Rachel, trying to keep the conversation neutral.

"Did you get your brother a present yesterday?"

"Yes, I did actually. He's very difficult to buy for, but I found a lovely old map of the town." She looked around us. "He loves collecting old maps. He frames his favourites, so I really hope he likes this one."

"I'm sure he will. Are you close to him?"

"Who wouldn't be? After what we went through as kids, it's a wonder either of us is anywhere near normal."

Hmm.

Rachel spoke more about Nathan, the fact he lived in Hampshire, not a million miles away from her own house, and that he ran his own little business, selling second-hand furniture which he collected from house clearances. She had set him up with a website too and said that had doubled his sales. I'm sure she had more to say about her brother but, even when I pressed the matter, she quickly changed the subject back to something more mundane.

We spoke a bit about my past and how I'd always wanted to live abroad. I didn't go into the detail of why I was there, that was personal. I just said the dream had become a reality and I hadn't been happier in years. Then I made my first Freudian slip of the evening. Nerves had got the better of me during a silent spell.

"All I need now is a woman to make my life complete."

I kicked myself under the table before Rachel could even reply. A huge smile spread across her face.

"Well now Daniel..." she held my hand across the

table, the same jealous faces from other customers staring in disbelief. "Is that a hint?"

Blushing, I tried to keep my composure.

"No, it wasn't, Rachel Brookes, and you know it wasn't." I gently pulled my hand away and immediately took a swig of my wine. Fortunately, Rachel kept the conversation light-hearted.

"If I didn't know you better, I could have sworn that was a pass, Daniel Kent."

The evening was still sultry as we walked back towards my house along the road out of town. The cicadas were in full chorus and the moon was doing its utmost to give enough natural light to guide us along the way. It was a perfect summer evening. As I smiled and gazed up at the stars, I felt Rachel link her arm in mine. Because we were nearly home to safety, I thought what was the harm spending the last few moments interlocked in friendship?

"Daniel?" Her voice had dropped to a whisper, almost inaudible.

Oh no, here goes.

"Tonight, can I stay with you? It's just that, you know, we may never see each again, and I believe we have become very good friends. I'm also a little down about going back home. It sounds silly, but I'm kind of scared and I don't want to be alone tonight."

She looked at me, fluttered her eyelashes and dropped her bottom lip. The perfect 'little child lost' look that would take somebody inhumane to ignore.

A voice in my head told me to see reason.

"I'm so sorry, Rachel." I looked directly at her, releasing her arm from mine. "It's not that I'm not attracted to you, Christ, I'd have to be mad not to be. But no, you go home tomorrow and..."

"And what, Dan?" Rachel looked sad.

"And I don't want to get involved. I've said it before, Rachel, I'm just repeating myself now."

The conversation was exactly what I'd dreaded that night. The evening had gone so well, right until the final few minutes. I braced myself.

"We *slept* together, Dan! Does that mean nothing to you? I see the way you look at me, I'm not stupid, I know you are attracted to me..." She had raised her voice and struggled to keep it from cracking. She looked genuinely distraught.

"Calm down, Rachel, it's–"

Her voice grew louder still. As she spoke, I noticed a light come on upstairs at the farmhouse at the top of the hill.

"Don't you tell me to calm down you, you fucking user!"

Shit, this is getting out of hand.

"I've not used you at all. We had both had a lot to drink that night and one thing led to another. It was enjoyable for both of us, but it happens all the time. One-night stands. Shit, I bet there's a thousand one-night stands going on right now across the world."

Rachel stopped as we reached my driveway, put her hands on her hips and turned to me, our faces inches apart. At least her voice lowered slightly, and she appeared to have calmed down a little.

"Listen to me, Dan. I came here to get away from Britain for a while. I had to, that's all you need to know. Then we met. At first, I'll admit, I thought you were okay, but a little timid maybe, not my type."

At least she's honest.

"Then I started to fall for you. I enjoyed working on your website and I liked your company. For me it wasn't just a one-night stand as you so eloquently put it."

She squared up to me, lifting herself onto her toes to confront me eye to eye.

"Tell me straight, Dan, are you saying you have no feelings for me? A simple yes or no will suffice."

She had put me on the spot, and I had to reply. I stumbled for the right words, but they came out at speed, leaving me hardly drawing for breath.

"Rachel, of course I have feelings for you. That night felt amazing, and all the help you've given me, and night's out like tonight. I will always cherish them. I was even hoping we'd keep in touch when you got back. You know, email, text. I thought you might even book up another week next year, you know, my first returning guest…"

"Fuck you, Dan! You can stick your gîte and your house and your 'French dream' right up your arse!"

Blotches had appeared on her neck and a thick bead of sweat stuck to her forehead. I'd never seen her so agitated.

She started to storm off towards the gîte. The light was still on at the farmhouse. I'd had enough.

"You know what, Rachel?"

"What?," she turned.

"You need help. You can't come over here and just walk into my life. You've used me, not the other way around."

"Fuck you!" She started to tear off again.

"Oh, and one more thing, Rachel."

This time she kept walking, but I hadn't finished what I had to say.

"If you've read my rules, you need to vacate by eleven o'clock tomorrow morning. At the latest!"

It must have been past midnight by the time I went to bed. I recalled slamming my door after my altercation with Rachel and then heading straight to the kitchen for my bottle of whisky. It was chilly indoors, but I didn't have the energy to light a fire, so I took the bottle upstairs and crawled into bed, genuinely feeling sorry for myself.

I'd given in, and fell into an alcohol-induced slumber. The crash of breaking glass awoke me sometime later. I struggled to find my bearings and my head swam between drunkenness and the onset of a hangover. Literally crawling from my bed, I followed the direction of the noise and made my way to the spare bedroom. Once I arrived, I pulled myself up and reached for the light switch. The bulb, which lay bare with no lampshade to protect it, momentarily blinded my eyes.

As I began to focus, I felt a gentle breeze brush past me. I walked over to close the window but, as I gingerly made my way, I stubbed my toe on something hard. Cursing loudly, I looked down to find the cause of my latest injury.

A single brick lay in the middle of the floor, surrounded by broken glass. It was a miracle I'd managed to avoid further damage.

26

Oh shit.

My head pounded. Rolling over, the first thing I saw was the bottle of scotch on my bedside table. The second thing I noticed was that it was almost half empty, a new bottle I'd opened after I'd stormed into my house the night before.

Recollections tumbled back into my mind, like an avalanche of events. Rachel nonchalantly strolling into my bedroom, watching me dress – she'd said she had called my name, but I no longer believed her; I know I would have heard her. Walking into town, the meal, the looks from both admiring and jealous people alike, the laughing, the interlocking of arms, the admission she liked me – even 'falling for me' – the argument, the shouting. *Be out by eleven o'clock, at the latest!*

I checked my phone. Quarter past ten. *Shit!* I leapt out of bed, my toe immediately sending pain waves to my brain. I yelled out and looked down at my bloodied foot.

What the fuck is that?

Then I remembered the brick, the smashed window, glass everywhere.

Throwing on a T-shirt and a pair of shorts, I hobbled into the spare room, trying not to smear blood from my foot onto the floor. The room was as I'd left it only a few hours before, large shards of glass spread from the window to where the brick still lay.

It would have to wait.

I hopped downstairs, flung the back door open and limped out onto my terrace. Rachel's car was still there. I turned to the gîte, but I couldn't see any movement there either.

Think, Dan.

I can't do anything until eleven o'clock at the earliest. If she hasn't gone by then, do I storm down and drag her out, or do I play it more diplomatically?

I needed to calm down, work things out logically. I went back inside and made myself a strong coffee. I searched for some paracetamol to ease the pain, which by now throbbed relentlessly on both sides of my head. I knew I would be in for a long day. I made time to phone Andy Jackson, and he said he could come over later to fix the broken window.

As I cleaned up my foot – fortunately it had looked a lot worse covered in blood than it actually was – and began to think as I showered.

What did Rachel want from me? It could be genuine, against all odds, she might like me. But, without trying to put myself down, I knew she could find someone better. Not only in looks but also professionally. There would be a queue of hugely successful businessmen waiting in line for a catch like Rachel. So, what else? Could she be running from something or someone? Then it hit me.

What she had said the night before. 'I came here to get away from Britain for a while. I had to, that's all you need to know.' Whatever she needed to 'get away' from she had found the perfect place. Nobody would find her for years if she kept her head down and made no contact with people back home.

It's not your problem, Dan.

The voices in my head overruled the thoughts of concern in my heart. I needed her gone. She was dangerous and my ex-fiancé was due in just over twenty-four hours.

Eleven o'clock came and went. I'd been sitting outside nursing my hangover with copious amounts of coffee. I hadn't taken my eyes off the gîte. There had been no sign of life and it was now over thirty minutes since she should have vacated.

The previous evening Rachel had clarified that she wanted more than just being a guest at my gîte. But how much more? Did she want a relationship and – I dreaded to think – even to move into my house, to start a life together? Or was it purely sexual, a physical affair? Whatever it was, it was the exact opposite of what I wanted. Sure, she was very attractive, out of my league even, but I found her so unstable. Besides, I didn't want any kind of relationship with anybody right at that moment of my life. I wasn't even sure how I would react to Emily arriving. A lot had happened back in England and I'd moved to France to start afresh, a brand-new challenge, an adventure, an escape. The last thing I needed was some crazy woman messing with my head and my business. *Shit!* Could that be it? Did she want to get her hands on my business? Had she seen an opportunity here that was too good to be true? Could she have seen the potential after building the website and then noticed one or two other bookings come in via the agency? Had it been it her who'd watched me looking around that other property a few days before? No, how could she get hold of a purple car and hide it away somewhere? Well, easily, now I thought about it. But then she couldn't have driven by twice, on my very first night here. Could she? My mind had gone into hyperdrive.

Deciding to play it as professionally as I could, I slid on my flip-flops and made my way down to the gîte. My toe felt fine, but my head hurt like hell. As I walked, I tried convincing myself I was well within my rights to ask her to leave.

My hands were trembling as I knocked on the gîte door. Rachel answered straight away. She was still in her dressing gown. She spoke as if I'd completely dreamt the previous night's events.

"Morning, Dan. Hey look, I just wanted to say–"

"You need to leave, Rachel. The terms are eleven o'clock–"

She interrupted me, her words hitting me between the eyes like a sledgehammer.

"I've booked another two weeks, Dan."

I recoiled, my hands grabbing the doorframe for support. Dizziness overwhelmed me. Rachel kept talking.

"You don't have anybody else due until July the fifth, so I thought I'd make the most of the opportunity. That will give me enough time to find somewhere else local."

Fuck it. I'd forgotten to book out the dates on my website after I'd asked Rachel how to do it the other day.

My blood boiled, and I felt the heat rise to the top of my head. My hands had inadvertently formed into two tightly clenched fists. I could feel my nails digging into the palms of my hands, yet I did nothing to take the pain away. I knew I needed to hold it together before I did something I'd really regret.

"You have no fucking right, Rachel..."

"But Dan, think of the money. Have you checked your bank account? Two more weeks' money has gone in already. And think of your reputation. People looking at your website will see June fully booked and now half of July. It's all good for business."

She was calmness personified. I couldn't fucking believe what I was witnessing.

"I want you to leave, Rachel. Now!" My temper was out of control and I took two steps back to stop myself from flying for her. This was turning into a sick nightmare. The tenant who would never leave. You read horror stories about this.

Will she ever fucking go?

"I'll leave in two weeks, Dan, sooner if I find somewhere more..." she considered her next words, "... more suitable."

"This is illegal, Rachel..." again she interrupted me, exuding calmness and self-control.

"Illegal, Dan? How? What are you going to do, go to the police and say this woman has made a booking on my website, paid for it and then refused to leave? Come on, Dan, you're making yourself look a little silly now."

She was right. What could I say? It had been me who had made the mistake of not booking out the dates on my website. There wasn't another booking for two weeks, so what had she technically done wrong? We both knew the truth was that I'd wanted her gone that day. I'd made no secret of that the previous evening. However, that would never stand up in a court of law. It would be her word against mine.

I also had the dilemma of Emily arriving the next day. I had intended her to stay in the gîte and, although that would be unnecessary because she was an invited visitor and not a paying guest, it still left me with an awkward explanation to make. Counting to ten, I tried to even my pitch.

"Okay, Rachel, not illegal, but you know I asked you to leave. What we had, or did, was a one-off, it will never happen again. I tried to end your stay as friends, but you wouldn't have that would you? No, you thought you were here for good. Well, I've got news for you, you will leave, and it will be on my terms."

She opened her mouth to speak again, but this time I held up my hand to stop her.

"Save it. We're done, Rachel. Keep out of my sight and out of my way from now on. As far as I'm concerned you have paid to stay in the gîte, and we don't have to have any contact."

Then I remembered the brick through my spare room window.

"Oh, and a good shot with the brick. I should make you tidy it up, but I don't even want you near my house."

She looked hurt and sorrowful. As she opened her mouth to speak, I held up my hand to stop her.

"Don't even talk to me, Rachel. You know what," I pointed at her face. "You mean absolutely nothing to me!"

My last words spat out of my mouth in uncontrolled anger. I could see how upset she was, and her bottom lip trembled, but I had to stick to my guns. However hurtful and spiteful my outburst had been, I'd had to make a stand, to get her off my back and to clarify that she wasn't welcome any more. Looking at her face at that precise moment, I'd achieved my goal.

Just as I was about to turn and storm back up my garden, I realised she stood motionless in the doorway. It was her turn to hold on to the frame as if to support her weight and stop herself from falling. She looked lost, frightened even. The last thing I noticed was a solitary tear running down her cheek.

27

After a restless night, I awoke on Sunday morning and cleaned up the mess in the spare bedroom. Andy had put in a new pane the night before, but there were still fragments of glass to vacuum. Emily would have to stay in there now that the gîte was out of bounds. My altercation with Rachel had left me incandescent with rage. How fucking dare she book two more weeks?

Because of your own ineptitude, Dan, that's why.

All I'd had to do was book two weeks on my website and there would have been nothing Rachel could do about it. But I'd fucked it up. And as I slowly cleaned the rest of my house, I knew she'd be down in the gîte, probably hatching her plan of how and when she would break the news to Emily that we'd slept together.

Following our doorstep fight, I'd seen no more of Rachel after I'd shut myself away for the remainder of the day. Laura came across during the afternoon to drop off more French cue cards. She'd suggested I look at them whilst she was there, but I just couldn't take any of it in.

Laura had asked if anything was wrong, and I'd told her about Rachel refusing to leave and booking two more weeks. My French neighbour and teacher did not like Rachel, but she surprised me by suggesting it all could have been of my making. "What do you mean, Laura?" I'd asked. She went on to suggest that maybe I wasn't cut out to run a business and my future may still lie back home in England. Why did she keep hinting that France wasn't for me?

The drive to Bergerac Airport took about forty minutes. I'd arrived in plenty of time before Emily's flight was due to arrive. Whilst sipping the red-hot café au lait I had purchased from the small airport shop, the tannoy announced that the flight from London Stansted had just landed. The excitement which had gradually built during the day turned to nervousness as soon as the broadcast was complete. *Get a grip, Dan, it's your ex-girlfriend, not the bailiffs coming to evict you from your home.*

Passengers started streaming through from baggage reclaim, and after several minutes I thought she might have changed her mind and not come over at all. After the final stragglers made their way through, I walked back outside, thinking I'd missed her. Becoming anxious, I returned to the terminal, my eyes darting everywhere for a glimpse of Emily. Just as I began to think she hadn't travelled, she appeared from the very place I'd been stood waiting moments earlier. She must have been the last person off the flight.

She pulled a very large suitcase behind her but, to be fair, I didn't pay much attention to that. There was something a little different from what I recalled, but I couldn't put my finger on what. Her short spiky hair was now much flatter and looked longer than I remembered, but it was still dyed blonde. Emily was wearing tight jeans and a denim jacket. Underneath she wore a T-shirt, no doubt depicting one of her favourite punk bands. Her look was complete with the all too familiar wireless headphones sitting over her head and pumping music into her ears – no doubt loudly.

As soon as she spotted me, she slid the headphones down around her neck before fumbling for her phone to stop the music. Although she looked happy to see me, her smile appeared forced, almost apprehensive. She walked patiently through the guide ropes before reaching me then let go of her suitcase and embraced me in both arms. I reciprocated even though it felt awkward. It was like meeting a relative or friend for the first time since their partner had passed away. A hug of tenderness and remorse. Taking one step back whilst holding her hands, I smiled and kissed her on both cheeks.

This seemed to lighten the mood.

"Oh, how very French, Mr Kent," she said, now smiling much more naturally. I could then see why I thought she looked a little different, and not just because of her hair. Emily had the first signs of ageing skin stretching from the corner of her eyes. She looked older, not much, but she had changed. She hadn't lost her good looks though – I had always found her very attractive – but she looked as though she had the weight of the world on her shoulders. It wasn't the Emily I'd been used to.

Not wanting to give any of my thoughts away, I hugged her again before holding out my hand to take the suitcase from off her.

"It's fantastic to see you Em. For a moment I didn't think you'd made the flight."

"Yeah, I got talking to one of the cabin crew. I was last off the plane. Anyway, it's great to see you too, Dan. I really need a break."

"Oh, nice to be used," I replied, pushing her arm. I felt more at ease with her than any other female I'd met in life.

"Isn't that what you're here for?"

It wasn't exactly comfortable, but we'd always had a rapport together. We had regularly played off each other, almost like a double act. It came naturally to us both. As we walked to the car, I could feel some tension releasing from my shoulders.

Driving back to the house, we tried to fill in the blanks since we'd last been together. We talked about Emily's business. She said it was going well but had become incredibly tiring. She told me how her parents were and how her older brother had moved to Australia. She said she was still single and had had no time for a boyfriend, which I found hard to believe. She asked if I was seeing anyone and I'm not convinced she didn't see me blush slightly as the thought of my night of passion with Rachel immediately entered my head. I looked out of the side window to hide my guilt.

"No, nobody," I replied, a little too late to sound convincing.

As we pulled into my driveway, I glanced over to the left to see if there was any sign of Rachel at the gîte – nothing. Next, I checked to see if her car was there, which it was.

I knew I had no choice but to strike up the conversation I had been dreading all day.

"Er, Em, I have a little confession to make."

"Go on," she said, looking intrigued.

"There's been a guest in the gîte for the past month, a woman called Rachel." I pointed at the gîte from the car and Emily followed my gaze.

"Okay, and?"

"Well, she was due to leave yesterday, for the second time in fact…"

Emily interrupted, "the second time?"

"Yes, she originally booked for a fortnight, then stayed another two weeks. Well, she was due to leave yesterday, but she booked another two weeks."

"And you didn't want her to I take it?" Emily knew me so well she could read my mind.

"No, she's kind of strange, a bit of a schizo. She's fine one minute and then the next she acts totally irrationally. Like somebody in one of those creepy movies."

We walked into the house, me carrying Emily's suitcase. Instead of commenting on my new property, Emily wanted to know more about my mysterious guest.

"Why are you letting her stay then, Dan? It's your place isn't it? Surely you decide who stays and who doesn't?"

"The thing is, Em. She has done nothing wrong. In fact, it's my fault. She wrote my new website for me, she's great at it, actually. I think that's what she does for a living. Anyway, because she knows my website address, she has used it to book direct, twice now. She hasn't had to go through the agency I'm registered with, so I've had no way of knowing, or blocking, her stay."

"But what has she done that's so bad that you want her out Dan?"

The conversation was heading in an inevitable direction. A direction I'd wanted to avoid.

"Nothing bad, as such. It's just as though she's in control of staying rather than me being in charge, and it's my business."

It was the best I could think of on the spot and it seemed to placate Emily, for the time being at least.

"So, where does that leave me, Dan? I take it I'm not staying in the gîte with *The Hand That Rocks the Cradle*?"

That made me laugh, although it also felt a little too close for comfort.

"I've got a spare room, Em. Besides, I've got another booking in the gîte in a couple of weeks and I'd sooner keep that purely for business. Are you okay with that?"

"Sure, I understand you would want to keep that separate."

Emily had taken it considerably better than I thought she might. In fact, her face had lit up when I'd told her she had to stay in the house with me. I had somehow convinced myself she would suggest staying in a hotel in town, but she seemed more than happy with the arrangements. Even if Rachel hadn't hung around, I must admit it felt much better having Emily stay in the house, anyway.

After a quick tour of my new home, I suggested we open a bottle of wine and take it outside onto the terrace. I wanted Emily to see the swimming pool and surrounding garden. I began to relax, and having my ex around made me feel much better. Within the space of a few hours in her company, it was as if we'd never been apart. Emily looked much more content too. It was great to have her back in my life, albeit only for a short while.

As we walked outside, I secretly prayed that Rachel didn't make an appearance that day. As I opened the wine, Emily still wouldn't let my unexpected guest drop.

"How long did you say this Rachel woman was staying for, Dan?"

"Another two weeks, why?"

"And you say she wrote your website for you?"

"Yep." I concentrated on the wine, unsure where the conversation was heading.

"So, she's got all your login details to your new website, and I take it emails and she can even get into the agency site you use?"

Feeling myself blush, I could have kicked myself.

"Well, yeah, she can."

"You idiot, Dan. What else can she access, bank accounts, credit cards…?"

"Oh fuck, you're right, Em. I emailed her the username and password for the two main sites but, you know me, I use the same password for everything."

"Get your laptop, you cretin. You have no idea who you're dealing with here."

Although Emily was right that I shouldn't have the same usernames for every site I visit, I didn't think Rachel would be the type of person who would hack bank accounts or other financial information. However, I did as I was told and fetched my laptop.

After about thirty minutes, we had changed the passwords to my online banking and email account. Although I felt it was all a little over the top, I went along with Emily's suggestion. The only thing left was to change the password to my new website so only I could get into the back end and make any alterations going forward.

"You sure that's everything, Dan? No other sites she could hack into?"

"No, that's it, just the new website left."

That's when I remembered I'd written the logon details to my gîte booking site in my notebook. I'd been going to give them to Rachel before she sarcastically reminded me, we had email nowadays.

"Hang on, before I forget, I need to destroy what I wrote in my notepad."

As I walked back outside with the book, Emily must have noticed the quizzical look on my face.

"What's wrong, Dan?"

I kept turning the first page over and then back again.

"It's the login details, Em."

"What about them?"

I passed the notebook to Emily.

"Look. The first page has been torn out."

28

I LOOKED EVERYWHERE for the missing page from my notebook. I couldn't remember if I'd torn it out when I offered to give my login details to Rachel. The more I thought about it though, the more I convinced myself I had waved the whole notebook to her the day she walked past my house. I'd searched everywhere, but to no avail. Where could it be and, more to the point, who could have taken it if someone had removed it?

Emily was sure that it must have been Rachel, but I wasn't so convinced. Maybe I was trying to protect her, but then I thought, how had Rachel set up my website without the login details? I must have emailed them to her. Again, I couldn't recall if or when I had. If I hadn't, then maybe Emily was right and Rachel had taken the page from my notebook, but when? As far as I was concerned, I'd always left the notepad in my living room, on the chest of drawers. Had Rachel been into my house?

That night, Emily slept in the spare room as planned. We had shared a couple of bottles of wine and chatted about the past – the good times – and reminisced about school and who was doing what now. Emily used social media a lot and had kept in touch with loads of people we both knew from our younger years. Although I didn't go in for all the Facebook and Twitter gossip, I must admit I found it fascinating what some of my old classmates were up to. She had photographs of a few of them too, and we fell about laughing at how some of them had changed. It had been an enjoyable night, and I went to bed happy that Emily would be staying.

Next morning, I decided it might be a good idea to introduce her to the Allaires. Emily thought it was good thinking too and added that she wanted to get to know everybody I had met since arriving in France.

Not Rachel you won't, I thought, not if I can help it.

I assumed it would stop the Allaires wondering about my new guest if I introduced her formally rather than them spotting Emily walking around. I also wanted to ensure that Laura knew I had no intention of moving back to England after her suggestion during our French lesson on Saturday afternoon.

As we started to wander along the road to my neighbours', I realised the only other time I'd turned up uninvited was after my car chase with the purple Peugeot. It made me feel momentarily uncomfortable, as though I might be trespassing and unwanted. I just hoped this visit turned out more amicable.

Walking up their long driveway, and quite a steep hill, I noticed a different vehicle parked in the yard. Laura couldn't drive, so I guessed they had visitors. Just as I was about to knock on the front door, I heard somebody call us from around the back of the house.

"Daniel, we're outside. Come around."

It was Laura, sounding much more cheerful than my last encounter with her. We made our way around the side of the house to the seating area where we'd had the barbecue a few weeks earlier. Laura stood to greet us whilst Jean-Pascal remained seated. Yet again, he showed no sign of pleasure at being in my company. He sat next to another guy, I guessed around their age. He was cradling a cup of steaming coffee and like Jean-Pascal, his mouth formed a hard, straight line.

I introduced Emily to Laura and the three of us exchanged hugs and kisses. Laura made Jean-Pascal stand, and he reluctantly shook my hand and kissed Emily on her cheek. There was a tension in the air, and I already regretted turning up uninvited. Laura and her husband kept looking back at their guest who had remained seated but hadn't taken his eyes off us. He didn't look too dissimilar to Laura, albeit a little older. You could tell he must have been a good-looking guy when he was younger. He was stocky, well-built, and had a full head of wavy light brown hair, tinged with grey at the temples. It was difficult to tell because he didn't stand at all whilst we were there, but he looked well over six feet tall. Not somebody I'd like to meet in a dark alley. Laura must have noticed me staring at him.

"Ah, Daniel, you have never met my brother, have you?"

Brother? She's never mentioned him before.

"No, I've not had the pleasure." I reached out my hand, but he continued to keep both of his around his mug of coffee.

"How are you doing?" he mustered, unenthusiastically. "I'm Robert, or Bob, whatever, Laura's brother." His English sounded as good as Laura's.

The similarity I'd recognised was confirmed by the close relationship; the same eyes, bone structure of the cheeks, and solid build. He shook Emily's hand too, again without standing. Emily wanted to know more about this sullen and rude individual. She'd never been one to hold back, always chatting to people at parties or in the pub whilst I stood a few inches behind her, hiding my face in my drink.

"Are you visiting from the UK, Robert?"

His abruptness showed no sign of abating.

"No, I live here. I moved here at the same time as Laura, actually." Laura seemed embarrassed by her brothers' brusque behaviour.

"Yes, we moved over when Dad died, and Mum decided she wanted to come back to her roots. Robert got a job at a local vineyard soon after."

Emily pressed him, although I could have kicked her for pushing this guy for more answers.

"And is that what you still do?"

"I have to pay the bills somehow, love, don't I?"

If there's one thing Emily could not stand, it's being patronised with sexist remarks like 'duck' or 'love'. If Robert had asked if she was any good at ironing or cleaning, I think she might have tipped the hot coffee over his head. Fortunately, Jean-Pascal spoke for the first time since we'd arrived.

"How's the house, Daniel?"

Thinking this was a strange opening question, I noticed a slight smirk across Robert's lips.

"It's great thanks. Couldn't be better." The grin disappeared off their guest's face as quickly as it had arrived. Laura looked at her husband and then at her brother, a scornful glance at each.

"Listen, Daniel, you've come at a bad time. We were in the middle of a..." she hesitated, "... of a family meeting, shall we say?"

"Yes," we all looked at Robert as he spoke again, still steadfastly anchored to his seat, "we're talking business."

"Hey, okay, sorry we came uninvited. Come on, Emily, let's leave these good people in peace." I tried to inject some cheerfulness into the proceedings, but it obviously fell on deaf ears. Robert spoke again as we went to leave.

"Talking of business, Dan," he stared directly at me. "I understand Laura is teaching you French?"

"Yes, Robert, yes she is."

"Robert!" Laura shot him a look.

"No, Laura, we're talking business, so this is as good a time as any."

"What is it?" Emily asked, matching the abruptness in Robert's voice.

"Well, what it is love..." *Oh shit.* "... is that we all have to make a living don't we, and I don't want my Laura being taken advantage of." Laura hissed something at her brother under her breath and then turned to me.

"What Robert's trying to say, Daniel is, well, what he's trying to say is that maybe a little gesture for my time wouldn't go amiss." She looked so uncomfortable and tears pricked her eyes. I saved her the embarrassment.

"Hey, listen, Laura. I've always thought I should pay you. Let me know what the going rate is and I'll see you right."

Robert's brusque reply was the final signal for us to leave.

"Plus, the back pay for all the lessons she's already done."

Emily grabbed my hand and started to lead me away. I looked at Robert, whose smirk had returned. I then turned to Jean-Pascal and finally, Laura. Jean-Pascal looked at the ground, obviously also very uncomfortable with the conversation, whilst Laura mouthed 'sorry' towards me ensuring her brother didn't catch her doing so. Despite Robert's attitude, I had no intention of falling out with my neighbours, so once again I apologised.

"Sorry to interrupt, it's my fault for coming around unannounced," I said, whilst Emily pulled at my arm to lead me down the driveway. I smiled back at Laura, but she had already turned and was saying something under her breath to her brother. Jean-Pascal collected the coffee mugs and started to walk forlornly back towards his house.

"Well, they're *nice* people," smirked Emily, as we returned to my house. It hadn't gone unnoticed by me she had held my hand all the way back from the Allaires'. However, my heart was still pounding from the unequivocal conversation at my neighbours.

"That was unreal," I replied, still catching my breath. "They have been so nice to me ever since I arrived; well Laura in particular. Okay, they haven't always been in a great mood but then again, who is? I know they've thought I wasn't the most talkative person, but her brother is a complete twat."

"Couldn't put it better myself... *love*." She air quoted the word 'love'. I smiled.

"Thought that would wind you up."

"So, what was that all about, Dan? You've not been taking advantage of her, have you?" Emily playfully punched my arm.

"Of course I haven't. She offered to teach me French soon after I arrived... oh, hang on." Emily noticed my tone had turned more serious.

"What is it, Dan?"

"Well, when I think about it, when I was at their house having a barbecue, we got talking about me wanting to learn French."

"And?"

"It might be nothing, but I remember Laura went to say something, but Jean-Pascal shot her a look, as if to say, 'don't you dare'. Anyway, she carried on and offered to teach me, over at my house."

"Don't you think he agreed?"

"Maybe not, or maybe he knew she'd do it without asking for money. It's obvious what her brother thinks about it. Perhaps Jean-Pascal thinks the same, but he's more placid or doesn't want to fall out."

That evening we shared a bottle of wine. Fortunately, we hadn't seen Rachel all day, and I'd noticed her car had been out when we returned from the farmhouse. Later, I'd driven into town and picked up pizza. Emily looked tired and, as I'd already noticed a couple of times since she'd arrived, seemed subdued and in a little world of her own. One thing she had never lacked was enthusiasm or a fervour for life, yet I watched her holding her wine and staring out of the window. She still looked beautiful though – I could stare at her for hours.

After we'd finished the first bottle, I told Emily to open another whilst I went upstairs to shower.

As I dried myself, I walked through to the bedroom then I heard footsteps running along the gravel outside. I stood still, trying to decipher what was happening. Next, the letterbox pushed open, a split-second passed, and the letterbox slammed shut again. Straining my ears, all I could hear was the blood rushing through my head.

Emily! I suddenly remembered that she was in the lounge alone.

I ran downstairs, holding tight onto my towel, which I'd wrapped round my waist. My eyes darted everywhere, trying to assess if anything was amiss. There sat Emily, still in the chair with her noise cancelling headphones on. She didn't even notice me, and her head nodded backwards and forwards in motion to whatever she'd been listening to. My eyes continued to move around the room, from the living room to the kitchen. Then I saw something on the floor; it was beneath the letterbox. I had to step closer to make out exactly what I was looking at. Laying there was a huge rat, its tail extending at least twice the length of the body itself. It had a sharp-pointed stick straight through its stomach and poking out the other side. A tiny pool of blood escaped from underneath its body. I'm sure it was still moving, breathing its last breath of air. It looked grotesque, and I felt myself gag as I held my chest in an attempt not to be sick. Emily's scream bought me out of my trance. She was now standing and following my stare towards the dead creature on the floor. Her headphones were still pumping music into her ears.

I made for the door, momentarily hesitating, thinking the perpetrator might still be on the other side. I held my finger to my lips and gestured for Emily to keep quiet. She removed her headphones slowly and held them by her side. Her mouth fell wide open, as she stared, aghast. I listened closely but I couldn't hear a sound. Only silence and the tinging noise coming from Emily's headphones.

Slowly, I opened the door. The heat of the night hit me before I tentatively stepped outside. Peering left and then right, there was nothing, no movement, and no sound. Emily joined me, gripping my arm tightly with her free hand.

The only thing breaking the darkness between my house and the town beyond was a single light in the gîte at the bottom of the garden.

29

"You look as though you got about as much sleep as me."

It surprised me to see Emily sat outside on the terrace after I'd clambered out of bed and made my way downstairs. I'd had an awful night with my mind racing over and over. Who on earth would do such a thing? Surely it had to be Rachel, she was the one with the vendetta. First wanting us to become an item, then booking the gîte after I'd made it clear that I'd wanted her to leave – twice. The brick through my window after our argument, plus the mood swings. She could be an absolute pleasure to be with one minute and then losing her mind over trivial matters the next. Then there's the fact that Emily had arrived, and Rachel would have known by then; she would have seen her. That would only make her even more irate, but would she really do a thing like that? The phrase Emily had said soon after she arrived kept swirling round my head – 'You have no idea who you're dealing with.'

"No, I couldn't sleep at all. Just kept seeing an image of that rat twitching…"

"Stop it, Dan. I don't even want to think about it."

Making us both fresh coffee, I joined Emily outside. I had to tip my head to shield my eyes from the dazzling sunlight. There wasn't a cloud in view. It should have been such a joyous time for me, but the list of concerns kept mounting up. In some strange way, though, I felt invigorated to fight back. Had it been the arrival of Emily or had my last encounter with Rachel finally thrown the shackles off?

"Don't let her destroy your dream, Dan," I whispered under my breath.

"Did you say something?" Emily looked up at me.

"No, sorry, miles away. So, what do you think of the pool, Em?" I tried to lighten the mood.

"Looks great. The whole house looks great, Dan, you've found yourself a slice of paradise here. Just one thing…" she looked over at me.

"And what's that?"

"Well, I can't vouch for the gîte, but the house needs a bit of a female touch."

She wasn't smiling; she wasn't frowning either. It was more of a neutral look; one I couldn't gauge. Emily looked back towards the pool.

"Can I go in later?"

"Of course you can, why not?"

Emily nodded at the gîte.

"I thought she might infest it with rats or something."

Although she laughed, I knew Emily had already made her mind up about Rachel. She hadn't even met her yet, but the light on in the gîte the night before had convinced Emily that nobody else could have fled so quickly after slamming the letterbox shut. My mind kept flicking to the thought of Rachel telling Emily about us and how she would react. The more I thought about it, the more my heart palpitated, and my palms sweated. I noticed my hand shaking slightly as I raised my mug of coffee to my mouth. Just as I sipped the steaming hot liquid, the door to the gîte opened.

Rachel appeared, dressed for spending the next few hours around the pool. Her hair was tied up, with the ponytail pushed through the space at the back of her baseball cap. She was wearing the same multi-coloured sarong which she had worn when I'd first seen her around the pool. Once again, even from this distance, Rachel looked staggering. Emily snapped me out of my trance.

"Put your tongue away, Dan."

Immediately feeling my cheeks burn, I looked over at Emily, hoping she was smiling. She wasn't.

"It's not that, Em. I'm just trying to see if she looks over here, you know, with any kind of guilt or expression that she may have been responsible for last night."

Emily followed my gaze and watched Rachel walk up to the pool and turn a lounger into the direction of the overhead sun.

"She's very attractive," she said to nobody in particular.

"Yes, well, I mean, I guess so."

"Fucking give over, Dan, you're drooling." There was a hint of malice in her voice which I didn't like.

"Leave it, Em. She's a paying customer. Do you want me to get potential punters to send their photos through before I allow them to stay, and then only accept the ugly ones?"

Emily knew she'd hit a nerve but at least I'd diverted the conversation away from Rachel's looks.

"And what does she do, you know, for a living?"

"She hasn't really said. Something about computers, website design, but nothing specific. She might be freelance if she can take this much time out."

"Hmm, let's find out."

Before I could react, Emily had stood and shouted out Rachel's name. Rachel was avoiding us. She hadn't waved when she'd first appeared from the gîte and was now ignoring Emily's calls. She just continued to set herself up on the lounger pretending to be looking for something in her bag. Emily walked down to the pool.

Oh fuck, oh fuck.

I quickly got up and stumbled after her. As we got within hearing distance, I thought I'd take over and try to keep everything on a neutral footing.

"Morning, Rachel," I said as cheerily as I could muster, although it came out more a quiver. It was as though it petrified me, which it did.

Rachel stood and faced us as we approached.

"Oh, hi, Dan. I didn't see you," she lied.

"Rachel, this is Emily, my friend." I looked at Emily, who just smiled at my introduction. She reached out a hand to Rachel.

"Nice to meet you, Rachel. I hear you've been here quite a while."

This will end in tears.

"Well, the gîte's been available and Dan's been such a great host, haven't you, Dan?"

They turned to face me in unison. I wanted the ground to open up and swallow me. When I spoke, it sounded as though I was thirteen years old and my voice was breaking.

"I aim to please."

"You sure do, Dan–"

Emily stopped Rachel in her tracks.

"What do you do for a living, Rachel? You must have an accommodating boss to allow all this time off?"

Rachel stopped smiling at me and trained her attention onto Emily. Her voice took on a much more sombre tone.

"I'm self-employed, if it's any of your concern. I sometimes even do some freelance work for free, don't I, Dan?"

Before I could reply, Emily spoke again.

"Oh yes, the website. Dan showed me. It's quite good, actually."

"Glad it meets your approval, Emily…"

"Is that what you do then, create websites?" Emily pushed it, although I couldn't understand why.

"That and other things, yes. Why the interest in what I do?"

The conversation was getting more and more acerbic with every second. I wanted to intervene, but I couldn't get a word in edgeways. I couldn't formulate a sentence, anyway.

"Oh, just curious. I like to know as much as I can about a woman who spends as much time as she can around *my* Dan."

'*My* Dan.' Did she just say, '*my* Dan'? What on earth was Emily up to? Was she trying to get at Rachel or was she suggesting something entirely different? This wasn't lost on Rachel either and she smiled directly at me whilst continuing to talk to Emily.

"And what do you do, Emily? Something exciting no doubt."

"I run a chain of recruitment agencies if you must know. They're based in the south of England..."

"Yeah? Where exactly? I'm from Dorking. Do you have a branch there? I might look in when I get back. I've been thinking of a career move since I've been out here." Rachel was probing; there's no way she was thinking of changing careers. For the first time, I noticed Emily clam up.

"We offer nothing computer related. You must look elsewhere, if you ever leave that is."

Shit, low blow from Emily. Rachel wasn't finished.

"Who said I wanted to stay in computers? Tell me, Emily, what's the name of your company?"

Emily went back on the defensive. She didn't want to give any more information away or at least she didn't want to divulge any further information to Rachel.

"As I said, there's nothing we can do for you." She turned to me. "Come on, Dan, let's go into town and have lunch out. The air around here is making me feel rather nauseous."

Emily stomped back towards the house without looking back. I hung back for a private word with Rachel. I tried to keep my voice low. It came out as a hiss.

"Was that you last night. Rachel?"

"Was what me last night, Dan?" Her demeanour had changed again, and she returned to her usual flirty self once alone in my company.

"You know very well what I'm talking about, Rachel. If I ever catch you, I'll..."

"You'll what Dan? Come down and give me a good seeing to?"

My blood was boiling, but I kept my voice low between gritted teeth.

"You really are pushing your luck. Anything else and–"

"I've really no idea what you're talking about. If you can't talk sense, then don't talk at all."

Rachel stood up and took off her sarong. I couldn't help but stare. She picked up her suntan lotion and offered it to me.

"Would you be a gentleman and apply this to my back again Dan?"

"Go fuck yourself, Rachel."

"Oh, Dan," she was loving this. "By the way, what's Emily's surname?"

"Her surname, why the hell do you want to know that?"

"Just interested, nothing more."

I didn't want to tell her, but something triggered inside me that made me curious as to Rachel's question. As soon as I told her the surname was Wilkinson, Rachel took out her phone and typed it into her Notes app.

30

I'M NOT sure what Emily thought, but she had only been in France for four days and she'd witnessed enough to make her question my being there at all. First, she couldn't stay in the gîte because Rachel had booked herself in again and then we'd discovered someone had removed the passwords from my notebook. Next, she'd had the misfortune of meeting Laura's brother Robert – also my first encounter with him – followed by the dead rat being shoved through the letterbox. To complete her warm welcome to France, she'd had a set-to with the woman who refused to leave my property. I'd told her I moved out here to live the dream; it felt more like a bloody nightmare at that moment.

The previous night I'd tried to reassure her, informed her this would all pass over once Rachel had gone, but there was no appeasing her. There was definitely something else on her mind and after her altercation with Rachel, she had crawled into her inner shell, something I wasn't familiar with. She sat on the sofa with her feet tucked under her backside and stared blankly at the television, which was showing a film on a British satellite channel. The rain poured outside and pattered on the roof tiles. I just sat in a separate chair and drank far too much wine, trying to blank everything out of my mind. Once the movie had finished, I was tempted to ask Emily if she wanted to share my bed, just for reassurance, but I thought better of it. Could it be the happenings since she arrived or was something else on her mind? I had definitely noticed a difference, even before the rat and the encounters with my newfound neighbours. Another thing that had struck me since she arrived in France was that she was spending very little time on her phone or laptop. Before we had split up the year before, Emily had lived and breathed her work and spent all hours addressing clients. After a couple of glasses of wine, I'd asked how the business was going and she'd said she delegated a lot of the day-to-day work to other staff now. She informed me she was keeping her eye on things, but it was a quiet time, anyway. I guessed she just wanted to unwind for a few days.

Emily's shouting woke me from my hungover slumber early the next morning. A quick glance at my phone told me it had just gone eight o'clock – Emily must have got up early to do some work – and I ran downstairs wearing only my boxer shorts. The door to the terrace was wide open and Emily stood at the far end looking back behind the house. As soon as I reached her, I could see what had made her shout my name in such panic.

Unaware that I was only in my underwear and with no shoes on my feet, I walked over towards the vegetable patch. As far as I could tell, every plant had been pulled up by their roots and thrown in various directions across the lawn. It looked like a bomb had gone off directly in the heart of the plot and had blown each plant out of the ground. The next time I registered Emily was there was when I felt her hand, cold, in the middle of my back.

"Who would do such a thing, Em?" I asked, trembling, both from the drop in temperature and also from the shock.

"You know my feelings, Dan. It can only be one person. She's really got it in for you."

Rachel. Why was she doing this to me?

"But we can't just throw accusations at her, Em. Yesterday, when you walked back to the house, I hung around for a chat with her. I asked about the rat and she denied everything. She sounded plausible, Em, honest."

"You're just being led by her looks, Dan. She's a lunatic. I'm looking at this from the outside, as a neutral, and I can tell you she's one unhinged woman."

"It's not fair to keep saying I fancy her, Em." I turned around to face Emily for the first time since we'd walked down to inspect the bomb site. Her hand rested on my shoulder, but she ignored what I'd just said.

"You're shivering, Dan, you'd best get dressed. I'll make a start in clearing this lot up. Do you have a wheelbarrow or something I can pick it all up in?"

I took her arm and pulled it from my shoulder. It annoyed me she'd deliberately changed the subject.

"There's one at the back of the garage," I said, and trudged off back towards the house.

. . .

Sulking in my room after I'd showered, I heard car tyres on the driveway. Looking out of my bedroom window, I saw Rachel's car driving off toward town. At least she's out the way for a while, I thought, and I lay down on my bed letting Emily clear up the mess on her own outside. I wasn't in the mood to help.

Voices from the garden woke me, floating up through the house from the open door downstairs. I'd been asleep about an hour, drifting off into a deep slumber and dreaming of giant rats ripping vegetables from their roots and slinging them across the garden with their mammoth teeth and jaws. I was sweating profusely and needed another shower, but the voices intrigued me. I was becoming a nervous wreck, anxious about whoever was around my house, thinking every one of them had a vendetta against me moving to France.

Once dressed and outside, I saw Emily talking to Brad. He was loading the wheelbarrow, and they had removed almost every uprooted plant from the lawn. Emily was raking the veg plot, it looked as good as it had when I first planted the vegetables a few weeks earlier. I felt a lump in my throat, maybe not everybody wanted me gone.

"Hey, Brad." I forced a smile, walking over to them.

"Here's Sleeping Beauty. How you feeling, mate?"

"I'm okay, a bit pissed off about this, but thank you," I turned to Emily, "and thank you, Em, you really didn't have to go to–"

Brad interrupted, "You didn't tell me you had visitors." He was looking at Emily.

"Didn't I say? Oh sorry. I take it you've introduced yourselves?"

"Nah," quipped Emily. "I just saw this stranger walk

past the house, grabbed him and told him to pick up mutilated vegetables."

"You've walked, Brad?" I couldn't help myself even though Emily had just lightened the mood, and they were both still laughing. Brad looked irritated by my question.

"Yes, stretched my legs and wandered out of town. I thought I'd call and see how you are, that okay?"

Emily looked at me gone out, impatiently waiting for me to reply to Brad.

"Dan?"

"Yeah, sure. It's okay. Sorry, it's just all this," I said, pointing at the area that was almost all cleared up.

"It's okay mate, you looked stressed. Emily told me about the rat. Shit mate, that must have really freaked you out. Any idea who it is?"

I thought about mentioning the brick through the window too and I looked towards Emily. She spoke before I could say anything.

"Dan has an idea, but he can't be sure, can you, darling?"

Darling now, *My Dan* yesterday and yet she'd pushed me away earlier like I was a drunk approaching her in a pub. Emily was becoming very difficult to read and I'd thought I knew her like the back of my hand. I also couldn't read her thoughts about why she stopped me saying we think Rachel is behind all this, but the look she gave me suggested I dare not let her down.

"Erm, no. I've seen a couple of people walking by recently and they had a good look into my garden. Could be them I suppose, but there's no proving it."

Emily smiled a 'thank you' towards me and I shrugged my shoulders in return. She looked at me and nodded at Brad. He hadn't noticed our exchange as he was loading the last of the destroyed plants into the barrow.

"Well, can't go accusing just anybody can we?" he said.

Brad stayed for a coffee after he'd tipped all the dead plants into a heap right down the far end of the garden. Emily had finished raking the plot and promised to go out with me later to buy more veg. I said I would see, but I didn't want to keep buying stuff for somebody else to ruin. What I'd really meant was let's wait until Rachel goes home next weekend and start again, but I'd avoided directing my anger towards Rachel in front of Brad.

Once he'd gone, I went straight into the kitchen where Emily was stacking the dishwasher.

"What was that all about? You didn't want me to mention Rachel, why?"

Emily looked towards the door as if Brad might still be there.

"Is he gone?" she whispered.

"Yes, you said goodbye, remember?"

"You idiot. I know I said goodbye, but has he definitely gone, out of earshot?"

I walked over to the door and looked down the road. Sure enough, Brad was turning the corner towards town, almost at the Allaires' drive entrance. I scuttled back indoors.

"Yeah, he's miles away. Well?"

Emily closed the dishwasher door and dried her hands on a towel which had been lying on top. She stepped closer towards me and kept her voice down, as if she thought the room might be bugged.

"Well, the thing is, whilst you were asleep, me and Brad got chatting. About all kinds of things to begin with, but he kept asking if Rachel was around. I said no, her car wasn't there, and I carried on gossiping about work, weather, you know, all the boring bullshit…"

"Yes, yes, go on."

"Calm down else I won't tell you." I loved that smile.

"Sorry."

"But every two or three minutes he directed the subject back to Rachel and asked something else about her. Where's she gone? What time did she go? When will she be back? Like it obsessed him."

"Maybe he just fancies her?" I began to lose interest in the conversation as he obviously just liked her and had walked up hoping to catch her sunbathing or something.

"That's what I thought, I even considered it was kind of sweet. Anyway, I then told him about the rat, and guess what?"

"What?"

"He didn't seem surprised, or at least he didn't flinch, just kind of took it in his stride. All he said was 'well, it couldn't have been Rachel, she's far too nice for such a thing'."

"I must admit, he's always stuck up for her. Once, when I went kayaking with him, he got defensive about her staying, saying she could stop as long as she wanted as long as she was paying. Then another time we had a beer in some village on the river and he defended her again."

Emily was deep in thought, still drying her hands on the towel. Finally, she spoke.

"And another thing, he said nothing about the veg patch. Just strolled up, introduced himself and said I should rake the soil whilst he cleared the mess up. Don't you think it's strange that he didn't even question when it happened?"

Emily was right, it was strange. And why did he constantly stick up for Rachel? Emily's phone rang and after looking at the caller ID, she mouthed the word 'work' to me and took the call outside. Her voice became fainter as she walked down the garden and out of earshot.

I carried on cleaning the kitchen, putting away the rest of the clean stuff that Emily had unloaded from the dishwasher before restocking it with more dirty items. I'd just put the last two wine glasses in when Emily came crashing through the door.

"Dan, Dan, quick," and she ran off back out of the house. I got to the door and saw her running down past the pool towards the gîte. Just to convince myself, I double-checked Rachel's car wasn't back on the driveway. It wasn't.

Running past the pool, I saw Emily pacing around outside the gîte, paying particular attention to the ground outside the entrance door.

Once I caught up, Emily was positively bursting.

"Look, look!" She pointed towards the ground.

Sure enough, there was mud everywhere.

"And look!" squealed Emily. I followed her around the corner.

Behind the gîte, out of sight, there was a pair of old boots. Also caked in mud.

31

IT WAS time to confide in Emily – well, most things. I'd lain awake most of the night, yet again, and I needed a friend, a close friend, to share my anxieties with. I was also desperate to share my plans for staying in France. She had always listened to me and she also had a very good business head on her shoulders. I was due to have a French lesson that night with Laura, and it was the first time I would have seen her since meeting her charming brother, Robert. Perhaps I would ask Emily what to do about paying for the lessons too. She'd heard Robert mouthing off – 'Plus the back pay for all the lessons she's already done.'

Brad phoned whilst I sat outside sipping my first coffee of the day. He asked if I'd had any more adventures since he'd left the day before. I said no and avoided telling him about the muddy boots outside the gîte. He'd have only gone all mushy about Rachel again, saying I couldn't go around accusing her. I'm sure if he caught her breaking into his house, he'd say she must have got the wrong property. Emily had her doubts about Brad and likewise, I was getting more sceptical of his intentions.

An hour or so later, Emily appeared. It was midmorning and the longest she had slept since her arrival. She definitely looked better for it, more colour in her cheeks and she'd made an effort with her hair, tying it up but letting straggles escape which overlapped other strands. The punk in Emily would never leave her.

I went inside, grabbed a coffee, put two croissants on a plate and moved back outside to join her. She was wearing a bright orange T-shirt and blue shorts which reached the top of her knees. She looked more colourful all round, and it suited her outgoing, fun-loving personality that I'd always admired. However, when I sat next to her, she still wore that haunted look and had the same worry lines around her eyes.

"Everything okay Em?"

"Yeah, sure. Feel better for a good sleep. I must have been shattered."

We made small talk for a while before both retreating into our protective shells. We sat in silence, admiring the countryside surrounding us and the beautiful town of Monpazier in the distance. Emily must have been thinking the same as me.

"I still haven't seen the town and I've been here almost a week."

"Yes, I know. There's been a lot going on and unfortunately, you've walked right into the middle of it. I'm so sorry, Em."

She reached her hand across the table and held mine.

It felt so good to be this close to Emily again, after all this time.

"Hey, it's fine, Dan. Just pleased to be here, away from it all."

What does she mean? Is everything okay back at home?

"Do you want to talk about anything, Em? You look as though you're carrying the weight of the world on your shoulders."

She took a deep breath and sat back in her chair, as if contemplating whether to open up and share all her woes with me. I tensed up, waiting for what might come, but then she exhaled all the air from her lungs and the distress escaped with it. Instead, she steered the conversation back to me.

"No, there's nothing. Anyway, tell me all about you. What are your plans now you've been here several weeks?"

Although I felt angry that she wouldn't share whatever had been troubling her, I was also glad of the opportunity to divulge my plans just to gauge her reaction. I told her of the house I'd found for sale and my idea of doing it up, bit by bit, and then renting that one out too. Maybe, in a couple of years, I would look for another and build up a small portfolio of rentable properties. My dreams were running away with me as I spoke, but I enjoyed watching the smile return to Emily's face as she sat and listened to everything I had to say.

"Sounds like you're going to take on the world, Dan," she smiled, "and I'm so pleased for you. You deserve a break and to do something you love."

I wondered if I should have asked her if she wanted to be part of those plans. Something stopped me. Did I want Emily back? There had been a lot of history and it wasn't as simple as just letting her slip back into my life. However, at the back of my mind, I knew there was nothing I wanted more.

We again sat in silence and my thoughts were spinning. Positive and negative ideas battled for my attention. Emily could see.

"What's wrong then, Dan, why aren't you doing cartwheels down to your swimming pool and back?"

The look of concern on her face tipped me over the edge and I stood up and started pacing around my garden. She was right. Why wasn't I ecstatic about my plans and ambitions? This was my escape, my new life and, on paper at least, everything was going in the right direction. Emily joined me and put her arm around my back, pulling me towards her.

"Hey, hey, what's wrong, what is it?"

Just feeling her close was the catalyst for me to blurt it all out.

"It's all going wrong though, isn't it, Em?"

She turned me to face her; we were inches apart. She ran her fingers through my hair, rubbing my cheek with her thumb as she did.

"What's going wrong, Dan? It's just somebody playing pranks on you and it's obvious who that somebody is. Don't let her get you down, this is your dream. Besides, she won't be here much longer."

I removed her hand from my face and held it by my side.

"There's been other things too though, Em, not just the rat through the door and the veg patch."

As I listed what else had gone on since I arrived, Emily held both of my hands and gently squeezed them the more I revealed. I told her about the purple car driving past my house several times, then the occasion the same vehicle happened to be outside the property for sale. I mentioned the subsequent chase afterwards and how I'd lost sight of it. I also told her about Andy Jackson, who he was and his comments the day he'd fitted my shelves. Emily had interrupted me and asked if the cupboard on the floor had been Andy's handy work, too. I explained about that and the day I'd been sure it was him who had driven his van right up my backside when I went to the garden centre. Another time when somebody watched me from the other side of the town square and when the contacts on my phone had been scrolled through. The brick through the window two nights before Emily arrived had shocked her the most. There were others that I couldn't recall but I could feel a huge weight lifting as I shared my experiences with someone I trusted. The list exhausted me and when I recounted them all together it almost overwhelmed me. What was happening to me?

"Wow. You're sure you didn't imagine any of them, Dan?"

"What, imagining somebody watching me from around the corner of a house and then getting in a purple Peugeot and me chasing them until I lost them? That's some imagination, Em."

"Okay, I'll give you that one, but somebody watching you across a crowded square, your contacts being scrolled through."

"A brick in the middle of the spare room floor? The white van? It was right up my arse, Emily. I could swear I could see Andy Jackson smiling…"

"It must feel like some kind of conspiracy, Dan, but I'm sure there's an…" Emily stopped in her tracks and let go of my hands.

"What is it?"

"There could well be a simple explanation for it, Dan."

What was she thinking?

"Could Rachel and Brad be in collusion?"

I tried to reason and speak at the same time.

"What kind of collusion?"

Emily looked over at the gîte to make sure Rachel wasn't around. She took my hand and led me back to the table on the terrace. Sitting down, she nodded at the chair next to her. I sat down too.

"Could Brad be the driver of the purple car? Is he keeping his eye on you, to see what you're up to? When you were looking at other houses and stuff."

"So how does that make them Bonnie and Clyde?"

"Don't take the piss, just listen."

That's me told.

"He's always sticking up for her, right?"

"Right."

"And now you've made it clear you want her to leave, he doesn't agree, thinks you're being too hard on her. Then things happen, a dead rat appears, your prize carrots are strewn across the lawn–"

"Hey, more than just carrots–"

"Shut up and listen. Is it also a coincidence that when I turn up, she gets jealous and they conspire to get at you? And judging from your reaction, they *are* getting to you, Dan."

Fuck, she could be right.

Emily continued.

"Have you ever seen Brad's car, Dan?"

"No, never. In fact, I think it's really weird I haven't. We once met in a village called Beynac-et-Cazenac–"

"Shit, your French is awful–"

"Piss off. Anyway, where was I?"

"Some village called–"

"Listen, Em, I'm being serious…" Emily stopped me, leant over and kissed me.

"I'm being serious too, Dan, but don't forget we go back a long way and know each other very well. I'm just adding a bit of humour before you scream the house down."

It was a kiss I'd never forget. It was only a peck, well, a long peck, but to feel her lips on mine again after all that time felt like touching velvet with my fingertips, so soft and so warm. But it was not the time, I was in full flow.

"It's okay, I'm calm, honest." My voice betrayed my words. "Anyway, this village I can't pronounce, it had a massive car park in the middle, with loads of empty spaces, yet Brad said he'd parked his car at the other end of town. Then another time he asked me to drive to kayaking, but wouldn't let me pick him up. Instead, he walked here to get a lift. Even yesterday he walked here from the village."

"There you go then. Ask yourself why you've never seen his car. Could Brad be the mystery driver and Rachel the rat catcher and vegetable destroyer?"

"Yes, but why did Brad help clean up yesterday?"

"He'd been hanging around to see Rachel you fool. He had no interest in helping to tidy up. She probably bollocked him last night for clearing up the mess she created."

. . .

It made sense. Rachel and Brad could easily have been in it together. I recalled the time when he suddenly appeared at the bar in town; it was only my second or third day after arriving. I remembered him ordering me a beer when I'd asked for a coffee. If he was the owner of the purple car, then he would have known I'd only just moved in. The very next day he could have followed me into town and joined me in the bar making it look purely coincidental. The following day, Rachel booked two weeks in my gîte. Fate or something a lot more sinister?

The pieces were fitting together, bit by bit. Just one thing was missing from Emily's fine piece of detective work.

Why?

32

My French lesson, or lack of it, with Laura the previous night had been taut with tension. Earlier, Emily had told me to offer to pay for Laura's time, as it was obviously a concern for their family. She also advised me to ask if she wanted back payment. I could always cancel if it became too expensive, anyway.

My attention had been drifting for the rest of the afternoon between Rachel and Brad being in cahoots and the kiss from Emily which had sent butterflies fluttering around my stomach. We hadn't spoken for months, yet, here she was, at my new home in France, leaning over and kissing me as if things were just the same between us. I didn't know what to think or what to do. I'd started a new life since we had split, and my depression was under control. The last thing I wanted was old wounds to reopen and a return to the rollercoaster life that had almost tipped me over the edge. However, Emily had been my rock, my soulmate. She had helped me through so much in the past. The kiss had made me realise that I definitely still had strong feelings towards her.

Just before Laura was due to arrive, Emily made her excuses and went outside to read her book whilst nursing a bottle of wine. I was pleased because anymore confrontation with Laura might have tipped me over the edge.

I hadn't been in the right frame of mind for a French lesson or seeing Laura at all. As soon as she arrived, it soon became apparent she wasn't in the mood either. Our acknowledgement on the doorstep was an air kiss on each cheek and no physical hugging which had been our greeting on every previous occasion. I wanted to get matters straight before we even began. I surprised myself as a newfound confidence gave me the courage to tackle things head on.

"Okay Laura, your brother made it clear that he thinks I should pay for these lessons and, on reflection, he's right. I did originally offer to pay you when you first agreed to teach me. I should never have accepted your offer to teach me for free. You tell me what you want, and I'll gladly pay, if we're in agreement, of course."

Laura evidently had come to talk to me too. She suggested we both sit down at the kitchen table.

"Daniel, I like you and I have enjoyed our lessons. However, it is probably best we stop now."

It felt like being metaphorically slapped around the face. It left me speechless, and I sat with my mouth wide open, unable to form any words at all. Laura spoke for us both.

"Robert can be a little crass, and I apologise for his behaviour. But, as you said, on reflection he is right. I shouldn't be giving up my time for free. I was just trying to be a good neighbour."

It was the complete change in personality that threw me much more than the content of her speech. Her eyes were piercing, looking straight through me. She constantly picked at her fingernails to the point I thought she would make them bleed. Now and then, she scratched her forearms leaving red marks and then she'd rub her neck with the palms of her hands, both sides and round to the back under her hair. Laura had taken on the actions of a nervous wreck. It was totally out of character and I was certain she was acting on instructions rather than her own wishes.

The next person to speak was neither Laura nor myself.

"Is everything all right?"

It was Emily, standing at the door. I'd no idea how long she'd been standing there, but it made Laura jump to her feet. The chair underneath her tumbled backwards and cracked to the floor, the sound amplifying the tension in the air.

"Oh, sorry, I didn't mean to make you jump." Emily walked over to her and attempted to put an arm round her shoulder. I stood with my hands on the table, perplexed by the situation. Laura brushed Emily's arm aside.

"I'm fine, just didn't know you were there, that's all."

Trying to keep my voice on an even keel, I offered Laura an easy get out.

"Laura, listen. Whatever you think is best is okay with me. Let's have a break from the lessons and I'll pay you for the ones you've already given me. How does that sound?"

For a moment, I thought Laura would be sick, and she made for the door.

"Pay me what you want, Daniel, I really don't mind. Listen, I have to go."

Emily would not let her leave so easily.

"Laura, whatever's wrong you can tell us. Dan has had nothing but good things to say about you since I arrived. Blimey, you must be a good teacher too because he can actually speak the language better than I ever thought he would."

Laura turned to face Emily and then glanced back to me. She stood at the door; half ready to leave with her hand resting on the frame.

"Nothing is wrong, nothing at all. It's just best we stop doing this, that's all."

Then came the bombshell.

"Maybe you could get your little tart down in the gîte to teach you. After all, she offered to at our barbecue and it looks like she's here to stay." She then turned to Emily before continuing. "And now you've got another one, Daniel. You're spoilt for choice."

Emily stared at me, but I was more interested in Laura. Before I could find the words, she had turned and marched across the garden towards the fence and the hill toward her farmhouse.

The encounter with Laura had weighed heavily on my conscience all day. I'd mowed the lawn, cleaned the swimming pool, and generally made myself busy around the house and garden. Earlier Rachel had driven her car towards town whilst Emily had stayed indoors doing some work on her laptop. Luckily, they had avoided each other, and I had avoided both. Female company had been the very last thing I'd needed that day.

As I walked back towards the house, I heard my phone ping in my pocket. It was an email from the agency confirming the booking for Saturday July the fifth was successfully cancelled.

What the fuck?

I raced inside and picked up my laptop. Emily stopped what she was doing and stared at me.

My laptop felt like it took an age to boot up, but I finally got into the agency page where I managed my bookings. Sure enough, the booking had been cancelled.

"Fucking hell!" I shouted.

Emily got up and walked behind me, her hand resting on my shoulder trying to see what I was looking at. That's when a second email pinged on my phone.

Booking cancelled

As requested by yourself, this booking has now been cancelled. The guest(s) have been informed

Dates: Saturday 2nd August to Saturday 9th August inclusive

Contact: Mr F. Moody

What the hell's going on?

Emily leant over and pressed F5 on my laptop. The page refreshed and sure enough, they had cancelled the second booking.

I turned to face her. She looked as shocked as I felt.

"What's going on, Dan? Have you cancelled these? It says requested by yourself."

"It isn't me, Em, why the hell would I do that?"

"But didn't we change all your passwords when I arrived last Sunday?"

"Yes, I'm sure we…" I racked my brain. "Hang on, I just logged into this account, the agency, with my original login details. I must have forgotten to do this one and the website after I found someone had ripped the details out of my notebook. Shit!"

"Oh, Dan, you idiot."

"Okay, okay, I don't need fucking telling, do I?"

"Well change it now, it's only two bookings…"

"Only two, only two? This is my livelihood, Em. I'll be going home with you at this rate. My plans are going down the drain."

"I'm sorry, I didn't mean to be flippant. I know you're worried but there's only one person who has access to your passwords."

Emily had a look of determination on her face.

"You need to get rid of her, Dan."

She was right.

"Yeah, but how?"

"Don't worry, I have a plan."

33

"What's the plan? Is it safe?"

I was desperate to know what was going through Emily's mind and also sceptical at what she could have been thinking.

"I'll tell you soon, but first you have to be honest with me, Dan."

Oh no, she looks deadly serious.

"Sit on the sofa, please. I'll make us coffee."

Doing as she said, I sat down, making myself as comfortable as possible. The mid-afternoon heat prickled my skin with sweat. Taking deep breaths, I tried to hold myself together. The whole situation was getting out of hand and, worse still, the one person I cared about the most was deep in it with me. My dream was turning into a living nightmare. Eventually, Emily sat next to me and put two coffees on the table in front of us. I desperately wanted to swap my drink for something much stronger. Emily turned to face me. With such a calm demeanour, I wondered for a second why I had been so worried.

"Tell me the truth, Dan. We can't put an end to this unless you are honest with me."

For the first time since the day my mum left me at the school gates, my bottom lip trembled. I so desperately didn't want to break the news to Emily, even though I was sure she'd guessed. I knew I had to be honourable to keep her on my side. She really was my only friend in France – the only one I could trust.

"Okay, Em. Yes, we slept together." I looked up to gauge her reaction, but her expression had not changed at all. She remained perfectly still and held my gaze. I had no choice but to continue.

"It was at the end of her first week here. We got drunk, very drunk…"

"Spare me the details, Dan. Has it happened since? Have you wanted to sleep with her again?"

"No, no, honest. I mean I could have done, she's like, crazy, you know." I babbled on but couldn't stop myself.

"And have you said 'no' purely because I'd been due to arrive?"

That question confused me slightly and for the second time in as many days I found some inner confidence growing. It was almost as if a great weight had been lifted and now everything else could escape from underneath.

"With all due respect, Em, we split up several months ago. It was amicable, for the best, we agreed. Why would I wait or put off another woman because you were due to visit me?"

My comment must have hit her like a sledgehammer. She looked hurt but remained calm, on the exterior at least.

"So why haven't you slept with her again?"

"Because I just told you, she's crackers, loopy–"

"Possessed?" Emily interrupted.

I hadn't considered such a potent description.

"I'm not sure if that's the right word. She definitely won't take no for an answer, but possessed might be..."

"Okay, fixated then?"

It was difficult to argue with that.

"But why, Em? Call me negative, but she's a good-looking woman who could find any single bloke. Why on earth would she be fixated with me?" I air quoted the word 'fixated'.

Emily leaned closer.

"Don't be so hard on yourself, Dan. You know my feelings for you have never gone away don't you?"

My heart began beating so fast I'm surprised it didn't show through my shirt. I leant forward to pick up my coffee, but Emily knew that it was just a diversion. She pulled me back, leant over and kissed me, long and hard. When she eventually removed her mouth from mine, it left me breathless.

"What the..." but Emily put her finger on my lips.

"One more question, Dan. If you had the choice of who stays between me and her, who would you choose?"

That's an easy one.

"Why, you of course, Em. What a... what a stupid question."

"Good. Now take me to bed and afterwards I'll tell you my plan."

The next morning, it pleasantly surprised me to be woken with a gentle kiss on the lips. The feeling of Emily's naked body next to mine immediately put me in the mood for more of what we had done the previous day. I put my hand under the duvet.

"Whoa, hang on, Casanova." She pulled my hand away, pushed the cover back and walked towards the bathroom. She turned around at the door and I took in the whole of her naked glory. She modestly tried to cover as much of herself as she could with both her arms. However, when she spoke, it brought my mood crashing back to the present.

"This morning, I want you to take me to see this property you've seen for sale. And then, this afternoon I have to see Rachel to put our plan into operation. We have to find out, Dan."

"Yeah, I know," I reluctantly replied. Right at that moment, I wanted to forget all about Rachel and cancelled bookings and dead rats and brothers of neighbours who wanted my money. I just preferred to wallow in self-congratulation at spending one of the nicest nights I'd had in months. Being back with Emily had been all I'd wanted ever since we'd separated. Maybe it was one of the main reasons I'd come to France in the first place, to escape the reality of no longer being with her.

As she left the room, and I heard the shower kick into life, I lay back on the pillow with my hands behind my head. Staring at the ceiling, I thought of the time that had passed since I'd arrived in France several weeks before. I deliberated on all the other reasons I'd wanted to leave my previous life behind, apart from Emily and all that had happened between us. I thought of the tube rides at eight o'clock in the morning, packed into the carriage on the Victoria Line going south from Kings Cross. Walking to the office in the pouring rain, waiting for the endless line of traffic to pass before the little man turned green on the crossing lights. Being bored stupid at work, clock-watching from the minute I sat at my desk to the minute I could pack away and leave. The hours, days and years I'd dreamt of this life. I glimpsed the azure sky through a gap in my shutters. As far as I could tell there wasn't a single cloud above. I rolled over and smiled.

Emily's side of the bed still felt warm, and I inched my head over onto her pillow. It felt so good to have her back and I knew she'd be on my side, ready to help. But there was still something not right, something in her manner. There were glimpses of the old Emily; fun, bubbly and an absolute pleasure to be in the company of. Then there was the other side, moody, distant and the look of discontent.

Whatever, she still likes me, loves me even. I liked her plan, and she had my best interests at heart.

After Emily had told me her proposal, I'd immediately phoned the agency to change the booking system for my gîte, so any future clients had to email me first to check availability. That way I could see who wanted the gîte and then verify with a yes or no once I knew who was behind it. It wasn't foolproof – Rachel could book under a false name for example – but at least I could be more vigilant. We did the same on my website, after I paid somebody online to work on the system, so bookings had to come via email. The first part of the plan was in progress to at least stop her from staying again.

My thoughts returned to Emily, and a notion entered my mind like a needle piercing skin. Why had I not thought of it before?

When is she going home?

I'd never asked how long she'd intended to stay but, thinking about it, it couldn't be long because of her business. The thought put me in a sullen mood. If she was going home soon, then what we'd had the previous twenty-four hours couldn't continue. So, did I need to decide? There was no way I'd ever go back to England. I loved it in France so much despite the protestations at the forefront of my mind. But there was no way Emily could stay; she was far too busy back home.

I must ask her later, sort it out once and for all.

Rolling over onto my back once more, my mind drifted to the pleasure I felt to have Emily back in my bed and back in my life. Could we ever start over again?

A stab of guilt ran through my head. Earlier I hadn't been entirely honest with Emily about Rachel.

When she'd asked me, 'Have you wanted to sleep with her again?', I had replied, 'No, honest'.

That wasn't exactly the truth.

In fact, it was a bare-faced lie.

34

THAT SATURDAY AFTERNOON, Emily had gone back to bed to have a nap. She hadn't been sleeping well since she'd arrived, and I agreed it would do her good to rest. We both had to be ready for the second part of the plan, but we knew we had to be patient and wait for the right time. I also wanted to take Emily out later that night for a meal in Monpazier. I yearned to celebrate our reconciliation, however long it might last.

The sun was boiling, around the mid-thirties, and I purposefully sat in the shade just messing about on my laptop, doing nothing in particular. A noise from the gîte caught my attention and Rachel appeared a few seconds later. She looked up and waved to me. I reciprocated, although not in an enthusiastic manner, trying to prove the point that she still wasn't welcome. Rachel scanned the rest of my terrace and looked for any sign of life behind me in the house. She was checking to see if Emily was around. When it became apparent I was alone, Rachel walked up the garden towards me. It was the last thing I'd wanted to deal with. Once she arrived, she spoke in a lowered voice.

"I know you have no time for me, Dan, and frankly I have got little time for you either. But I think you should know what I've found out, you know, before I leave next weekend. I promise to keep out of your way until then, but you need to know this. Can I have a word, in private?"

"What's it about, Rachel? Don't tell me, you've booked the gîte for another twelve months?" I added sarcastically.

She ignored my response yet appeared keen for the conversation to continue. She looked deadly serious. It made me feel uneasy.

"I could easily book the gîte for another twelve months, Daniel, that's easy once you know how. However, that's not what I need to talk to you about."

Either something genuinely troubled Rachel, or she was a fantastic actor. Given past episodes, I leant towards the latter. She asked if I would walk around the garden with her to 'keep away from prying eyes and ears.' Reluctantly, I agreed, if only to stretch my legs and not to wake Emily when our voices inevitably became raised.

"What did you want to talk to me about, Rachel? I haven't got all day."

She strode off along the garden and I had no alternative but to run after her. I hated the way she dictated my movements and had me chasing after her like some schoolkid with a crush.

"Don't interrupt, okay?" She stopped, momentarily, and looked directly at me. I unwillingly nodded my agreement. Rachel carried on walking, once again leaving me scurrying to keep up.

"On Tuesday, just after you told me to *go fuck myself*, if you recall, I asked what Emily's surname is." She waited for my acknowledgment. "Hmm," I replied, now mildly anxious where this might be heading.

"You told me *Wilkinson*. Emily Wilkinson. So, I did some investigation Dan–"

"You have no fucking right–"

"Hush, hush, Dan. You promised to let me finish. Once I'm done, you can make up your own mind." She continued in the same level voice that now began to grate on me, more in fear of what she would reveal than any other reason.

"Emily Wilkinson is director and owner of Wilkinson Recruitment Limited, registered in Surrey, England."

"And?" Rachel shot me a look to keep quiet.

"I doubt you know this, Dan, not being a businessman–"

"And you build websites, Rachel. You're not a fucking detective, are you?" My interruption made me feel better about myself, until Rachel responded that was.

"Yes, I build websites, Dan. I'm also a freelance journalist if you must know. I have connections–"

I interrupted for a second time.

"You're a what? Journalist? Are you fucking spying on me?"

My emotions were blocking any logical response. Could she really be a journalist?

"Of course I'm not spying on you. I told you, I *had* to get away for a while. I'm on holiday but I have very good connections back at home and I know how to find things out. I told you I do other things apart from design websites."

I stood facing her, seething, both at her smugness and

her revelation. She continued to speak whilst walking away from me.

"As I was saying, there are ways of finding out online if a company is in trouble," she stopped and turned to face me, "such as issuing an insolvency notice."

"No way, Emily's–"

"Emily's what, Dan? A brilliant businesswoman? Think again. Wilkinson Recruitment Limited filed for insolvency on Monday the fifth of May this year. She's finished, Dan, it's why she's here."

It couldn't be true. Emily would have confided in me, wouldn't she? Is that why she'd been so quiet, staring into space half the time? Snappy one minute, laughing the next? With this going on in her life no wonder her behaviour had been so erratic. It was so unlike the person who had always picked me up when I was down. Rachel continued strolling, and we were now at the bottom end of my garden, past the house.

"She would have told me." I was talking out loud, more trying to convince myself than anybody else. "She's always been honest with me."

Rachel laughed.

"You think so, Dan? Listen, I know you love her, it's obvious, and maybe that's why we could never get together. But you have to listen to me. All I'm saying is tread carefully. I know what this move means to you and you have made it clear you don't want me interfering with your plans. Will you allow Emily to get in the way?"

She walked away whilst I stood rooted to the spot. I knew Emily as well as anybody and I knew it would be her pride that was stopping her from telling me of her business troubles. She would be embarrassed and just waiting for the right time to break her news. It's not as though I'd throw her out or think anything less of her.

Looking at Rachel walking away from me, I tried to think what she could possibly gain out of this. Revenge? She couldn't know Emily and I had slept together the previous night – or could she? – but it could still be jealousy. The only thing Emily hadn't done was tell me what was going on back in England. Was that such a crime? This was just Rachel shit stirring, wallowing in somebody else's misfortune. She hated Emily and was trying to turn me against her too. That would not work. The more I thought about it, the more obvious it became that Rachel was now seeking to destroy everything I was attempting to build. She'd just said so herself; she can't have me, so she didn't want Emily in my life either.

What a mess.

The sensation of somebody watching me interrupted my thoughts. I spun around, searching all directions but couldn't see anyone. Rachel had now reached the gîte door. What I saw made me realise more than ever that I'd been right.

She didn't know I was looking at her but, as she disappeared inside, I could see she had a huge grin on her face.

35

I KEPT Rachel's revelations to myself for the rest of the day. I needed time to work out in my mind what I should do next and how I would approach Emily to seek the truth. She didn't surface from bed until early afternoon and I knew it would be fruitless to have a deep discussion with her. She had looked spaced out for the rest of the day. We postponed the meal in town as she 'didn't feel like socialising'. The day dragged on for an eternity and I was pleased to go to bed early and I fell asleep before Emily came upstairs. I didn't even hear her get in or if she even slept in the same bed as me because she was up and about before I awoke.

It was a new day, and I had to talk with her. I patiently bided my time and grew more and more apprehensive as the day drifted aimlessly by. Mid-afternoon I asked if she felt up to going out that night, thinking neutral territory would be the best setting to tackle such a sensitive subject. Mercifully, she agreed.

. . .

Emily looked lovely when she emerged from the house just before we were due to walk into town. It was still very warm, and the sun was reluctant to call it a day. As we walked, I noticed Rachel standing at her window in the gîte. She stared directly at us and I felt unnerved by it. I'm guessing she was trying to work out if I'd said anything yet, and when Emily put her arm through mine, she maybe drew her own conclusions. She pulled the shutters together with such force I'd half expected them to fall in a heap by her feet. Emily said nothing, but I glanced at her from the corner of my eye and she had a wry smile etched across her face.

We made for the main square. It was my favourite part of town, the hub, and for the last day of June, it was busy, albeit on a Sunday night, which was normally the quietest evening of the weekend. The restaurant I'd frequented with Rachel had a couple of tables spare and we made our way to one near the back. After we'd ordered food and our first drinks had arrived, I got the matter out in the open. I was almost at bursting point.

"Em, can I ask you something?" She immediately looked defensive. I already dreaded the outcome.

"Okay, what is it?"

"I know something's wrong, Emily. I know you better than I know anybody else and you've just not been yourself ever since you arrived. You know you can trust me, there's nothing you can say that will make me think less of you."

She took a large gulp of her cold beer, almost drained it in fact. Looking around the restaurant and then back at me, she leaned across the table and put her hand out for me to reciprocate. I squeezed, waiting for the response. It was not what I had hoped for.

"There's nothing, Dan, just tired, that's all."

She was lying. I played mind games too.

"Another thing I've noticed is that you're hardly on your phone, Em. No emailing either. I thought you'd be inundated with stuff from the business. In fact, I thought I'd barely see you once you arrived."

Her palms were sweating, and she immediately pulled her hand away. She signalled the waiter, drained her beer and promptly ordered another without asking me if I wanted one or not. I pressed on.

"You've not told me when you're going back either. How long do you plan to stay away? Surely the business–"

"The business, the business, is that all you can say?" she snapped at me; teeth clenched in an attempt to keep her voice low.

"Tell me, Em, I know."

"You know what?"

"Rachel found out about your business." I held up my hands to diffuse the mention of Rachel. "I know as well as you, she had no right to interfere, but that's the way she is."

"And what exactly did Rachel find out?" Her cheeks had turned bright red and tears pricked at her eyes. She looked like a cartoon character whose ears were about to emit steam.

"She looked you up, your company. She said something about looking up information online and that your company is in trouble. Then she mentioned insolvency..."

That word shattered Emily's resolve. She broke down in tears, sobs escaping, and her shoulders juddered up and down. I passed her a napkin off the table which she refused, and instead she took a packet of tissues from her shoulder bag. Some guests looked over, but as soon as I stared back, they instantly understood that it would not be not in their best interests to keep on gazing our way. I reached out my hand again and a wave of emotion hit me smack between the eyes when Emily eventually held her hand out too. We sat for several minutes allowing her to compose herself.

"Why didn't you tell me, Em? It's not an issue and I wouldn't judge you at all."

Regaining her composure, she took another gulp of her newly replenished beer.

"I'm just so ashamed, Dan. I've failed…" she momentarily lost it again but the worst of the crying seemed to abate.

"You've not failed anything. What are you talking about? You gave it a good go, made some good money. It's the economic climate that's all. If there're no jobs out there, how can you advertise them?"

It was my way of involving politics, a sure-fire winner for any failed business. I did not understand what the job market was like, if I told the truth. I'd never really paid too much attention to it.

"But what about the staff, Dan? I've had to let forty something people go."

"Well, they're the best qualified to find other work, then, aren't they?"

Emily choked a small laugh, then another, like a car starting on a cold morning. She suddenly became serious.

"But what about you, well, us, now, Dan? You must think I'm completely using you."

"Are you? I must admit it's crossed my mind since Rachel told me yesterday…"

"You knew yesterday? Why didn't you say anything?"

"You just looked so out of it all day, Em, I couldn't bring myself to mention it."

"You are so kind to me. I really don't deserve you." She withdrew her hand for a second time. "I'll pack first thing tomorrow, find a flight or look for some accommodation elsewhere."

Were we breaking up for a second time? The circumstances were not dissimilar to the first time. Job losses, feeling depressed… a ghost walked over my grave. I had to get back to the present.

"You'll do no such thing. I want you to stay." I checked myself. I didn't want to seem too eager. "If you're staying for the right reasons, of course."

"I promise I am. I must admit I needed to get away from England, from the business. There's still so much paperwork to address but my solicitor is doing most of it. But now I'm here, and now I'm back with you, I can't think of anywhere else I'd sooner be. I wish we'd never split up in the first place, Dan. I've never stopped thinking about you."

She sounded so genuine. I knew how gullible I could be, but if I told the truth, I wasn't even that bothered if Emily was being honest or not. I knew she had strong feelings for me, and I knew how hard it had been for her when we'd separated before.

"We were both idiots, that's all," I joked. "As long as you've come to your senses now…"

"Rachel!" Emily's expression suddenly glazed over.

"Sorry?" The same faces turned to look at us.

"Rachel. The shit-stirring little cow. I could kill her, Dan, I really could."

"Leave it, Em, please. She goes home this weekend. She's just weird."

"Well, I still aim to find out more about her and why she's doing those horrible things to you. And we must find out Brad's involvement too, especially as he's not going *home* this weekend."

We strolled home in the balmy air; arms interlocked once again. There was still a light on in the gîte when we walked by. I could feel a pair of eyes on us all the way to the house, but I wouldn't give Rachel the satisfaction of turning around to see.

I'd forgotten to leave any outdoor lights on, and I fumbled around with my key to unlock the door. As soon as I reached inside for the kitchen light switch, we both jumped in unison. Emily, for the second time since she arrived, let out a high-pitched scream and stumbled backwards with her hand over her mouth.

The slow crawling larvae blanketed the kitchen floor. They became disorientated with the sudden dazzle of light. Little white legless creatures looking for safety. Once Emily had stopped screaming, I swear I could hear them shrieking back in unison.

"What the fuck are they?" Emily whimpered behind me.

Walking on tiptoe between the hideous little things, taking deep breaths to stop myself from vomiting, I reached the under stairs cupboard. There, I stretched for an old wooden broom the previous owners had left, and set about sweeping and swatting them towards the door.

"I said what the fuck are they, Dan?" Her hand still covered her mouth.

I swished the broom backwards and forwards like a demented fool. Some were getting trapped in the stiff fibres and crawled upwards along the handle towards my fingers. I panicked and brushed them off, one clinging onto my hand and whirling itself in and out of any nook it could find.

"They're maggots, Emily, dirty fucking maggots."

Emily screamed again.

"How the hell did they get in?" This time I ignored her as I imagined them crawling up my arms and under my shirt sleeves. I yelled out as I furiously started stamping on as many as I could whilst sweeping the squashed carcasses outside.

Once I'd swept away all those I could see, I filled the kettle and boiled it. I did not know if you could kill maggots with boiling water, but I had to try something. Emily came back inside, slammed the door shut and pushed a towel as tight as she could under the gap at the bottom.

"Dan, how did they get in?" She was trying her utmost not to cry.

I lifted the boiled kettle and walked towards the door.

"I'm guessing the same way as the rat did."

36

EMILY MADE me go downstairs first the next day. I'd been under strict instructions to remove any maggot, large or small, and not to give her the go ahead until they were all gone. Secretly, I knew it was an impossible task. Some of the filthy little things had wriggled sideways and backwards, out of my sight. They could be under the cupboards, hiding amongst the furniture and even have made it into the next room, waiting for nature to take its course and morph into flies. I would have to buy some proper powder to kill them off completely. By the time I'd reached the back door with the boiling water the previous evening, there were none in sight. I'd made a show – mostly for Emily's sake – of emptying the kettle near the entrance, but it had been a futile effort that must have had them laughing at me from their secret hiding places. Once we went to bed, Emily had asked if they could climb stairs. My reply hadn't been entirely honest, mostly because I didn't know the answer myself.

Once I was downstairs and back in the kitchen, I

wasn't sure exactly what to expect. I removed the towel and opened the door and the coast was clear. Thankfully, there wasn't a bug in sight. I involuntarily shivered as though somebody had walked over my grave.

Now it was time to play the waiting game and put the second part of our plan into place. I took a coffee outside.

Emily joined me sometime later.

"Any sign?," was the first thing she asked.

I'd been keeping my eyes locked on the gîte ever since I'd come outside. We needed Rachel out of the way but, so far, nothing.

"Not yet," I sighed.

"I meant the fucking maggots, Dan." She sat in the seat next to me and followed my gaze down the garden.

"Maybe staring at the gîte isn't helping. You know she looks out of that window all the time, don't you?"

Emily was very shrewd. She had worked Rachel out in just over a week whilst it had taken me two months. In fact, Emily had always been the astute one. Even at school she knew she would one day be her own boss and had dreamt of running a business. At the time she had no idea what that business would be, but her determination would always win the day. At exam time she studied and studied whilst I played music, wearing extra grooves in my vinyl collection. During break periods Emily sat on the school field, reading or writing in a journal. Other girls hung around in groups talking about boys and what clothes they wanted. I always used to watch her, from a distance, never having the courage to talk to her. Whenever a girl spoke to me, I just went red. A couple of girls who knew Emily used to tease me saying they knew I fancied her. When they threatened to tell her, I said something nasty to put them off the scent. I'd soon gained the reputation of the boy who girls didn't go anywhere near, including Emily. In fact, we didn't even speak until a house party when we were both seventeen. Afterwards, she said how surprised she was that I was quite nice, especially after all the rumours she'd heard about me. My shyness held me back in so many ways back then.

"What do you suggest then?" I asked. "She knows I sit out here on the terrace. I thought it would look more conspicuous if I made myself scarce."

Lunchtime came and went. I mowed the lawn. That way it wouldn't appear obvious I was watching her, but I could see if she left.

Just as I rounded the pool for the final time and about to give up hope, I saw the door handle turn and Rachel appear. Thankfully, she wasn't wearing a swimming costume, and she had her car keys in her hand. My hands trembled, but I needed to hold myself together. I turned off the mower engine.

"Going somewhere nice?" I enquired, kicking myself for sounding so unnatural. My voice had inadvertently risen several octaves.

Rachel looked at me blankly.

"I'm going to look in the estate agents, Dan, see what I can find."

What the fuck?

"Oh, okay. I thought your flight was booked for Saturday though?"

"Don't worry, I won't be staying here beyond Saturday, Dan, but, you never know, you might get lucky and have me living close by." She laughed, blew me a kiss and sauntered off past the pool up towards her car.

She has got to be fucking kidding me.

Having finished the lawn, giving Rachel time to be far away, I parked up the mower and ran back into the house. Emily sat patiently on the sofa. I noticed her feet tucked underneath her body and she kept looking at the floor for intruders.

"She's gone out, but guess what?"

"Tell me," Emily replied, with obvious trepidation in her voice.

"She's only going to look in the fucking estate agents…" I stopped myself, staring at the ceiling deep in thought.

"What is it?"

"Hold on, you don't think she will look at the house I've found do you? Brad might have tipped her off when he followed me that day."

"You might be right, but that can wait. We have to act now."

She sprang to her feet, inspected her sandals and slid them on.

Emily's plan was to get into the gîte as soon as Rachel wasn't around. She said we must find evidence it's her who is trying to frighten me or, worse still, drive me away. I wasn't sure what we should be looking for, but Emily was convinced we would find something incriminating.

With the key to the gîte in my hand, we slowly crept out of my house and walked down the garden. We glanced at each other every few steps, both trying to convince ourselves that it was a good idea.

Turning to look in all directions, I slid the key into the door and slowly turned it. The click sounded as though it had amplified itself ten times louder than normal and again, I looked around.

"Get in!" Emily growled under her breath.

Rachel had pulled the shutters closed, giving the place a solemn feel. I recalled going to my granddad's house soon after he died, and my gran had drawn all the curtains. "It's a sign of respect," she'd told me later.

"Check upstairs, Dan," Emily instructed.

"What am I looking for?" I whispered back.

"Anything, you idiot. If you find it, you'll know. Just look."

Anything? What the fuck is anything?

It immediately felt wrong and a pang of guilt shot through me. Suddenly, Emily's plan didn't feel so good. What could we possibly find that would incriminate Rachel? I pulled out the bedside drawers, looked in the wardrobe, and went through all the pockets of her clothes. Was I expecting a note with 'put rat through the door' for one day followed by 'dig up vegetables', 'infest with maggots', 'ruin his business', 'throw Dan down the well', all listed neatly and in date order? This was crazy.

"Dan! Get your arse down here."

My heart skipped a beat. I put everything back as best as I could remember and ran downstairs, taking two steps at a time. Emily stood in the middle of the room holding some kind of book. She looked deep in thought, flicking through the pages as fast as she could, hesitating now and then to read a few lines and then skip to the next.

"What is it?" I whispered.

"It's a diary, or more like a journal." Emily turned to face me and even in the gîte's gloom, I could see she had turned ashen white. I joined her but couldn't keep up with the pace as she was taking it all in.

"Slow down. I can't read at that pace." I reached out to turn the last page back.

Emily slapped my hand.

"I'm quicker than you. I'll tell you later. Look for the muddy boots or something else."

Look for boots. What kind of crap job is that?

I prowled around like a demented ostrich, stretching my neck this way and that.

Then I heard the car.

I stopped mid-step, like an adult game of musical statues. Emily held my stare. We listened for the car, dreading the crunching sound of tyres on gravel.

It was going so slowly, almost crawling. I was convinced it had slowed down to turn into my driveway. We held our positions until the car went out of hearing distance. It must have driven past.

"Come on," I said, "we need to get out of here."

"You go, I have to finish this. Keep watch outside and cover for me if anything happens."

Pouring us both a glass of wine, we sat on the terrace in silence, both deep in thought as to what to do next. It wasn't incriminating evidence, but it also filled us both with fear.

Emily had continued to read the journal and emerged from the gîte about thirty minutes later. It had felt like an eternity as I pretended to pull weeds from the lawn and drag the net up and down the swimming pool to give the impression I was fishing out flies. When she finally appeared, she locked up the gîte and walked back to the house, ignoring me.

I'd chased her up the garden, angry that I'd been treated as no more than a lookout. She told me to grow up and explained all she had read. Rachel had been married although we couldn't tell how long. However, over the last year or so there was a mention in the book of another man and, as Emily turned the pages, this man became more and more prevalent. The book included pictures of both her and her husband but no photos of the new guy. Emily said there were several pictures of her husband and newspaper clippings throughout which she hadn't had time to digest. She'd only wanted to read the recent articles. I'd asked how she knew it was her husband and she told me there was also a wedding photo in there. Emily asked if she had a brother and I recalled Rachel telling me about him, Nathan, rescuing her from her dad when they were in their teens. Emily nodded as I passed on the information. There were several photographs of Nathan according to what Emily had found.

As the new guy became more and more involved in the story, Emily said that Rachel's comments became more and more disturbing. From, '…this cannot carry on…', to '…I need to stop him, one way or another…'.

It bought back memories of the day Rachel said something like 'we'll see about that' after I'd told her of Emily's imminent arrival.

What is she capable of?

Towards the end of the journal, Emily had found newspaper clippings dated from the year before. They were taken from a local newspaper in Dorking and began with 'Inquest into Man's Unexplained Death Begins' and had kept track of the five-day court case. They had banded all kinds of accusations around during the hearing, but it looked as though nothing definitive could stick with any individual.

Finally, the judge delivered a verdict of suicide and the empty packets of paracetamol and the bottle of Jack

Daniels pointed to a fair decision, at least in the eyes of the local press.

The final clipping in the book was taken from the obituary column from the same newspaper.

Brookes, Patrick

Passed away at home on April 22, aged 37.

Beloved husband of Rachel.

Finally, at rest, without the demons.

37

"SHE KILLED HIM, DAN." Emily was adamant.

It was impossible to argue with. I'd always been brought up with the saying 'innocent until proven guilty' and Rachel had stood in a court of law and they had attached no blame to her. However, I agreed, one hundred per cent, that the journal made for grim reading and, the more the 'new' guy came onto the scene, the more Rachel seemed to want rid of her husband. However, that could just be natural, couldn't it? Married, at first happily, a new man arrives, affair, no longer happily married, eventually wants husband out of the way. Still doesn't mean she killed him… still doesn't mean she didn't.

The one thing neither of us could determine was, where did Brad fit into all of this? There were no photographs of the new man on the scene, no names mentioned, just 'him' and 'he' scribbled amongst the ramblings. We still couldn't pinpoint Brad as having any close connections with Rachel if he had any at all. However, it didn't rule him out either.

Also, how did it fit in with her being responsible for all the horrible things taking place recently? Emily was convinced it proved she was unstable, capable of anything. "It's an obvious sign of jealousy," she'd remarked as we discussed nothing else for the rest of the day and long into the night. Again, it was no actual proof. Where were the muddy boots we thought we'd find? It was impossible to find evidence of her cancelling my bookings or attracting rats and maggots in large numbers. If Rachel had been behind all those things, she was covering her tracks very well. Then again, if she had anything to do with her ex-husband's death, getting away with digging up vegetables would be child's play in comparison. She was due to go home in four days' time. Right then, I didn't believe that would happen for one minute.

Later that day, I'd shown Emily the house that I'd found for sale. The main reason we went was to take our mind off things, if only for a few hours. We had driven into town and got the keys from the estate agent so we could look inside. I wasn't sure if they would just give them to us but it was for sale with the same agent I had bought my house through and they seemed very trusting of my motives – in fact; it wasn't far from the truth anyway – I was very interested in it.

Emily had liked it, a lot, and could see the obvious potential. The house even had a cellar which I hadn't known before just from looking through the windows. It was also plain to see that Emily was still skirting around issues where my future was concerned. She found it awkward, thinking I believed she was just using me. Despite constant reassurance, she kept changing the subject, even though I had decided I wanted her to stay around forever.

We drove aimlessly back not following any road signs. The countryside around was delightful. The fields full of sunflowers bowed and nodded at us in unison as we drove by. The yellow flowers gave way to endless rows of vines and then deep wooded copses which cast shadows across the narrow roads. The French marked each river or stream with a small black sign depicting the name of the water that flowed below us, every one looking inviting enough to stop and take a paddle in. The wider rivers often had youngsters splashing around or the odd yellow or orange canoe paddling slowly with the flow.

Emily smiled at every turn, every undulation and at almost every house we passed.

"I'll have that one," she'd say, "no, that one," or "oh wow, Dan, did you see that one?"

Cyclists waved, farmers nodded, and hikers stepped aside and smiled as we drove on. It was the paradise I'd longed for all my life. If only the circumstances were different.

As we eventually arrived home, late in the afternoon, our moods were dealt a sickening blow as Rachel sat at the table on my terrace. She was reading her journal. The back door to my house ajar. Had I left it open?

"Hi, you two. Nice day?"

As soon as we got out of the car, Rachel stood, with a

beam across her face totally contradicting her clear underlying mood. I spoke first.

"Hi, Rachel, what are you doing here?" Both myself and Emily were looking at the book on the table, completely bypassing Rachel and her false impression. She caught our eyes and turned her head slightly to look at the book too.

"Ah yes, my personal organiser. Every good journalist has one you know." She looked back up at us. "Did you find what you were looking for?"

"I don't know what you're…"

"Save it, Dan," her previously hidden disposition now surfacing faster than a salmon on its journey to spawn. Emily intervened before either of us could say anything else.

"Actually, Rachel, I read it, well, bits of it, yesterday."

Emily shot me a look as if to say, 'don't you dare contradict me'. I stood silent.

Rachel's full attention now lay with her antagonist. She stepped by me towards Emily.

"And why did you do that, Emily?"

"All I wanted was to find something that pointed to you doing horrible things to my Dan. The maggots were the final…"

"What maggots? What the hell are you talking about? You're as bad as him accusing me of things." She glanced at me, but only a quick peek. Her gripe lay firmly with Emily and she looked as though she was enjoying it.

Emily took a step back as Rachel crunched her heels into the gravel. I stepped towards them; it looked like it could turn nasty.

"We know all about you, Rachel. Tell us, what really happened to your husband, the truth?"

Oh shit, straight for the jugular.

"My husband killed *himself,* Emily. Happy now?"

Emily looked back at the journal lying on the table, hoping it would speak for her.

"So, who's the other man? Who did you have an affair with, Rachel? Something made your husband kill himself, if that's what he did."

No, no, no, Emily.

"You interfering little cow. Your business fails and you come running back to the guy who dumped you. Then you interfere in my life, breaking into my holiday home, going through my stuff, accuse me of murder." Rachel turned to me. "What do you see in her? She's a failure and now she's using you. It wouldn't surprise me if it's her trying to drive you away so she can get her hands on your property. She knows how much you love her, you'd do *anything* for her, wouldn't you, Dan?"

Racking my brain, I tried to think of something to diffuse the situation. Before I could think of anything, Rachel swung between me and Emily, a wry smile had returned to her face.

"You know what? You two deserve one another. Go, Emily, take him, ruin him like you did your business!"

Emily took a step towards Rachel, but I grabbed her arm.

"Let it go, Em."

Rachel picked her journal up off the table, opened it, and flicked the edges of the pages over and over.

"You know what? I have kept diaries all my life. This one contains the latest chapter of my life. A life that's never been pleasant, but I've always tried to see the positives. This journal…" she held it aloft, "…this journal depicts when it all went wrong again." She looked all around her, taking in the surroundings. "This, this was supposed to be my new life, a new chapter shall we say," she laughed, "but even this has gone wrong. Accused of everything, yet innocent again. Maybe that's the story of my life, eh? Maybe I'm being punished for something I did in a previous life."

Rachel was already walking towards the gîte when she turned to ask me a question.

"What day is it, Dan?"

"Tuesday, why?"

"Only four more days and I'll be gone. Don't worry, I won't stay around here. I've hired the car for another few weeks. I'll just drive, searching for another new start."

"Looking for what exactly, Rachel?" Emily asked, now holding my hand. It didn't go unnoticed by Rachel.

"Who knows what I might find, Emily. Peace, love, solitude. Hold on to what you've got, he's a good one."

She was too far away for me to be sure, but, as she swung back round towards the gîte, I'm certain a tear rolled down Rachel's cheek. I think Emily saw it too.

Next morning, I had to force myself out of bed. The prospect of lying there and not allowing anything to prise me away from my dreams felt so inviting. I'd slept well all night, the deepest and longest sleep I'd had for ages. Maybe it was the bottle of wine Emily had insisted I have to help knock me out. She had come back from town with pizzas and drinks after dropping off the keys for the house with the estate agents.

As I showered, I recalled what had happened once we returned from the viewing. It sounded like a farewell speech from Rachel and it had pulled at my conscience all night. Emily was unperturbed, 'good riddance' was the most positive thing she'd had to say. We both knew that Rachel could be the perfect actor, always 'Little Miss Innocent' when, in fact, she was behind everything. "Let's look at the evidence," Emily suggested. "Who was this mystery guy then, Dan? Why was the light on in the gîte when the rat came through the door? Why was there mud and boots outside her gîte? How did a million maggots appear from nowhere? Who could have thrown a brick through your window in the middle of the night?" They were all questions we had no answers for, apart from the obvious. As I deliberated about the last one; someone had thrown the brick through my window two days before Emily arrived – a sure sign of jealousy at the forthcoming visit of my ex-fiancée, the evidence against Rachel seemed overwhelming. The worst thing of all was when Emily said, "I'm scared she will never leave at all, Dan."

Walking out onto the terrace, I knew immediately something was wrong. First, my eyes turned to the driveway, Rachel's car wasn't there. Then I looked down towards the gîte and that's when I noticed the next thing. The glistening multi-coloured sheen on top of my swimming pool. Walking down the garden, I felt tears prick behind my eyes and an overwhelming desire to throw myself in and sink to the bottom, never to return.

Once I arrived at the scene, I could see the whole pool had been contaminated, but with what? It looked as though a million rainbows had descended on the surface and bobbed up and down with the motion of the water, disturbed by the slight breeze.

A large black patch at the far end of the pool caught

my eyes, and I walked round to inspect it. That feeling again of somebody watching me, but I couldn't see anybody in my immediate view.

As I reached the other end of the pool, I found a large black slick of oil on the ground. Two footprints were embedded into the grass behind it. Two footprints, made by what looked like boots, which were staring back up at me.

Behind the footprints were two more, then another. I traced them with my own feet. Two by two. Again, I had the strangest feeling I was being watched, but this time I didn't look up or even care. Eventually, the footprints led me directly to the front door of the gîte. However, something didn't add up.

38

"That's it. I'm selling up."

I was almost in tears when I got back to the house. It was too much. Somebody was trying to destroy me. Buy why? Did Brad drive here overnight and tip oil into my pool? Had Emily been right and Rachel was doing her utmost to get back at me for not welcoming her into my life with open arms? Whatever, or whoever, I'd had enough.

I considered my options. Sell up and move elsewhere in France or sell up and move back to England. The latter sent a shiver down my spine. *Oh no, please, not back to England after only three months.*

What about the length of time it takes to sell a property in France? It's not like England, you don't put up a 'For Sale' sign and start getting enquiries via your friendly estate agent within days. It can take months, years even, and that's just to get an enquiry. *What if I can't sell it and I'm stuck here for good? Stuck with whoever is doing this to me?*

Emily's voice roused me from my horrific thoughts.

"Whatever's the matter, Dan, you look awful?"

Without saying a word, I took her by the hand and led her outside to the pool. She walked round to the far side, following me, saying nothing. Her mouth fell wide open but not a word escaped. We arrived at the spot where the deep black puddle had soaked into the grass, complete with two footprints. Emily looked down.

"It's her, Dan, look, boot prints."

"Yes, and look at the size of them, Em. Rachel's feet would fall straight out of them."

Emily considered the options. She told me all the reasons it could still be Rachel, she could wear thick socks, she could try to put us of the scent. She wasn't even convincing herself though. Then another idea popped into her head.

"If it's not Rachel this time, then it has to be Brad. His feet would need bigger boots. He could have done it in the night, Dan. Shit, if you think about it, we'd had enough drink to knock us out for weeks last night. We wouldn't have heard a thing. You were snoring like a train before I even climbed into bed."

She was right. I wouldn't have heard a burglar if they'd been in my bedroom. I'd already considered Brad too. Emily spoke again.

"We should keep quiet and not accuse her or Brad. That's what they want, the attention, to drive you out. Let it be and she'll leave on Saturday for good. Her and Brad will be out of our lives."

The rest of the week passed slowly. I'd not slept during the nights so made up for it during the day. I hadn't shaved and only crawled into the shower twice after

Emily told me I was beginning to 'acquire an odour'. My enthusiasm had diminished and even little jobs around the house had become too much. If it wasn't for Emily, I'd have been living on dry bread and wine. It was her who got me out of bed late Friday morning, and told me to wash and change because I needed to go into town to buy some fresh food from the market. She suggested that I stop for a beer and cheer myself up. Only weeks ago, I'd have given my right arm for such an invitation, but right then the comfort of my own damp sheets seemed much more enticing. Emily walked around to where I lay, kissed me on the mouth and asked if I would make the effort for her.

As I wandered around the narrow streets of Monpazier, I became a little more positive. I ambled slowly down towards the town square. Occasionally I would stop and look in the cute shop windows, marvel at the cakes on display in the patisserie, baulk at the pigs' heads in the bouchére and smell every flower head at the fleuriste. Emily had been right; the fresh air and company of strangers was doing me the world of good.

When I reached the square, I felt parched and desperate for a beer. I made for the bar at the far end, my thirst increasing my stride with every single step.

Just as I sat down, something, no somebody, caught my attention. I looked up, right at the other end of the square. "It's Brad, over there in the arches," I said aloud.

The couple on the table next to me stared in my direction. Only days before I would have gone bright red, prior to excusing myself in deep embarrassment. But right then, I had a renewed vigour. If it was Brad who was helping to destroy my life in France, then I needed to stop him.

The waiter appeared at my table, but I was already standing, not taking my eyes off the other end of the marketplace.

"Erm, be back soon. Sorry, pardon." I don't think my French lessons had impacted my pronunciation.

Taking to the very perimeter of the square, past the multi-coloured brickworks of the buildings, I ducked in between the arches and soon I found myself only feet away from where I'd spotted Brad.

Shit, I've lost him.

"There!" I said to myself through gritted teeth. I even pointed through an archway towards the church just beyond. If anybody had been watching me, they would think I had completely cracked.

I sneaked through the arch and stood in front of the church, my eyes darting up and down the narrow streets. I spotted him to the right, walking away from town. If he had any idea I was behind him, he showed no sign. I could make out small white earphones and the wires dangling down to the phone in his pocket.

Following at a safe distance, I ducked behind parked vans and cars. I must have looked like I was shooting a poorly acted spy film from the 1950s.

He turned left past another church and headed further out of town. I had to back off more because there were now only the two of us in the same street. If Brad turned around, he would see me straight away. It could only be because of his music that he didn't hear my foot-steps echoing off the houses either side of the road.

It felt like an eternity before he turned down a narrow side street. We must have been on the outskirts of town and it was an area I had never visited before. He nodded to a passer-by who said something in return. The said person now approached me and looked me up and down. He said something in French, something I didn't understand. I looked towards Brad, convinced he would hear the same guy talking to somebody else right behind him. I nodded a 'hello' in the stranger's direction and he raised his voice to repeat exactly the same words as he'd said before, annoyed I hadn't addressed his original question. I shrugged my shoulders this time. He tutted, mumbled something under his breath and continued to walk by. If Brad hadn't had earphones in, he would definitely have heard that, but he carried on walking. He headed directly towards three caravans parked up in a yard.

What the fuck? I whispered to myself.

Brad made for the one at the far end, the scruffiest one of the three and put a key into the door. I hid behind a car, now knowing he wouldn't be going any further.

What the hell's he doing here? He surely can't live here. He speaks so well, dresses so smart. But *you've never seen his car, Dan, never known where he lives.*

Once the caravan door slammed shut, I stepped out and had a good look around. His mobile home looked disgusting from the outside, green mould covering over half the exterior. The metal-framed windows were rusty and the frosted glass to what must be the bathroom contained a crack from top to bottom. There was some graffiti sprayed in blue paint at the end near the tow bar. Next to it was a blue Citroen which looked as though it would fall to pieces if anyone ever attempted to drive it, let alone try to tow the caravan. It had a soft top, but the canvas was torn and peppered with mildew.

The situation paralysed me. It knocked me sideways. My immediate thought was what my next move should be. I couldn't just go walking up and knock on his door and embarrass him. He'd also know that I'd followed him. Then again, I needed to understand if he'd been behind what was happening to me and also how well he knew Rachel. It was time to grow some balls and take a grip of my life. The old Daniel Kent still tried to convince me to stop, walk away and enjoy that beer in town whilst the new Dan found himself knocking on Brad's caravan door.

A soon as he had opened it and saw who was there, he immediately tried to slam it shut. I'd half expected that response and already had my foot jammed in the doorway. Brad kept slamming the door against me but there was more chance of the caravan falling to bits than it hurting me. I pushed by and forced my way in.

The stench hit me before I could take in the surroundings. There were empty tins of food left on the work surface near the cooker, their lids open at the same angle making them look like a row of smiling oversized cats. The bin overflowed, and beer cans were strewn across a makeshift coffee table in the centre of the room. Brad tried to tidy in front of me, but it was a futile attempt and he soon gave up.

"What do you want, Dan?" He looked everywhere but into my eyes. I struggled to find the right words myself, but I knew I had to tackle this once and for all. A little white lie wouldn't do any harm I thought.

"I was strolling around town, going down all the side streets and stuff, you know? I, kind of just saw you, around the corner there." I pointed back up the road, "and I called you, but you didn't hear."

It was quick thinking and Brad looked as though he'd accepted it as the truth. He removed the earplugs from his phone.

"Yeah, I had headphones in." He slumped to the only spare space on the sofa. "So now you know where I live. Bet you're surprised, eh, Dan?"

"Why didn't you say, mate, it's nothing to be ashamed of?"

"Nothing to be ashamed of? Fuck you, Dan. Look at your pad and compare it to this."

It was impossible to argue with that, so I cut to the chase.

"But I thought you were well off, Brad. You speak well, dress well. I thought you were a man of leisure living the high life."

Brad was almost in tears as he told me his story. He came from money, in fact his father still had money, and he sent some over now and then when Brad got desperate. He had fled from England when a local thug had threatened to kill him after Brad slept with his girlfriend – a one-night stand. Since arriving, he'd told his dad he was doing well and was setting up a vineyard which he constantly needed money for until the first harvest came in. It was all a lie. All he'd done since he arrived two years ago was work in a bar. He'd been sacked from that job two months previously for dipping his hands in the till.

As he told me his story, I looked around, taking in the surroundings. I spotted something on the windowsill at the far end of the van. I walked towards it; Brad oblivious as he carried on with his life story.

"What's this doing here, Brad?"

I turned back to face him. I held a photo frame in my hand, and I rotated it towards Brad so he could see the picture. His face gave away that he knew very well what I was looking at before I'd even shown him.

"What the fuck is this, Brad?"

That was the catalyst for the tears to flow. He became incoherent in his reply, just jumbled words interspersed with sobs.

In my hand, I held onto a photo frame containing several pictures of Rachel. Rachel, sunbathing on a lounger; she was lying next to my swimming pool.

I crouched down next to him.

"Why, Brad? When even?" I was blabbering as much as him.

"Please don't tell her, please." He looked directly at me for the first time since I'd arrived. "I took them one day when I passed your house. She was just there, around your pool. I guess I find her attractive, but I know she wouldn't fancy a loser like me." He pointed to the four walls of the caravan. "How could I ever ask her to come back here?" That's when I remembered the clicking noises in my garden. The day I'd been mowing the lawn and Rachel had stopped me to put suntan lotion on her back. I recalled the weird clicking sounds and the footsteps running when I'd gone to retrieve my phone. It was Brad. Brad fucking Jones taking photographs of the woman who was staying in my gîte.

I slowly made my way back towards the town square. I needed that beer more than ever. I'd promised to keep the photograph quiet from Rachel and assured him I'd tell nobody of his circumstances. He asked me not to tell

Emily either – I'd said okay but I hadn't made my mind up if I would or not. Brad also confessed to not owning a car and the day we had met in the village for lunch, he had caught a bus there and back. Everything had been for show, a front. Brad Jones was destitute – it was so sad.

As I left, I'd said I'd help him find work once I'd sorted a few things out myself. I wondered if Andy Jackson might have something for him and then I remembered the new kitchen cupboard falling off my wall – did that put Andy into the frame? I gave Brad a hundred euro's cash as I left. "Get some proper food, Brad, and for fuck's sake tidy this place up." That had made him laugh between stifled sobs.

As I eventually reached the town square, I made my way back to the same seat I'd left an hour earlier. The couple who had stared at me before had moved on and a much younger couple occupied the table. They were sharing a bottle of wine.

I'd stopped at the tabac in town and bought myself twenty cigarettes. I hadn't smoked in years, but I fancied one more than at any other time in my life.

As I drank my beer and lit up my second cigarette in as many minutes, I contemplated what had just happened. At least one thing was for certain, Brad had absolutely nothing to do with what had been going on.

39

THE NEXT DAY was noticeably cooler, and the skies were overcast. I was purposefully avoiding getting out of bed. Emily had got up very early and the coffee she had brought me sat stone cold in its mug on my bedside table. I'd only drunk about half before I crashed back into a deep sleep. She said she was walking into town to have a good look around Monpazier and to stroll around the shops at her leisure. Emily had always hated me shopping with her as I got bored so quickly. She could browse for hours.

I hadn't mentioned Brad to her when I returned home the day before. I'd decided to keep it quiet until after Rachel left, thinking it would only confuse the issue more and I didn't want to embarrass Brad any more than he already was.

Eventually, as I showered, I let out a huge sigh of relief that Emily wouldn't be around for Rachel's departure. She had made herself scarce to avoid further confrontation.

Thank you, Emily.

I still felt groggy even though I'd drenched myself in the shower for a good ten minutes. The notion of crawling back into bed was incredibly tempting. I hoped I wasn't coming down with something.

As I dressed, I thought of Brad and his desperate situation. I'd completely misread him, although I wouldn't chastise myself for thinking the way I had. His outward persona gave the impression he was a big hitter in the city, and he was on holiday to unwind from executive burnout. The truth, however, was somewhere near the opposite end of the spectrum. He was down on his knees and struggling to make ends meet. I would love to help him get back on track. Maybe Emily would think of something. I just prayed Rachel would leave before lunchtime with no confrontation. Afterwards, we could help Brad and get on with the rest of our lives too.

I'd lost all track of time as I aimlessly drifted around the house, emptying the dishwasher and putting on a new load of laundry. Emily wasn't back from town and it was almost lunchtime – she must be staying out to eat and making sure the coast was clear before she returned. I moved outside to see if there was any sign of life at the gîte. It was now after eleven o'clock.

Once outdoors, the chill of the breeze went straight through me. I'd become so used to twenty or thirty degrees of heat every day that the temperature caught me by surprise. It must have dropped to the mid-teens and the thick cloud overhead threatened rain any moment. I immediately turned to go back inside to fetch my hoodie when I noticed Rachel's car was no longer in the driveway.

Has she gone into town or has she already left?

Looking over towards the gîte, exactly the same as I had done two weeks previously, it looked empty, subdued even. There were two rubbish bags outside the front door. Something didn't seem right. Surely, she wouldn't have left without even a goodbye.

Do I wait for Emily to return or do I check it out alone?

I'd had enough of depending on others. Brad's situation had made me realise how lucky I was. It was time to stop feeling sorry for myself and pick up the baton.

I fetched my hoodie and pulled the zip up so far that it caught the skin on my neck. Instinct made me feel for blood but there was nothing.

As I walked towards the gîte, a feeling of fear crept through my body. It reminded me of watching a horror film when you plead with the main character not to go into the woods when he hears voices beckoning him. The only thing missing was mist swirling above the pool and a rook or raven perched on the fence, daring me to progress forward.

Again, I forced myself to take matters into my own hands. I took on a more purposeful pace and soon found myself outside the front door.

Taking a final look around, I willed Rachel's luggage to be waiting in the front room and her to return to collect it all any minute now. I was getting an overwhelming feeling she had just taken off. I knocked gently on the door.

Nothing. Not a sound.

I knocked again, this time a little firmer.

Silence.

"Rachel, it's Dan. If you're in, can you open the door, please?"

I was unconvinced I would have heard that myself if I'd been the other side of the door.

My fist banged much louder the next time. It would have woken Rachel if she was still in the gîte. The fact that her car wasn't there and there was no response from inside made it obvious she wasn't in.

I scrambled round, trying to look through the downstairs windows, but she had pulled the shutters closed from the inside.

Looking back up towards the house, I checked if her car had miraculously returned, thinking for some bizarre reason I must have missed it when I got my jumper. It wasn't there.

Something felt amiss, and I ran back to the house to grab my spare key. That's when I saw some marks in the grass on the far side of the pool. The morning dew still hadn't evaporated in the shade of the trees and it looked as though somebody had been walking around the other side of my garden. There was a thin line too, running parallel with the footprints. Could that be from whoever carried the oil to pour it into my pool? That had to wait.

First, I needed to check on the gîte and I returned a few moments later with the spare key. I struggled to stop my hand from shaking as I inserted it into the lock, my head frantically looking around for unwanted visitors. A snapping noise alerted me, somewhere past my house, towards the very end of my garden. It sounded like a foot standing on a fallen twig. I stood frozen, watching, listening.

Silence.

Scrambling to open the door, I was pleased to be

inside. I shut it behind me with a thud and instantly locked myself in. I removed the key and gripped it in my hand, immediately feeling its jagged edges dig into my palm.

Now what?

"Rachel, it's me, Dan." Why was I still calling her?

It didn't take long to cover the gîte, the open plan living room, and the kitchen downstairs with two bedrooms and the bathroom upstairs. All of Rachel's clothes had been removed, from both the wardrobe and chest of drawers. She had made the bed, the bathroom shelf was empty and, once I went back downstairs to check, there was nothing in the fridge or cupboards. A single plate on the table contained crusts from her morning toast. Next to it sat a half-drunk cup of coffee. I felt the mug, stone cold.

Could she have driven into town to pick some things up? Emily had gone into town. Surely, they hadn't travelled together. No way, they couldn't stand each other.

My mind was going crazy, and I scrambled around the gîte looking for any kind of clue as to Rachel's whereabouts. She knew she had to vacate by eleven o'clock and I'd fully expected her to push that timeline to the limit.

Running back upstairs, taking the steps two at a time, I looked from left to right, then back again. Scanning every single surface.

I've no idea why but instinct told me to look under the wardrobe, the drawers, the bed. It was when I bent down onto my knees, that I noticed one of her suitcases, pushed right to the back of the bed, almost out of sight. *Why on earth would she forget that, it's half of her luggage?*

Quickly, I looked out of the window. There was still no sign of her car, so I heaved the case out and onto the bed. It was full and just as heavy as the day she'd arrived. I recalled that I'd ended up carrying it to the gîte for her. I felt for the latches to spring the case open, but she'd locked both with a three-dial combination code. I left it alone as I knew I didn't have time to try multiple sets of numbers.

Thinking she could return any minute to collect it, I panicked and pushed it back under the bed. My back creaked as I stood back up.

Footsteps outside!

Shit! She's coming back.

I quickly smoothed over the quilt and fluffed the pillows for some unknown reason. I scanned the window to look at the driveway next to my house, but her car still wasn't there.

That's when I saw Emily marching down the garden towards the gîte.

40

I OPENED the gîte door just as Emily was placing the other spare key into the lock. She jumped back with a look of absolute disbelief on her face.

"Fucking hell, Dan!" she exclaimed; her hand placed firmly on her heart as if to stop it exploding out of her chest. "What the fuck are you doing?"

Emily rarely swore, especially to that degree. She hadn't seen me in the bedroom window and was oblivious that anyone could be inside.

"Well, *I'm* looking for Rachel. Can I ask what you're doing here? And where did you get that key?"

She looked sheepish and her eyes drifted from the key in her hand and back up towards me. She regained her composure before speaking again.

"The keys are hanging up in the spare room, Dan, you know, exactly where you put them?"

"Okay Em, but why are you here?"

"The same reason as you I'm guessing. When I left

the house this morning, her car wasn't there. I thought it strange that she would go without saying goodbye." She looked directly at me and smiled sarcastically, "without saying goodbye to *you* that is, Dan. So, I went into town, fully expecting her car to be here when I got back and when it wasn't, I thought I'd check if her stuff had gone. I thought you were still in bed."

I stood there, staring at Emily. My mind was all over the place. She spoke again to snap me out of my trance.

"And?"

"And what?" I replied.

"Has her stuff gone, Dan?"

"Erm, yes, as far as I can tell."

Emily tried to push past me.

"It's all gone, Em, all her clothes." I kept it from her that one suitcase had been left under the bed. I secretly hoped that Rachel would realise and come back for it. Whatever had gone on, and whatever she had done to me, I had wanted to say goodbye, one last time.

Emily put her shopping bags onto the sofa and walked into the kitchen to put the kettle on. She noticed the concern etched across my face.

"Just accept it, Dan. The other day when we last saw her it wasn't exactly a joyous occasion, was it?"

She was right. I recalled the last time I saw Rachel. She'd walked away from me and Emily after the altercation over her journal. I'd thought she was crying as she went. It was plain to see that she had avoided me for the rest of the week.

Think, Dan, think.

"I need to find out what's going on, Em. It's not Rachel leaving, but all the other things."

"Well, I bet you all the other things stop now she's left." Emily air quoted 'other things'. "She wanted you to herself, Dan. Her sulking off like this has only proved the point."

"I think you're right, Em." I picked up my car keys from the table. "Don't mind if I go for a drive, do you? I just want to be alone for a bit."

Emily looked a little hurt, but she kissed me on the cheek and said she'd cook something nice for later once I returned.

Andy Jackson didn't live far away, and I arrived within twenty minutes of leaving home. I remembered I'd written his address on the back of the business card he had given me. As I pulled up outside, I was pleased to see his white van on the driveway. It looked like a modest house and not particularly well kept on first impressions – something which surprised me for an all-round handyman.

He appeared both perplexed and worried in equal measure when he opened the door and saw me standing there.

"Hello, Dan. What are you doing here?"

"Can I come in, Andy? It's important."

His wife wasn't at home and he had been watching English sport on television. He muted the sound and threw some clothes and bags off a chair for me to sit down.

"I haven't got time to stay, Andy. I just need you to be honest with me."

He had gone white, as if half expecting this very conversation but dreading it at the same time. He spoke before I asked him anything. What he said caught me totally off guard.

"Okay, I admit it. I knew you were too shrewd to not work me out, that's why you haven't been back to pay me isn't it? It was a childish prank, anyway."

I sat in one of the chairs without further invitation. What was he talking about? I'd completely forgotten about paying him, a genuine mistake.

"What was childish, Andy?"

He looked directly at me, blankly.

"You don't know? Isn't that why you're here?"

"Just tell me." I became impatient. I was dreading what he had to say. *Was it Rachel? Is that why she's missing?*

"Your cupboard, Dan, in your kitchen. Your fucking cupboard."

I came to my senses, almost with relief. The cupboard had completely slipped my mind too. It still annoyed me now he mentioned it.

"You what, Andy? You *sabotaged* my kitchen cupboard? You knew it would fall down?"

"Yeah, it's an easy thing to do. Put it up and then as soon as you put weight on it, it will fall–"

"Wait!" I stood again, not giving a shit about a stupid fucking cupboard. "It was you, wasn't it? You drove that van the day you nearly forced me off the road? That day I went to the garden centre?"

He sat down on the sofa and stared at the flickering TV. He didn't have to say anything; I knew he'd been behind the wheel. It made complete sense; how else could his white van have turned up just two minutes later? The bastard!

"Why, Andy? Why?"

He looked suitably embarrassed as he told his story of wanting my house. It was him who had outbid my original offer by two thousand euros, but that was all he could afford to go to. I'd immediately increased my offer by five thousand and he'd had to pull out of the auction. He said his wife had been heartbroken, and he'd lost his chance of owning a property with a ready-made business on the side. I recalled how he'd said it was a bargain the day he came around to do the kitchen.

"You could have killed me, Andy." I was angry with him, but it muted my feelings as it at least cleared up a couple of issues.

"Nah, you're a good driver, Dan."

He smiled when he left the room and returned seconds later with two cans of cold beer. He passed one to me.

"Hey, listen, I'm sorry, mate," he continued. "I was just pissed off that you've got exactly what I'd wanted. That day I fitted your kitchen really made me realise what we could have had. You going on and on about it wound me up. I stood there thinking how I could get my own back on this guy. But I didn't, did I? It was just a prank, and the driving thing. I promise it's nothing personal, you're a good bloke. Can you forgive me?"

I tugged at the ring pull on my can of beer, allowed the gas to hiss and escape before taking a big gulp. I couldn't help but smile back.

"Hang on, Dan, if you didn't come here to beat me up for fixing you up with a dodgy cupboard, then why are you here?"

I almost laughed as it had completely slipped my mind why I had called round.

"I need to know why the previous owners of my house left." Andy considered his response whilst taking a long swig of beer.

"I don't know why, they just..."

"You owe me big time, Andy. Just tell me the truth please and I'll leave you in peace."

He left the room to fetch two more beers, he'd already drunk his first. I stood and caught myself in the mirror. The confidence flowed through my veins and I felt a determination inside that I hadn't felt for years and years, if I'd ever felt that way at all.

A few minutes passed before Andy came back into the room. I doubted if he would tell me, but I knew deep down that he was well aware of why they'd left. He passed me the second beer which I placed on the table next to me. I wanted to keep my head straight and filling myself with alcohol was not the best thing to do. Andy sat back down, opened his can, and told me all he knew.

The couple were called James and Grace Langton. Andy didn't know where they had moved to, or if they were still in France. He said they had told him about things that happened at the house. First, somebody slashed the tyres on their car whilst they slept. A few days later, the lawn mower and other garden implements were stolen from the garage. That would explain why there was a brand-new ride-on mower left behind.

"The final straw for them was when Grace was riding her bike home from town and a car drove up behind her, swerved and clipped her handlebars on the way past. The impact threw her from the bike into the hedge on the side of the road."

"Shit, was she hurt?" I asked.

"Hell, yeah, she bust her arm in two places," Andy replied, pointing at his forearm.

He went onto tell me that as soon as she got home from hospital, James had phoned the agent to put the house on the market. They'd had enough and wanted to get away and start afresh.

I needed to know if he had done anything else to get back at me. I mentioned my destroyed vegetable patch, the dead rat through the letter box and the brick through the window. He looked genuinely shocked and concerned. I didn't know Andy very well, but I had believed him when he'd pointed out the driving and cupboard were more in jest and tomfoolery than trying to frighten me away from my property.

He explained he had done some final work with the gîte, decorating and fixing up the satellite TV to make it a more attractive proposition.

"They had made little from the gîte as far as I can remember," he continued, "in my opinion, they never saw the potential."

"But you did, eh?" I quipped.

"Of course I did. That town is a tourist magnet. With the right marketing I think you could fill it over half the year, at least."

As soon as he'd said it, he looked downbeat again. I didn't have time to feel sorry for him and took it as my cue to make a move. I shook Andy's hand on the way out and just before I left, I remembered something else.

"Oh, Andy, some bastard has tipped oil into my swimming pool. You don't know anybody local who could drain it and clean it for me do you?"

He replied almost instantly.

"Yes, I can do that," he stopped in his tracks, "if you trust me that is."

I walked away but turned to challenge him. My face bore a sarcastic grin.

"Oh, I trust you, Andy. I also know you'll be very cheap, won't you?"

41

Next morning, I woke well before Emily. When I'd arrived home from Andy's, I had wanted to check if Rachel's suitcase was still in the gîte. However, Emily had gone to a lot of effort in cooking me a meal and I didn't want to spoil the ambience by talking about Rachel again. Instead, I took my phone into the bathroom and dialled Rachel's number – it rang and rang without reply.

I'd told Emily all about Andy and his antics. She said it didn't surprise her as I'd given the impression he was a bit of a prankster. "Typical cockney cowboy," she'd joked, which I thought was a little harsh.

Emily had been more upset that I'd gone off to see him without telling or inviting her. "I could have come with you, Dan," she said. "I'm in this with you, you know." She was right, but I'd found a whole new energy and I'd needed to tackle things alone. Besides, whatever I thought or said, Emily always came back round to Rachel being behind everything. It looked that way, but something still niggled inside about why Rachel hadn't said goodbye. There were other things I'd wanted to tie up too – now that Rachel had left.

Before Emily had woken, I'd sneaked down to the gîte. I quickly checked under the bed and the suitcase was still there. It was only on my way out that I noticed the kitchen table. It had been cleaned; no plate with discarded toast crusts and no stone-cold coffee in a mug. I looked in the cupboard and the full complement of crockery was in place. Six big plates, six small, six cups, six of everything, just as it should be. Surely Rachel wouldn't have come back just to finish tidying up – no, there was only one person who could have done this.

"Why did you tidy the kitchen in the gîte, Emily?" I asked when I took her coffee in bed. She was already awake and sat up looking at her phone.

"Sorry, what?" she asked, glancing up and taking her coffee from me. I repeated the question, annoyed, as I knew she'd heard me perfectly well first time.

"Oh that. Well, when I saw you in there yesterday, I noticed she'd left some stuff lying around. I just made myself useful whilst you were out at Andy's and went down to tidy up." She looked up at me, "Surely you don't mind me doing that, Dan, do you?"

I relented. What was wrong with me? It was a nice thing to do, nothing sinister. I left her to shower after she'd agreed we'd go into town together. I wanted to show some solidarity, and I knew a good walk always helped me to think.

We made our way into the centre late morning. Being Sunday, there was a small flea market in the main square. Most shops looked as if they were open and a steady flow of both locals and tourists meandered around. The heat had returned with the sun whilst the occasional translucent cloud did its best to cast a shadow.

After we'd covered the market and strolled along the two or three main shopping streets, I led the way out of town, the opposite way from my house. My aim was to do a full circle of Monpazier's perimeter before returning home. Emily stopped a few metres behind me.

"Where are you going?" she enquired.

"Let's just do a loop, Em. I'm really in the mood for walking."

Reluctantly she followed, always lagging a few paces behind. I didn't care though; I hadn't wished to make idle conversation but wanted to take in what had happened since I'd arrived in France.

"Dan!" Emily ducked behind a parked car, pulling me down with her.

"What the fuck…"

"Shh," she whispered, poking her head slowly up above the car.

"What's wrong?" I hissed.

She crouched back down next to me, her face only inches from mine.

"The car you said has been following you, the Peugeot…"

"Yes," I said impatiently.

"There's a Peugeot parked over there." She pointed beyond the car we were crouching behind. "A purple Peugeot."

I went to stand straight up, but she pulled me down.

"Fucking hell, Dan, don't be so stupid. The driver may be sat in it for all we know. Now, slowly poke your head up and see if it's the same car."

Doing as I was told, I gradually lifted myself by my

knees. There it was! It was the same car that had been driving me crazy since the day I'd arrived. I lowered myself back down, my back pressed against the car we were hiding behind.

"Shit, that's it, Em." I was bursting with excitement without considering the consequences. The owner of that car had followed me to look at the house that's for sale. And the same owner had been keeping their eye on my comings and goings for weeks and weeks, including my very first day in France. I stood to walk over. Again, Emily pulled me back.

"What the hell are you doing, Dan?"

"I'm not running anymore, Em, I need answers."

"Well, I want nothing to do with it. You heard what Andy said, somebody knocked that poor woman off her bicycle, and they've been following you since you arrived. Let's go, Dan, it's not safe."

She looked genuinely concerned and began moving back in the direction from which we had come. I tried to think on my feet.

"You go home. I'll find somewhere to keep out of sight where I can see the car. I just want to know who it is, but I promise not to confront anybody. It will be easier with only one of us here, anyway."

Emily told me I was crazy but accepted my assurances that I wouldn't do anything stupid. She walked off toward town, occasionally turning her head to see if I was still hiding.

After an hour, I decided that whoever the owner was, they would not return soon. I'd found a small alleyway to hide in and, apart from a couple of passers-by looking at me bewildered, nobody else had even known I was there. Reluctantly, I trudged home.

Eventually I arrived in my driveway, by then feeling exhausted. I jumped when I saw Brad sat at the terrace table opposite Emily. He looked up but struggled to manage a smile.

"Hey, what's up, Brad?"

He stood and shook my hand.

"I just thought I'd walk up to see you." He looked at Emily, "to see you both."

"Brad's been telling me you went to see him the other day, Dan?" Emily forced a smile for Brad's sake, but underneath I could see she was seething with me. I tried to remain calm and cocked my head nonchalantly.

"Oh yeah, didn't I tell you, Em?"

Before she could reply, Brad interrupted.

"Sit down, Dan, please." I did as I was asked, and my eyes darted between him and Emily. Brad was there to tell us something. Something significant by the look on his face.

"I've told Emily what you found, you know, where I'm living, my caravan, my lack of job and money."

He didn't mention the photographs of Rachel. I glanced at Emily and then back at Brad. He looked at me with begging eyes. I nodded.

"Anyway, there's something else I didn't tell you. Now Rachel has left I feel I should come clean."

"Hang on, mate," I said, standing. I came back with three beers. Emily shook her head, but I left the third bottle on the table in front of us, anyhow. I opened two and passed one to Brad. He guzzled it down like it might go off if he didn't drink it really fast.

"Go on," I said, "you know I won't judge you."

Brad told us he hadn't been entirely honest all along, and he knew Rachel, in a roundabout way. More precisely, he knew her brother, Nathan. They had been friends, neighbours, back in Hampshire. He'd never met Rachel but had seen loads of photographs of her in Nathan's house. He said they were very close.

I'm not surprised, I thought, after what they'd been through.

"Anyway," Brad continued, "back in May, a few days before you arrived, Dan, Nathan called me. We've kept in touch since I've been in France, mostly on Facebook. The couple of times I've been back to England, Nathan has put me up." I was getting impatient.

"Why did he call you, Brad?"

Emily shot me a look, but I ignored her and continued to stare at Brad.

"He told me that their uncle, a fucking lunatic apparently, had tracked Rachel down, knew she was living near Dorking. It was only a matter of time before he found her house. It scared Nathan, and he wanted to know if I could put her up in France." Brad looked downtrodden again. "I've never admitted to Nathan where I live so I told him I already had somebody staying with me and said I'd keep my eyes open."

He took another huge swig of beer, draining the bottle. I opened the other one and slid it across the table to him. I hadn't even touched mine yet.

"Then I saw you, Dan. Walking across Monpazier square like a startled rabbit. I hadn't seen you around town before, and I thought you must be a newly arrived tourist. So, I followed you…"

"Hang on, you followed me?"

"Yeah, you remember. You sat in the bar in the corner of the square, knocked your chair over," he attempted to force a laugh, lighten the situation, but nobody was in the mood for joviality.

"The day I asked for a coffee and you bought me a beer? I remember. But what's that got to do with Rachel?"

"Well, if you recall, you told me you'd just moved into a local house. You also told me you had a gîte to rent out. That's when I thought…"

"You'd tell Nathan so he could tell Rachel?" Emily was one step ahead of me.

"Yep," said Brad. "I immediately called Nathan, he phoned Rachel and told her the rough address, and she found it online. She's a right whizz with the internet, apparently."

I remembered now, the very day after I'd bumped into Brad, I'd had my first gîte booking. My first guest, arriving only four days later. I wanted to know more about Brad now.

"Tell me Brad, now it's all out in the open, why is it you were so shy around Rachel then? I know now that you're attracted to her, so why didn't you ever make a move?"

He looked at Emily, then back to me. He explained that he found her very attractive but would do nothing that might piss Nathan off. He thought she was far too good looking for him anyway and looked upon her more as a sister than anything else. "I just wanted to look out for her really," he said.

I knew it was bullshit, and he was protecting himself in front of Emily. He may have wished to preserve his friendship with Nathan, but deep down he didn't have the confidence to take things further. The situation of where he lived didn't help either.

Silence fell around the table, each of us deep in thought. Then Brad looked up at me, suddenly looking very concerned.

"Where has she gone now, Dan?"

"I've no idea, mate. She left yesterday before I even got up."

"What, she didn't even say goodbye? That's a bit fucking weird."

Brad looked at Emily and issued a silent apology for his language. I looked at Emily too; she looked spaced out.

He was right; it was *fucking* weird.

"Fuck it," Brad continued. "I'll have Nathan on the phone soon, asking me where she's gone. What the hell do I tell him?"

"You tell him she moved on, to look around the area, find different accommodation," Emily replied. "He can't expect you to watch her every move, Brad."

Brad looked at Emily as if she didn't understand. He then looked back at me for some kind of moral support. I nodded once in recognition that I fully understood his predicament.

42

BRAD HAD STAYED OVERNIGHT in the spare room. Emily had taken pity on him and had cooked us all a meal. Brad and I had moved on from beer and polished off two bottles of red over the course of the night. Emily left us to it and went to bed early.

Next morning, me and Emily sat outside on the terrace. Brad was still in bed. As we ate breakfast, I noticed Jean-Pascal out in the field on a tractor. I hadn't seen Laura for over two weeks now, and I felt a sudden urge to talk to her.

"Em," I said, still looking up at the farmhouse.

"Ugh, ugh," replied Emily, reading something on her phone.

"I still haven't paid Laura for those French lessons. I think I'll walk over whilst Jean-Pascal is out of sight and clear it up. That okay?"

Emily looked up from her phone and saw Jean-Pascal weaving up and down his field on his tractor.

"Whatever, Dan, but don't pay too much, okay? I really don't like that family."

I walked up to the farmhouse via the driveway, keeping their property between me and Jean-Pascal. I wanted to see Laura alone. I knocked firmly on the door.

"Oh, hello, Daniel." It wasn't the most pleasant of greetings, but I hadn't been expecting anything more.

"Hello, Laura. Look, I know we haven't spoken since, well, since our last lesson. However, can you spare me five minutes? There's something I must ask you."

She looked left then right, and then stood motionless. No doubt listening for the distinct sound of her husband's tractor.

"Quick, five minutes, that's all."

There were no pleasantries or coffee or fresh bread, not that I would have accepted, anyway. We both sat at her huge kitchen table. I cut to the chase knowing time was against me.

"Laura, I've been told of why the previous owners left my house. There were, shall we say, issues?" I scanned her face for any sign of guilt before continuing.

"They had things stolen from their garage, a lawn mower, other things. Someone had slashed their tyres on the car overnight. Then, one day, Grace was knocked–"

"Off her bicycle?" Laura interrupted.

"Yes…"

"And you want to know if we were responsible?"

Fuck, this is not going to plan.

"Well, I guess so, yes."

Laura stood up and walked over to her sink. She

placed both hands on the edge and stared out of the window. She stayed with her back to me as she spoke.

"Yes, Daniel, my brother was responsible." She turned around, her face had turned crimson and she looked close to tears, "and do you want to know why?"

I was speechless. Such an admission with no look of regret or remorse etched across her face. She spoke before I could form any words.

"Your house, Daniel, your little gîte and all your land, do you know who that once belonged to?"

I shook my head, dumbfounded by how quickly the conversation had moved on.

"Us, Daniel, yes us."

"I don't understand, Laura, I…"

"We sold it to a property developer. The house fell into disrepair and the gîte was crumbling to pieces. We had a family meeting, and between myself, Jean-Pascal and Robert, we agreed to sell it. We thought they had offered us a good price."

"Isn't that good, Laura?"

She stepped closer to me; her fist wrapped tight around the towel she'd picked up from the sink. I could see the white of her knuckles. I leant backwards in my chair.

"Good? Did you say good? We had been completely ripped off, Daniel. It turned out they'd paid us a pittance. The developer came back, fixed up the house, fixed up the gîte in no time and then put it all up for sale. And do you know how much for, Daniel?"

"I have, erm–"

"A fucking fortune, Daniel."

I had never heard Laura swear before. Her words were incandescent with rage.

"And then Grace and James bloody Langton turned up, with their posh car and posh clothes."

She took a deep breath and sat back down next to me. She must have seen the fear on my face. She calmed herself down before continuing.

"Oh, Daniel, it's not your fault. You see, it was Robert, my brother. He knew we had made a terrible mistake. He's always had an awful job at that vineyard, working all hours for so little pay. Our farm hardly breaks even. And then we see people walking around your property, *our* property, with guests in the swimming pool, playing and laughing. We know how much you charge for a week in the gîte, Daniel, we know everything. And Robert was angry, he's always angry."

It took me by surprise when she reached across the table and took my hand in both of hers.

"I tried to warn you, time and time again. You must remember?"

Be careful, Daniel. People are set in their ways.

"You saw how angry Robert was when you turned up at our house that day? And the time you came running to me and Jean-Pascal when you wanted to know who owns a purple car. My husband and my brother have no time for you, Daniel, or anybody else connected with your house. You must accept this. We have lost everything and every time we look down our hill, it reminds us of what we could have had."

"So why aren't *you* angry with me, Laura?"

"I'm not an angry person, Daniel. We made the mistake and we have to live with it. I tried to warn you to get away peacefully. I wanted you to leave before anything happened to you. I have spoken many times with Robert.

He is calmer now, just don't upset him." Laura smiled for the first time since I'd arrived.

What does she mean, 'before anything happened to you'?

"So why did you want to stop teaching me French?"

"Ah, that was my pact with Robert. He said if I didn't teach you French anymore then he wouldn't do anything else to drive you away. He said–"

"Hang on," I interrupted, pulling my hand away from Laura's. "What do you mean, anything else?"

Laura looked to the door. She listened for the tractor. We could still hear it in the background.

"There was one thing, Daniel."

"Go on," I said.

"Do you remember our second lesson?"

I couldn't off the top of my head.

"Well, you went to fetch a drink from the kitchen, and when you returned, I was looking at the photographs on the wall."

I recalled the moment she was talking about, and I remembered thinking something was strange. Laura stood again and went to a drawer at the far end of the kitchen. She took something out, something I couldn't see, and walked back to the table. Then she opened her hand and let it drop in front of me. I picked up the piece of paper, already knowing what it was. I unfolded it and immediately recognised the front page of my notebook, complete with logon details to my website. I looked up at Laura, a solitary tear suspended on her cheek. It seemed to lack the desire to end its journey.

"You stole my login details, Laura? Why?"

"Robert made me. I knew you had a website and that Rachel woman was helping you with it. Robert said I should take something that would affect your business."

"And did he cancel my bookings with these details?" I held the piece of paper aloft. Laura snorted a laugh.

"Oh, I doubt that very much. None of us can even switch a computer on, Daniel. That piece of paper hasn't moved from that drawer since I put it there. I remember Robert being mad that I'd chosen to steal passwords to a computer. He said I may as well have stolen a key to a house on the moon," she laughed. "It was a just a stupid idea. Besides, Robert has calmed down since our lessons ended."

Then I recalled when the gîte cancellations took place.

"But the two bookings were cancelled the day after you stopped our lessons, Laura. Surely…"

"That must be purely coincidental, Daniel. If you have had booking cancelled, then somebody else is behind it. I can assure you it wasn't us."

The sound of the tractor engine cutting out brought us both to our feet.

"Can I have your word, Laura, that you know nothing else about what has happened to me?"

"Why, what else *has* happened?"

"I'll tell you another day."

She took my hand again as we neared the back door.

"You have my word, Daniel; we haven't done anything else. I like you; I like you a lot. It's why I didn't want you to get in with that Rachel, she is far too full of herself. And now you have Emily with you, be careful Daniel, just be careful. I can always smell trouble."

I smiled. Laura did not understand my past or my history with Emily. I kissed her on both cheeks and reached for the door.

"Oh, Daniel, that reminds me."

"What is it, Laura?"

"That Rachel, has she left now?"

"Yes, you'll be pleased to know she left on Saturday, why do you ask?"

"Well, we didn't see her leave and, well, we see most things." She blushed ever so slightly as I returned her smile, "so she must have left very early?"

"Yeah, I guess. I must admit I was very surprised that she went without saying goodbye."

A look of disbelief shot across her face.

"Yes, that is strange. You were, how do you say, very good friends, weren't you?"

It was my turn to blush, and I quickly opened the door to leave. Laura wasn't quite finished though.

"But surely Emily knows why she went so early?"

I stopped in my tracks.

"Emily? Why would she know?"

"Well, it may be nothing, but when you were out all Friday afternoon…"

Shit, she really does miss nothing. Friday, where had I been Friday? Oh yeah, the day I followed Brad to his mobile home.

Laura cleared her throat to regain my attention.

"Yes, go on, Laura."

"Well, when you were out all afternoon, Emily was down in the gîte with Rachel."

I looked at her surprised.

"Emily with Rachel? Are you sure, Laura?"

"Oh yes, quite sure. In fact, she was down there a very long time."

43

The idea of Emily and Rachel being in the gîte together had sent a shiver down my spine. What could it have been about? Who would have initiated the meeting?

I'd tried to read Emily's mind all night after I returned from seeing Laura, but there was nothing to scrutinise, no signs, no hints. She'd asked if I'd paid Laura – something that had completely slipped my mind – to which I'd replied 'yes', and I explained about the house and land once belonging to the Allaire family. I skimmed over the details, incriminating nobody. I'd wanted to gauge Emily's reaction, which was non-committal. She had been surprised that they had sold so cheaply, and she had showed some compassion towards their predicament. It must have been hard for them to accept after they had originally assumed they'd achieved a top price. I left out the part about Laura seeing her and Rachel in the gîte – I needed to continue to ponder that alone, without my thoughts being impeded.

. . .

The following morning, I again woke early, leaving Emily in a deep sleep. It was before six and there was something I needed to do. I had to find some clue or reason why Rachel had left so abruptly. The only place I could think to look was back in the gîte.

The door clicked open and once again I found myself alone, not understanding what I was looking for. I went through the place room by room, item by item. I lifted the toaster, the kettle, every kitchen implement. I crawled on my hands and knees, shining my phone torch under every single piece of furniture. The sofa, the chairs, underneath the cooker, the dishwasher, but I found nothing. Exasperated, I dragged myself upstairs.

I stripped the bed bare, picked up the pillows and then the mattress. I pulled the cupboard drawers out completely, and I shifted the wardrobe far enough forward to peer behind. Once again, I crawled on all fours, shining my torch into every crevice. The only item that glared back at me was the suitcase.

Sitting next to it on the bed, I stared at the combination locks. Clicking them one digit at a time, I soon realised it was a fruitless task. How many three-digit combinations could there possibly be? I ran back to the house, checked Emily was still asleep, stopped off at the garage and returned to the gîte armed with a hammer and screwdriver.

Prior to setting about the task at hand, I tried to call Rachel's mobile again. It must have been the fourth or fifth time I'd tried to call her since she'd left on Saturday – three days previous. As before, the response was a soulless ringtone. I placed my phone on the bed and stood over the suitcase, ready to smash my way in, one way or another.

I tapped the screwdriver head underneath the lock on one side. Satisfied the tool could only bore itself further below the bracket, I pulled the hammer behind my head and struck the handle with all my force. As I expected, the blade slid deeper underneath but still not far enough. After two or three further blows, the screwdriver went straight through and the lock spat into the air before landing on the floor beyond the end of the bed. I jammed my fingers under the ledge and felt the lid move, but only as far as the second latch would allow. Within minutes I'd removed both locks.

After looking out of the window and back towards my house, I satisfied myself that there was no movement and Emily must still be in bed. I had no expectations that the suitcase contents would give me any further clues than I already had – precisely none at that point. I lifted the lid. That's when I saw the envelope laying on top – it had a single word written in neat handwriting directly across the middle – *Dan*.

I've no idea how much time had elapsed between me finding the letter and reading it several times over, but I sat on the edge of the bed dumbstruck. I searched the suitcase contents for more clues, but in my mind, it satisfied me. I didn't need any further details than I held in my hand – not from Rachel at least.

I returned Rachel's clothes to the case and crudely pushed the lid down until it clicked over the metal rim. I pushed it back underneath the bed, with its missing locks hidden against the wall. I collected the broken pieces from the floor. Returning the hammer and screwdriver to the garage, I walked back into my kitchen; the letter tucked deep into my back pocket. I was startled to see Emily sat at the table.

"Hi, where have you been so early?" Emily looked directly at me. I made for the kettle, desperate to avoid her stare and attempted to compose myself.

"Oh, just in the garage. I was checking how much petrol was in the mower, the grass needs cutting."

"Wow, I never knew it could take that long, Dan."

She was being facetious, but I had no time for her games. I turned to face her.

"Well, it did Em. I had a bit of a tidy up whilst I was there too. Is that a problem?"

Emily went back to scrolling through her phone. The wry smile on her face made my blood boil. I gripped the edge of the work surface and forced all my aggression down my arms and through my hands.

"Doing anything today, Em?" I asked, as politely as I could muster.

She stood up, pushing her phone into her dressing gown pocket, the smile still etched across her face.

"Nah, no plans. I could help you tidy the garage if you like though?"

With that she turned to leave the kitchen.

"I'm going to take a shower, Dan. I thought we might view that house again today. I've got some plans I wanted to share with you."

"Yeah, sounds great, Em," I replied, without even thinking what I was saying.

As soon as I heard the shower, I walked outside and took out my phone. I knew I had to make the call and time was against me. He answered it on the second ring.

"Holy shit! Daniel Kent. How the devil are you?"

"Hiya, Rick." I immediately looked back at the house, straining to hear the shower. "Listen, I don't have long. Can you talk?"

I hadn't spoken to Rick since I'd arrived in France. We had become close again after I'd left Emily back in England. It was just the two of us who had met up a few days before I'd left for my new adventure in the sun. I knew I could trust him with my life.

"Of course I can talk, Dan. What the fuck's wrong?" He had picked up the obvious concern in my voice within seconds.

"Rick, it's about Sue…"

"Sue Wade? Your old neighbour? You're the second person to call me about her. Some bird called, hang on…"

"Rachel Brookes?" I filled in the blanks.

"Yeah, that's it, Rachel. Well, she phoned me earlier this week. She said you and her were close. What the fuck's going on over there, Dan?"

"Yes, Sue, my old neighbour. I can't say much more yet but, can you remember when she died, you know, got knocked down?"

"Course I can. You were pretty upset if I recall. Her husband was beside himself–"

"Yeah, yeah, Mike, her husband. We were all upset." I looked back at the house. I couldn't hear the shower anymore. Walking further away, I lowered my voice.

"What do you remember of the accident, Rick?"

"What, apart from the obvious?"

The night Sue Wade died would live with me forever. It was a cold, wet October evening. The clocks were due to go back an hour that weekend and it was already dark soon after six o'clock. Sue had been to the gym and was jogging home. The heavens had opened, and the rain lashed down. The streets were quiet, everybody huddled up indoors. Sue had made it to only two streets away from our houses, herself and Mike living next door to me. The road she died on was tree lined and unlit. Emily had told the police she hadn't seen a thing and the first time she knew anything was amiss was when her car hit something. The force sent Sue cartwheeling over the top of the vehicle, only her head coming into contact with the windscreen before being propelled at least ten metres behind. The only glimmer of good news was that the ambulance crew had said it must have been instant and Sue wouldn't have felt a thing.

Rick, mentioning how upset it made me, caused it all to come crashing back. I'd had to put on a facade at the time, especially in front of Mike and Emily. It was only when I was alone with Rick that I could let all my emotions escape. I didn't tell him everything, but it had always surprised him how upset I'd been. He knew Sue used to come around, bring me meals when I was at my lowest and generally make a fuss of me. He also knew Sue and I used to take their dog for long walks. The one thing he knew nothing about was our affair. Until I'd read Rachel's letter, I didn't think anybody knew about our affair.

"Yeah, apart from the obvious."

The phone went quiet as Rick was deep in thought. I kept ambling slowly down the garden, further away from my house. Eventually Rick replied.

"Nah, nothing, mate. Just the terrible accident and how shook up Emily was. Talking of which, she's with you isn't she? Does she know you're calling me about Sue?"

"No, no, she doesn't even know I'm on the phone to you, Rick. And yeah, Emily arrived, let me think, she arrived just over three weeks ago now."

I knew Rick couldn't help me with any further details about Sue. I needed to end the call promptly. The silence on the phone was my prompt to go. However, Rick spoke before I could.

"Three weeks ago, you say?"

"Yeah, I picked her up from the airport on a Sunday."

Rick repeated his question, this time the emphasis very much on the first word.

"*Three* weeks ago? Are you going mad, mate?"

I needed to get off the phone.

"What the fuck are you talking about, Rick?"

"Hang on, let me check the calendar on my phone…" Rick went silent and I could hear him walking around his house.

"… yeah, thought so. Dan, you there?"

"Yes, I'm still here. What is it?"

"Dan, I've just checked my diary. I saw Emily in the pub in May, yeah, Wednesday the fifteenth of May."

Wednesday the fifteenth of May was four days before I arrived in France. Rick continued.

"I was on a night out with my company. She was drunk, out with some girl she works with, I think. I remember asking her what she was celebrating."

"And?" I was looking back at the house now. Emily appeared on the terrace, searching for me.

"She said she was going out to France the next day. That would have been Thursday. She had a flight booked. I knew you were going out on the Sunday because we'd been out for the beers on that Monday night, remember?"

Emily spotted me and started walking.

"Yes, I remember. What are you getting at, Rick?"

"Emily's been in France for weeks, Dan, a couple of months even. I just took it you'd been together all this time, and that's why you've not sent me a single message since you got there. Not sure where this Rachel bird fits…"

Emily was hurrying across the lawn now, directly towards me.

"No way, Rick, she only arrived…"

"Dan, Emily arrived in France three days before you did."

44

My Dearest Daniel

It is now Friday, the day before I am due to leave your beautiful gîte and, of course, the day I leave you forever.

I so wish it hadn't ended like this and we could have found a way to be together. However, since your ex fiancée has arrived, it has been impossible to be close to you and tell you exactly how I feel. Hence, I hope you find this letter first and allow me to explain my situation before and after arriving in France.

First, a little confession, Dan.

I came to France because I had received a letter from my uncle. You may recall me telling you that my uncle is a violent man. Myself and my brother Nathan have avoided him for years, in fact, ever since running away from home. We heard he had been in prison for beating someone to within an inch of his life. Somehow, he tracked me down and I knew I had to get away. I was hiding at Nathan's house when he took a phone call from his good friend, Brad Jones. Nathan had told Brad of my situation and asked for his help. Brad called a couple of days later. He said he had bumped into somebody in France who had a gîte for rent, so Nathan and I spent a few hours surfing the web until we found you. It looked idyllic, and I booked it for two weeks and a flight the very next day. I am sorry I never told you this, but I doubted you would let someone stay who was 'on the run' from her crazy uncle!

My second confession is more personal, and I hope you can bring yourself to forgive me and understand what I am saying.

Dan – when I first met you, I thought you were a little strange. Don't misunderstand me, I immediately found you attractive, but you were so insecure that I imagined you to be weird – does that make sense? However, after a while I warmed to you. You are a vulnerable person, Dan, and I guessed you must have had a rough time back in England. It's why I tried to warn you away from Laura – because of your vulnerability. I thought you were liable to share everything with everyone – you deserve so much more.

My feelings for you grew and after our night together I knew we were a good match. We'd both had our difficulties in life, and I felt we could help each other. Being in France, away from all our combined history, I hoped it gave us the perfect opportunity.

I know you like me too, Dan. The way you look at me, the way you touched me when I asked you to apply the sun cream. I honestly believed we could have had something special.

. . .

Then she arrived. Or has she always been here? As soon as I saw Emily her face looked familiar. I thought I'd seen her in town before – watching me, watching us.

Okay, confession number three, Dan.

One day, as I went to get something out of my car, I spotted your mobile phone left on your outside table. I looked at your contacts. I wasn't sure who or what I was looking for, but I noticed a 'Rick Morley' in the list. I recalled you saying that you and he confided everything in each other. I took down his number, you know, just in case I ever wanted to find out more about you. I guess it's the journalist in me! I'm so pleased I did. You must read the rest of this letter, Daniel!

I phoned Rick two nights ago. I explained everything to him, who I was, what had happened between you and me and the fact that Emily had arrived and ruined everything.

It took Rick by surprise. He couldn't understand how you and I could ever have got together with Emily staying in your house at the same time. I told him Emily arrived weeks after me, but he said she had flown out a long time before. Again, my journalistic instincts took over, and I asked more about your past, Dan. He told me about you losing your job, becoming depressed and finally separating from Emily soon after the death of your neighbour, Sue Wade.

You never mentioned Sue to me, so I investigated further. Because of my background, I have good contacts at Surrey Police. I phoned a female officer who has worked in that area for years – she did me a huge favour and looked into the death of Mrs Sue Wade.

I guess you already know this part, but Sue had been knocked down and killed by Emily Wilkinson. However, my police officer friend told me that there were no witnesses on the night of the 'accident', BUT the police were also convinced it was no 'accident'. There were no tyre marks – something normally very common at the scene of a pedestrian being hit – no signs that the car slowed down at all. The lack of concern, or interest, from Emily when they interviewed her also bothered them. However, it was Emily's word against nobody else's, and the court found her not guilty and put the incident down as a terrible accident. The police have always 'known' differently, Dan.

Please be careful. You may just consider this to be sour grapes, jealousy even. In part, that is the truth. I want you to myself, but time has told me this can no longer happen. But the real reason is that I care for you, deeply, and I am afraid for you. I'm also afraid for myself; it's why I have packed my bags and am ready to leave tomorrow. I need to get far away, especially if that is what she is capable of. I will come to say goodbye and tell you where I have hidden this letter.

In the meantime, I so hope you have come to see me and told me you've made a huge mistake.

All my love
Rachel.
xxx

45

"Who was that?" Emily asked as she reached me on the lawn. I was still staring at my phone, several moments after Rick had hung up.

"Erm, that, that was Rick. Just calling to check up on me."

My false laugh even embarrassed me. Emily could see straight through it, but she played along, anyway.

"Ah, okay. Hope he's all right. I haven't seen Rick for a while now."

No, not since the day before you left for France.

"So, are we going to look at the property that's for sale, Dan?"

Again, without thinking, I nodded my approval, and we walked back towards the house. The feeling of somebody watching us was again overwhelming. This time I saw who it was. Laura stood outside her home at the top of the hill, her arms folded. She stared down at us. Something about her whole demeanour concerned me.

. . .

After we had eaten breakfast, in total silence, Emily agreed to walk into town to collect the house keys from the estate agent. I needed to shower anyway.

As I walked upstairs towards the bathroom, something caught my eye on the bedside table. It was on Emily's side of the bed. I approached slowly, still in a state of shock with all that was happening and unfolding in front of me. Just before I reached the table, Emily came bounding into the room behind me. She physically pushed me aside and picked up whatever it was from the surface. What was it? Where had I seen that motif before? It was all a blur. Emily kissed me on the cheek and said she'd be back within half an hour. She instructed me to be ready when she returned.

Whilst I luxuriated in the shower, I tried to assess exactly what was happening to me. Had Emily been responsible for Sue's death; I mean, on purpose? That's murder, not manslaughter, not accidental, that's unmitigated fucking murder! And also, where was Rachel?

And had Emily really arrived in France three days before I had? The feelings I'd been getting of somebody observing me I'd always subconsciously blamed on Rachel, following me wherever I went. Then I recalled the time when someone watched me in town, the day I'd stopped for a beer. Somebody wearing white training shoes. I'd never suspected Emily because, until an hour ago, I had no idea Emily could have been in France at the time. I thought of Rachel's car bonnet being warm when I stroked the cat. I had convinced myself she must have followed me into town and driven back before me. But she could easily have been out shopping or for one of her drives around the countryside. Then the day Brad and I had been kayaking. I'd known somebody was watching us from the trees, high on the riverbank. Somebody had been walking in tandem with our canoes before disappearing deep into the trees.

Could it be true?

Back home in England, when I had been suffering from depression, I had been getting a constant feeling of being watched. Whenever I ventured from my house, I could have sworn somebody was there. I'd mentioned it to my doctor, and he said it was a classic sign of depression and a mild form of paranoia. The feeling of paranoia had been especially strong whenever I had popped next door to see Sue.

Fucking hell, Dan!

I turned off the shower and dried myself as quickly as I could. Glancing at the time on my phone, I couldn't recollect how long it had been since Emily went into town.

After dressing in a matter of minutes, I ran outside and peered down the road towards town. There was no sign of Emily returning. I had to act immediately.

Taking the stairs two steps at a time, I rushed into the bedroom and straight for the wardrobe. I took Emily's suitcase from the bottom and threw it onto the bed. Unlike Rachel's, this one had no lock, and I'd soon thrown the few random items of clothing in the air. And there they were, at the bottom of the case. A pair of white training shoes.

Fuck, fuck, fuck!

Hurling everything back into the case, I tried to think on my feet. Rushing back downstairs, I found myself outside on the terrace again. A quick look towards town and still no sign of anyone.

What now, Dan?

For the first time since she'd suggested it, I wondered why Emily was so keen to have another look around the house that was for sale. I went to the garage, looked around and put a small screwdriver into my shorts pocket. What the hell I thought that would achieve I didn't know. Nonetheless, it felt right having some kind of self-defence tool at my disposal.

I caught myself smiling. Surely Emily wouldn't hurt me.

Would she?

A flash across my mind. I searched deep in my memory for whatever had interrupted my thoughts. I quickly backtracked on everything I'd done since coming off the phone to Rick. It was like one of those movies which puts all your actions into reverse, all at warp speed.

Running backwards upstairs, the suitcase back in the wardrobe, replacing the items of clothing, the white trainers sat at the bottom, throwing everything out of the suitcase, getting dressed, standing in the shower, Emily kissing me on the cheek, her pushing me out of the way, the item on the bedside table… that's it, the item on the bedside table!

Think, Dan, think.

A key of some sort, maybe. Yes, silver with a black top. The black top, plastic. The motif.

Think.

The motif. A tiger, no, a lion.

Are you sure?

Yes, a lion.

Got it!

A lion on a key. It was a car key. A Peugeot car key.

I walked down to the gîte and doubled back to the terrace, thinking all the time. Emily was in town now, it's where she'd left the Peugeot. That's why she was so keen on getting back home the other day when we saw the car in town. I recalled she hadn't wanted to walk that way and had lagged behind me. And then when we spotted the car, what had she said?

'Let's go, Dan, it's not safe.'

I'd stayed over an hour, waiting for someone to return to their vehicle. All along, Emily was back at the house knowing very well that nobody would come. She'd let me hide there, in that alleyway, like an idiot.

Pacing up and down the garden I saw the well down the far end, beyond my garage, hidden in the trees. Something pulled me towards it but I did not understand what.

As I got closer, I noticed my footsteps inadvertently slow down. I felt my heart beat a little faster and the palms of my hands sweat. The feeling of someone watching this time submerged me, weighed me down, leaving me struggling for breath. I had no time to look back. I dragged myself forward, my feet felt like lead weights.

That's when I recalled seeing the footprints in the dew on Saturday morning. The thin line that accompanied it along the edge of my garden, the far side of the swimming pool. What direction had the footprints been heading?

I knew exactly what direction. The same direction as I was walking now. Towards the well.

The sound of Brad throwing rocks inside came cascading back through my thoughts.

Thud.

I was only meters away. I felt for my phone as I knew I'd need my torch.

Thud.

My free hand reached out. My knees were like jelly, but the support of the wall felt good and secure.

Thud.

I peered over the edge, my torch beam ricocheting off the inner bricks, trying to find some focus.

Thud.

The light struck the bottom. I had to strain my eyes and focus all my attention just to get my brain to collate the information it was receiving. A distinct smell of petrol wafted from the base of the well.

The flies swarming towards me almost knocked me off my feet. It felt like hundreds of the little shits, banging into my torch, my hand, my face. I stifled a scream and gagged on my vomit. Concentrating all my efforts, I gripped one hand onto the well edge, trying my best to ignore the intense buzzing of the creatures constantly flying around my head, my ears. Finally, the torch beam found the culprit, a large bone in the well's base, a massive bone covered in hundreds of slippery fucking maggots.

Then I saw the boots, filthy muddy boots. Next the oil canister. How the hell had she got that down there? And what's that? I strained my eyes, my feet now lifted off the floor as I leaned deeper inside the well. I could just make out the writing on the white box, 'humane rat catcher'.

I stepped backwards, my mind spinning. The beam

from my phone was still pointing towards the well. The odd fly buzzed around my head.

No… no… this can't be happening.

As I continued to walk backwards, I heard the swish of the iron bar through the air. It felt like seconds before it connected with the side of my head and instantly knocked me unconscious.

46

The combination of a watery haze of daylight filtering from somewhere above and the sound of relentless rain outside woke me from my slumber. Instinct made me feel the side of my head, which I instantly regretted. A huge bump protruded just above my right ear. It felt perfectly round and hurt like hell at the merest of touches. Taking my hand away, I noticed dried blood on my fingertips and recoiled back onto the icy concrete floor beneath me.

As I felt for my phone in my pocket – which wasn't there – I tried to recall the last memories I had before I'd found myself in this freezing cold – where? The buzzing of flies was the first thing that came back, making me retch and realise just how thirsty I was at the same time. The recollection of being hit whilst walking from the well accounted for the massive lump on my head. I remembered being bundled into a car, half helping and accepting my fate. I felt like shit.

Reluctantly I lifted myself up, my head throbbing harder as I made it onto my knees. I noticed the light attempting to crawl in through an iron grill next to the ceiling. It looked partially blocked from the outside and let in very little brightness. Where on earth was I?

I stood up and gingerly made my way around the room, whatever room it was. There were sheets everywhere, like in a haunted house protecting old furniture from the damp and cold. I rifled through drawers in an old cabinet and picked things up before sighing and putting them back down. Eventually, I sat down on a chair, again protected by a white sheet. Directly in front of me, there was a staircase leading upwards to a closed door. Several balusters were missing from the handrail, and the carpet on the steps was threadbare.

Am I in a cellar?

Trying desperately to think of a property with a cellar, my mind came up blank. I cautiously walked up the steps, darkness almost completely enveloping that area of the room. I tried the door handle, an old brass knob that wriggled precariously in my hand. As I'd expected; locked. Maybe bolted and also with a key. It hardly moved.

Banging on the door reaped no reward and everything was deathly quiet on the other side of the cellar door. My head hurt so much now that I needed to sit back down. I reclined in the chair as far as I could to get comfortable and drifted in and out of sleep.

My mind wandered to the night I had spent with Rachel and all the times I'd tried to force her to leave. I'd been convinced for weeks it was her trying to force her way into my life, my business. I'd satisfied myself something had unhinged her, that she was deluded, but even if she had been highly strung, it now looked as though she had nothing to do with this. It must be Emily; everything pointed to her now.

Please let Rachel be safe.

Time passed by. Two more hours of sitting, sleeping, and pacing the room trying to think. I was parched and my stomach was constantly reminding me I hadn't eaten for ages. After relentlessly banging on the cellar door, I knew I had to be alone in the house. I had to take bathroom breaks in the furthest corner of the room.

Rain lashed down outside mixed with an infrequent rumble of thunder. The weather had finally broken, and the summer storms had reached the Dordogne.

Eventually I heard a car outside. It sounded as though it was on the far side of the property – maybe on a drive-way? I tiptoed over towards the grill, straining to hear. A single door opened, hardly audible from where I was, and seconds later it slammed shut. Then very faint footsteps, walking at first before breaking into a run, towards the house and out of the rain. Positioning myself at the foot of the stairs, I heard someone walking above me. Cupboard doors opened and then crashed closed. Was that the fridge door next? It was hard to distinguish between the sounds.

A few moments later, the footsteps were right above my head and I heard a key being inserted into the door at the top of the stairs. It turned intermittently, jamming once or twice. Next two bolts slid open with a crack and the doorknob wobbled under the force of somebody trying to click it into position to connect the inner workings.

As soon as the door opened, a beam of light shone

down. Dust particles danced in the haze, and I quickly turned my head to confirm I was in a cellar. With the light shining on the far side of her, I could only make out Emily's distinctive shape. Her spiky hair created an amazing silhouette against the wall behind her. It was impossible to see her face, but she could see mine. She also carried a large iron bar in her hand. I went for the bottom step.

"Stop!" Emily ordered, raising the iron bar above her head. Immediately I backed off. She told me to stand still whilst she put the iron bar down, bent behind her and lifted a tray from the floor. Without taking her eyes off me, she placed the tray onto the top step before retrieving the bar again.

"You must be thirsty, Dan, and hungry. I can't let you starve to death so you can eat whilst you think."

"Think what exactly, Emily?"

"Of a way out of this, Dan. You've got yourself in a right predicament, you and that interfering slag Rachel. If you can't think of a solution by this time tomorrow, I must get rid of you too," she paused for dramatic effect. "Oh, Dan, it could all have been so different."

"What the fuck have you done with Rachel? The same as you did with Sue?"

Emily laughed, or cackled would be a better description. Her silhouette made her look creepy, ghostlike.

"There's a theme here, isn't there, Dan? Sue was a slag, and she had to be disposed of. Rachel was a slag so, well, you get the idea."

"But how did you know about me and Sue? Nobody knew about us."

"Oh, my poor Dan. That's where you're wrong you see. I knew everything. When you thought I was at work, I was in my car, watching. At first, I assumed you were just friends, but no, you wanted more, didn't you? I set up a camera in our bedroom, Dan. I watched you sneak into her house when Mike went to work. I watched you fuck her. You thought you had it all worked out…"

Whenever I'd ventured from my house, I could have sworn somebody was watching me.

"I was suffering from depression, Emily. Sue was a shoulder to cry on, someone to share my thoughts with. It was a huge mistake sleeping together, and we both knew it. Why didn't you talk to me instead of, instead of what you did?"

"It was perfect, Dan, nobody suspected anything. Fancy going out jogging on a night like that. She was asking for trouble."

"And Rachel? We didn't sleep together, we were…"

"Spare me the bullshit, Dan. I've been watching you two for weeks, months even. From the very first time you took her into town…"

"Into town? Rachel had only been here three or four days?"

That hideous cackle again. Where had she learnt to laugh like that?

"Surely, you've worked it out, you're not that stupid. I followed you into town when you walked, and whenever you drove out somewhere, my little purple Peugeot followed you everywhere."

"Fucking hell, Emily, you really did arrive in France before me, didn't you?"

My head throbbed, and I desperately wanted the glass of water I had spotted on the tray. Emily waving the iron bar around told me I had to be patient though.

The white trainers I'd found in Emily's suitcase had

already persuaded me she had followed me into town that day, but what about the other things?

The rat? I recalled the humane trap in the well just before the iron bar hit me from behind. When had the rat been pushed through our letterbox though? I'd been into town to get the pizza, and after eating I had showered, only to come downstairs and see the rat hanging underneath the letterbox. I tried to picture Emily. Yes, sat on the sofa, her headphones on, supposedly oblivious to the creature on the floor behind her. She fucking well planted it there!

The vegetable patch? Emily had found it dug up whilst I slept off a hangover. She said she had got up first to do some work, but that's bullshit, she didn't have any work to do. Why hadn't I thought this through before? She got up early and dug up the vegetables. Later she had taken a phone call outside, more than enough time to plant muddy boots outside the gîte. The maggots followed suit, get a large bone covered in meat and let them breed like rabbits. Then, whilst I'm in the shower, place the meat at the back door and let the maggots make their way in. She probably shook most of them off in the living room before putting the bone back outside.

The brick though the window? I'd thought it happened two nights before Emily even arrived in France but now, I knew different. Had she watched Rachel storm to the gîte after our argument on the terrace? It would then be so easy to blame my guest for hurling a brick in the dead of night. The swimming pool contamination, too. The cancelled bookings.

Oh shit, it's true.

Everything that had happened to me had pointed to

Rachel, when, in fact, Emily had done it all, incriminating my guest at the same time.

"Why, Emily, why go to all the trouble to blame her?"

"I did nothing, Dan..."

"Liar! All those things, just to set her up."

"Dan, don't be so foolish. All I did was see you falling for her, just like you did with Sue. The way you looked at her that day when you introduced us..."

Put your tongue away, Dan.

"... it was obvious you had already slept with her. But this time I couldn't just run her over, that would look far too conspicuous. No, I tried to do the decent thing this time, tried to make you see sense."

"But she was due to leave on Saturday, Emily. She hadn't booked the gîte–"

"Oh, save the fucking speech, Dan. She had no intention of going. She would have asked you if she could stay in your spare room because she couldn't find anywhere else. She had it all worked out."

Was Emily telling the truth? It sounded like something Rachel might do but was Emily still trying to turn me against her?

"And when did you find this out, Emily?" I asked sarcastically.

"Friday. I told you to go into town if you remember? The previous day Rachel had seen me in the garden and asked if I would pop over to the gîte the next morning, alone. I got you to go into town and made my way down there. I think your nosey farmer neighbour saw me – she misses nothing, does she?"

Oh yes, sure. In fact, she was down there a very long time.

"What did she want?" I asked, already knowing the answer.

"Oh, she was quite the detective. Her contacts in the police had informed her of all she needed to know about Sue, and she had already come to her own conclusions. She was very silly, Dan, because I told her to go, get away whilst she could. That's when she went on and on about persuading you to let her stay and that I could never come between you. You had yourself a nice little catch there, I'd have thought she was out of your league."

I stepped forward again, this time out of pure hatred for the woman standing at the top of the flight of stairs in front of me. How had I ever fallen for her, she's evil, disturbed. She lifted the bar again.

"Steady, Dan, the clock is already ticking. You need to think."

Emily took a step backwards out of the door and closed it behind her. She raised her voice so I could hear.

"Now, eat up, get some rest and start putting your brain into gear. You are in a bad place and only you can come up with the solution."

47

Sleep came in fits and starts. I'd drunk the glass of water straight down as soon as Emily had left. I'd immediately regretted not making it last. She had brought me fresh bread and cheese, something I would have devoured in different circumstances. However, I just picked at it before dropping the plate on the floor next to my chair. The seat was also my makeshift bed.

In between dozing, I recalled the smell of petrol from the well in my garden. Emily must have planned on burning the evidence she had planted there but hadn't yet had the time. Maybe, after she dumped me in the cellar, that was where she had gone?

What time is it? I didn't even know what day it was.

Sitting in the chair, staring into thin air, trying to think. What was I supposed to be thinking, anyway? There was no reason I could give that would make Emily allow me to leave and live a normal life without her presence. I was trapped either way.

The sound of tapping on the iron grill made me

jump. The room was covered in a blanket of darkness and the iron bars shed no light at all.

"Psst. Are you in there?"

It was Brad!

I scrambled out of the chair and crept over towards him. I was at least three or four feet below the grill separating me from the outside.

"Brad," I whispered, convinced somebody else would hear me. "Is that you? I can't see a thing."

"Yes, it's me. Your neighbour, the French woman at the farm–"

"Laura?" I interrupted, suddenly feeling the urge to hug my one-time French teacher.

"Yeah. Well, I went around earlier, you know, to your house. There was no sign of anyone until I noticed her walking down the hill towards your place. She beckoned me over and told me all about a house you had seen for sale. That's how she could give me precise directions."

Laura had told Brad where she thought I might be and for him to be very careful, especially of Emily. I recalled the time I went around to her house and Laura nodding and saying she knew exactly what house I'd been talking about. I remembered the look of concern the last time she had seen me and Emily in the garden. She had also seen Emily go to the gîte to visit Rachel.

"That's where I am now? At the house for sale?"

Of course, the house has a cellar! We had seen it only the previous week when Emily had got the keys for us to look around. Shit, I bet she'd even had a copy cut for herself before returning them to the agent. She'd had no need to walk into town to fetch them.

I asked Brad how he'd got out here and he admitted to taking my car. He'd parked it on the far side of the woods and made his way through the trees, stopping on the periphery so nobody would spot him.

"She left mid-afternoon, soon after she'd arrived with a couple of bags of shopping. I've stayed undercover until dark."

As Brad spoke, I dragged the wooden cabinet across the room and placed it directly underneath the grill. Brad had stripped away all the debris from the outside and the dim moonlight offered some respite from the darkness. I stood on the cabinet, now face to face with Brad on the other side of the metal bars, although he was hardly visible. There was a thin strip of Perspex on the outside, obviously to keep water out. I felt like I was in prison.

"I didn't know where you were, or even where to look, but when I saw these bars, I crouched down and thought this is exactly where I'd hide someone."

"Can you get me out?" I enquired, sounding almost polite given the circumstances.

Brad said he'd checked all the doors and windows but couldn't find a way in. The iron grill we were at was on the far side of the house, away from the main entrance and the driveway.

Without thinking, I tapped the bars with my fingertips. It appeared to wobble. We stared at each other.

Brad hit it harder and the plastic cover cracked straight down the middle. As he pulled it apart with his hands, the sound of the rain rushed through the open space and the fresh air that hit me had never felt so good. I could now see Brad properly for the first time and not his shadowy outline. The rain had drenched him from head to toe. I swallowed hard as an image of his filthy caravan entered my head. This guy deserved so much more.

"How can we get the bars off?" Brad jolted me out of my trance.

Think, Dan, think.

Brad was struggling to peer through.

"Is there anything in there? A crowbar or something?"

I quickly surveyed the room and then looked back at the grill, trying to figure out what it would take to move this thing. I walked back towards Brad and I saw the screws, one in each corner of the grill.

"The screwdriver!" I exclaimed, a little too loud.

My shorts had front and back pockets and one more on each side of my thighs. I scrambled in each, panicking that it had fallen out during Emily's assault and subsequent transporting of me to the cellar. It wasn't until I checked my final pocket that I felt the small screwdriver. I climbed back onto the cabinet and tried it in one of the bottom screws. Fortunately, it fitted, not perfectly, but it would move them if I could get them started. However, they were rusted beyond their years and I couldn't shift them at all.

Brad passed me his torch through the bars.

"Look for something, Dan. There has to be something in a cellar to help you."

Jumping off the cabinet, I told Brad to keep his eyes peeled for Emily's return. I couldn't imagine she would leave me there all night, alone.

Just as I was about to give up, I noticed a can of something on the floor at the far side of the cellar. It sat next to several paint pots, all rusted concealing what colours were originally inside. I picked up the can. It felt empty, but when I shook it, I could distinctly hear some liquid sloshing around the bottom. The label was rusted over too and the only words visible were in French. I ran back to join Brad holding the can up for him to see.

"Squirt some on one of the screws," he instructed me, "it looks like that stuff that eases rusted things loose, like an oil."

I did what I was told, careful not to use much, as I knew I'd have to get at least three screws out to twist the grill wide enough for me to crawl through.

After a couple of minutes, and allowing the liquid to work, I tried the screw. It still wouldn't move. I tried the second and left that one for a few moments. It turned, albeit only about a quarter of a circle, but it still moved. My hands were sweating, so I grabbed a rag, wrapped it round the screwdriver handle and pushed it as deep into the groove as I could. It turned again, a full circle this time.

"Yes!" I heard Brad cry under his breath, "try another."

The third and then the fourth both shifted. It was painfully slow, each screw turning only ninety degrees at a time. Once I'd moved three out of the four, I needed to take a break. My hands were trembling, not only from fear but from squeezing them so tightly around the screwdriver. I soon started again, and they were moving easier now. When I got them so far out, I continued with my fingers. Each screw was at least two inches long, but at last, three of them were out.

The grill stayed in place.

Shit!

The years of neglect had rusted it to the wall.

I moved swiftly around the room again and returned with one of the fuller tins of paint. I jammed the small screwdriver behind the grill and hit the handle with the paint pot.

The first two times nothing happened, apart from me getting plaster splinters in my eyes. The third time, I hit it as hard as I could, the anger now rising from within. The grill made a high-pitched scraping noise against the wall and it definitely moved a fraction. I hit it again and again. Perspiration trickled down my forehead and I could feel my shirt sticking to my back, cold and uncomfortable. With all my energy, I hit the screwdriver as hard as I could. The paint tin flew out of one hand and the screwdriver from the other, both crashing to the floor. At first, I thought I'd missed the target completely, but when I looked up, I saw the grill swinging down, held up only in the bottom corner by the screw I hadn't been able to move. The hole looked tight, but I knew I could squeeze through if I went head-first, on my stomach and Brad pulled from the outside.

We both froze as a car pulled up on the opposite side of the house. A door slammed shut followed by the now familiar sound of footsteps walking towards the house.

We stared at each other, each waiting for the other to speak.

"Quick," I whispered, "this is my only chance."

Without hesitation, I lifted myself up, so my top half was horizontal with the open space. I pushed my arms through first and Brad took hold of my hands. My head fitted through after I'd turned it to one side. I tried to lift my legs to make my whole body streamlined with the opening, but I had no way of leveraging them up. Instead, I shifted myself forward the best I could and, with the help of Brad pulling my arms, my chest was on the base of the grill. This made it much easier to tilt my legs horizontally and Brad could pull harder without fear of decapitating me.

The key rattled in the cellar door.

After a few scrapes, I inched forward.

The cellar door opened, and I could hear footsteps slowly coming down the stairs. Emily must have already guessed that something was awry.

It was a tight squeeze, and I was making painfully slow progress.

Fuck it!

My belt snagged on the grill.

A light from behind shone directly into the hole I was crawling through.

"Just fucking pull, Brad!" I yelled.

As Brad dragged me through, I felt a hand grab my ankle. I instinctively kicked out and Emily lost her grip and fell backwards. Her scream of anger filled the night air, echoing off the basement walls and deep into the woods beyond.

Just as Emily came at me again, the belt snapped, and propelled me outside into the pouring rain.

As I attempted to find my bearings, we heard footsteps ascending the cellar stairs and then a door slam shut. Emily shouted something indecipherable inside and we immediately ran for cover behind an old outbuilding. It looked like a disused coal bunker at the far side of the house which I hadn't noticed on previous visits. It gave a little respite from the weather as we tried to gather our thoughts. Soon afterwards, Emily emerged outside. My optimism grew slightly. There were two of us now and her iron bar couldn't take us both at once.

Minutes passed, and although we heard muffled cursing as Emily ran around searching for us, we drew a collective intake of breath once we heard the door to the house bang shut again. She must have gone back inside, maybe to get her car keys and make her escape, thinking we were well on our own way to safety.

How wrong we were. The door may well have slammed closed, but it was from the outside. It had been an intentional ploy to lure us out from wherever we were hiding.

As soon as we stepped out from behind the coal shed, we were standing face to face with Emily, several metres apart.

She grinned. An unrecognisable look of anger and holy damnation written across her face. The rain had made her dark make-up run down her cheeks. She looked deranged, unhinged and utterly horrifying.

The shotgun in her hands pointed directly at us.

48

THE TWO OF us stood motionless, our eyes transfixed on the gun. It was only a few metres from where we were standing. The rain lashed down, huge droplets soaking us to the skin. I could feel the cold seeping into my flimsy canvas shoes. Emily spoke first, her voice calm and level yet revealing a hideous undertone of intent.

"You wouldn't listen, would you? You always know best." She took a stride towards us, the gun now trained directly on me.

"Daniel, all you had to do was get that bitch to leave and we could have lived the perfect life over here, away from everything," she paused, "away from everyone."

Out of the corner of my eye, I noticed Brad take a small step forward. What was he thinking? I attempted to keep Emily talking.

"Where's Rachel now? What have you done with her?"

Emily grinned, amplifying her monstrous features.

"She's gone, Dan, far away by now I should think. You'll never see her again."

She was lying. I knew she had killed Rachel, just as she had killed Sue. Emily, the one person I had fallen head over heels in love with, was a born murderer. Could she have done this before, prior to me even knowing her? I shivered involuntarily.

Emily continued to talk, but she just repeated herself, round and around in circles. How it could all have been so different, how I wouldn't listen and how I'd had my opportunity to end all this amicably. My mind drifted, tuning in and out of her mumbling whilst my eyes darted around looking for anything I could use in defence. There was a block of wood near my feet, about three feet long. It would be nothing against what Emily was holding, but would she really use the gun?

Brad inched ever closer to her, his eyes concentrating on the weapon. Emily continued to stare at me, her lips still moving yet all sound had now evaporated. She was tuned out from reality and I knew dialogue was no longer an option. I edged sideways so the block of wood was within reaching distance. Emily was in such a trance she didn't seem to notice either of us moving. Until I stepped on something loose and a large rock crunched against the somewhat smaller stones beneath it.

Emily snapped from her stupor, swinging the gun wildly from one of us to the other. Brad took this as his cue, and he lunged himself forward at her.

The noise of the gun was deafening, reverberating around the outbuildings and dense trees beyond. I'm sure I heard bird wings flapping in the distant woods before Emily's piercing scream drowned out all other sound.

It had blown Brad backwards, about ten feet, and he

lay motionless on his back. There was a huge hole in his stomach, blood pouring to the ground and immediately forming a crimson puddle. This soon mixed with the rain and trickled in all directions as the water found its natural course. He stared at the sky. But he did not blink, even though the rain splashed relentlessly into his open eyes.

I looked around. Emily had stopped screaming, but her hands trembled, and the gun shook violently in her grip. She gazed at the corpse on the ground and the unbelievable amount of blood gushing from the hole in Brad's stomach. This was my only opportunity.

Crouching down, I picked up the block of wood. Inching towards Emily, I lifted my weapon over my shoulder, ready to deliver the fatal blow. She slowly turned to face me.

The gun was still smoking from the end of both barrels and there was an acrid smell of gunpowder hanging in the air. Emily snapped out of her trance. Unbelievably I found my voice and spoke as calmly as I could.

"What now, Emily, will you kill me too?"

Her grin returned, coupled with white spittle that formed in the corners of her mouth. She pointed the gun directly at my forehead and squeezed the trigger. I stared, waiting for the final click.

Although the gunshot didn't seem as loud as the previous one, it still echoed around the open countryside and shook the old timbers of the building surrounding us. I waited for the pain to hit me, but Emily dropped to the floor instead, knees first with her head bent hideously backwards at the neck. She buckled under her own weight and finally her face smacked against the stones with a sickening blow.

Totally confused, I spun around. Brad still lay motionless, staring at the open sky. I looked back at Emily, blood poured from beneath her torso. Somebody had shot her in the centre of her back, a smaller hole than Brad's, yet big enough to tell me she stood no chance of survival.

"Daniel." I heard a whisper from the darkness on the far side of the house. "Is she dead?"

Laura stepped out of the shadows, and just like Emily a few moments before, she held a shotgun aloft, ready to squeeze the trigger at any sign of movement.

"Laura," was all I could manage. I repeated myself immediately but this time as a question. "Laura?"

"Is she dead, Daniel?"

I looked back down at Emily's body. I nudged the side of her ribs with my foot. She was literally a dead weight.

"Yes, Laura, she's gone. How did you…"

Laura stepped closer, examining Emily and then Brad. After convincing herself, she eventually dropped the gun to her side. She spoke slowly, evenly, and without taking her eyes from the two corpses.

"Brad called round to your house, Dan. I spoke to him and told him where I thought you might be. I waited all day for you to return but when nightfall came, I knew something was wrong."

She began shaking, violently. The shock was coming out, and I moved closer to comfort her. She allowed me to wrap my arm around her shoulder, still staring at the two bodies.

"I drove to the edge of the woods. When I reached the woods, I saw your car, and I knew Brad had taken it."

Something made me stop her in her tracks.

"How did he get my keys; they were in the house?"

Even in those dire circumstances, Laura appeared to blush.

"We owned the house once, Daniel, remember? The previous owners never changed the locks, and I knew for a fact that you hadn't."

With that, she moved my arm from around her shoulders and slowly walked away, back toward the woods. I couldn't be sure, but I believe she turned and gave me a wry smile and a slight nod of the head before she completely disappeared into the darkness.

The following morning, I sat silently on the terrace. The storm had abated, and the sun was doing its best to disperse the clouds and add some heat to the day.

After Laura had left me alone the previous night, I'd found my phone in the empty house and alerted the police. An ambulance had taken the bodies away, and I was questioned time and time again about what had happened. The police promised another visit the next day and instructed me to go nowhere. They said they would visit Brad's caravan to find identification and if he had family anywhere who would need contacting. When I arrived home much later, I noticed two police cars outside the Allaires' house.

A doctor had checked me over at the scene and said I would inevitably suffer from shock but he hoped it would soon pass over the coming days. He gave me some sleeping pills to help me through the first few nights.

I transfixed my eyes on the gîte. Even though it is impossible to explain, some kind of sixth sense made me stand and walk over to the building at the bottom of my garden. The door was unlocked, and I guiltily let myself in, with a strange feeling that I was trespassing on my own property. Moving from room to room, my thoughts drifted to Rachel. I stood and stared at the places where we'd been intimate, all kinds of memories coursing through my mind.

Then I saw the guest book on the table in the living room. Just as all those weeks ago, when I was checking over the gîte before Rachel arrived, the book lay open. There was still nothing written inside, but I knew it had been closed when I was last in there – it's something I would notice. Had Emily been back in whilst she had me locked in the cellar? Now I knew she had arrived in France before me, I suddenly realised it could easily have been her who had been in the gîte whilst I'd prepared Rachel's welcome pack.

Instinct made me run upstairs and directly into the main bedroom. I dropped to my knees and looked under the bed.

Gone, the suitcase was no longer there.

What the fuck is going on?

Sprinting outside, I ran the length of my garden and down to the well. The overwhelming feeling of being watched again spread from my head to my toes. Just as many times before, there was no sign of anybody in the vicinity.

Paranoia, Dan, just what the doctor had said.

A steady plume of smoke drifted from the well, but the fire was already out. Peering inside, I could see some burning embers and a pile of ash. The overnight rain would have distinguished the flames, but the odour of petrol told me that the fire would have destroyed almost everything within minutes.

I turned my torch on and leant over as far as I dare. The oil canister had survived the best and I could just make out some cardboard of the rodent trap packaging. The boots had appeared to melt rather than burn, but there was no suitcase as far as I could see. I climbed back off the wall, exasperated. I needed to calm myself; it was all over now.

"Leave it to the police, Dan," I muttered to myself as I traipsed back to my house.

49

Several days later, and after various visits from the police, life resembled some kind of normality, as normal as could be that is.

The police had contacted a member of Brad's family back in England, an aunt, I believe they said. They had pronounced both him and Emily dead at the scene, a single gunshot wound to each would be the coroner's report. Laura had been questioned, but following both of our statements, they informed us they would take no further action.

The noise of motors outside awoke me and I pulled on a T-shirt to investigate what was going on. The sun blinded me as soon as I opened the back door, and I immediately shielded my eyes from the glare. It was already boiling, and I guessed it was close to midday given the intensity of the heat. I reminded myself not to take a sleeping pill that night; they were making me crash out for far too long.

"Morning, Dan." Andy Jackson checked his watch. "Just!"

The motors were draining the swimming pool and Andy was being true to his word in helping to get the water changed and the pool back in use before my next guests arrived in just over a week.

There had been three new bookings for the gîte for the rest of the summer and a couple more in September and October once the kids had returned to school. It had helped take my mind off events and force me back into the real world – just what I needed according to the same doctor who had visited me the previous day to check on my recovery.

"Morning, Andy, thanks for sorting this out." He waved and went back to work. I returned to the house to take a shower. I needed to go into town to visit the estate agents. Although the house with the cellar was out of the question, I still had a hunger to look for a second property. It would help focus my attention and increase my earning potential. I had already visited the Allaires and agreed to let Jean-Pascal and Robert help me renovate any future purchase and get it ready for the paying public. It pleased me they both saw the funny side when I'd suggested I would even pay them for their troubles.

The walk into town helped clear my mind, and I knew I had to focus on the present. I'd been through a traumatic time and the doctor had warned me I might suffer from flashbacks and nightmares. Two nights ago, I had phoned Rick back in England. He had agreed to come out and visit me in a few weeks' time – I was already looking forward to that immensely. Rick suggested I went to stay with him straight away, but I knew that would be running from the truth. No, I wanted to face this head on. My shy, vulnerable days were behind me. This was the new Daniel Kent.

After my visit to two local estate agents in town – unsuccessful on this occasion although both reassuring me they acquired new properties on a weekly basis – I carried on wandering and exploring.

As I approached the town square I turned and walked into the church. Notwithstanding that I'm not a religious person, I felt a sudden urge to go inside a place of worship to think and to collect my thoughts. Dropping a euro coin into a tin box, I lit a long thin candle before placing it precariously into a metal holder. Sitting down, I stared at the flickering flame; the wax melting fast. I thought of Brad and then of Sue. Closing my eyes and cupping my hands, I said a silent prayer to whoever might listen. When I opened my eyes, floods of tears ran down my cheeks. At last the grief began to escape, and a weight felt as though it was gradually lifting from my shoulders. I whispered "God bless" to the dancing flame and stood to leave.

Soon I found myself sat on an old rusty bench on the outskirts of town. It was next to a children's play area, but the soaring heat meant no parents would be out with their kids until much later. It felt tranquil, and I let my thoughts drift along with the afternoon haze.

I took a deep breath and made a promise to myself that France was my new home and my new life started there and then. Nothing could follow me now, I'd escaped my foes, my demons. Any such thoughts would be pure paranoia. I'd suffered with it all my life. Even being picked last for most sports at school had me lying awake all night, thinking it was a deliberate ploy for me to self-harm. The fact was, I wasn't very good at most sports at school.

I'd had multiple jobs and held none of them down. Did every single boss have a personal vendetta against me or was it because I just wasn't interested in any of them enough to progress my career?

Satisfied with my self-observations, I ambled back towards town. I needed a long cold beer.

Just before I arrived in the square, I found myself on the same street where I'd spotted Emily's purple car. I recalled hiding in the archway, passers-by raising their hands to their mouths to hide their obvious smirking beneath. I even found myself smiling until I saw the black BMW. It was literally feet away from the spot where Emily's car would have been the day I'd waited.

Looking around, assuring myself nobody was watching, I approached the vehicle. I couldn't be sure it was the same hire car that Rachel had picked up at the airport, but it looked identical in my eyes. I circled it twice, looking for any telltale sign – nothing was obvious. A black BMW is a black BMW, there are hundreds, thousands of them.

Again, I twisted my head in all directions before crouching down to look in the front driver's side window. Placing my hands either side of my forehead, I squinted to peek inside. There was nothing that pointed to Rachel. An almost empty packet of chewing gum on the passenger's seat and a CD case in the glove compartment.

Taking a couple of steps back, I repeated my actions in the back window. Jumping backwards, I almost crashed into an old lady carrying two plastic bags full of fresh vegetables.

"Pardon, madame," I said, "pardon."

She tutted and continued to walk along. I let her disappear down the street and bent back down to look in the rear window a second time. Sure enough, there was Rachel's suitcase, sitting proudly on the back seat.

I walked away, my head darting from side to side.

Think, Dan, think.

There was only one explanation. Somebody had parked the car right behind where Emily's Peugeot was days before. Emily must have driven the BMW into town and parked as close to her own car as possible. That way she could transport items or other things – my body shivered – from one car to the other. She must have come back whilst I was in the cellar, started the fire in the well and then removed Rachel's suitcase from the gîte and put it in the back of the BMW. That was also how she would have been able to take Rachel from the gîte to her own car and dispose of the body at will. There were a thousand forests around where you could easily hide a dead person.

Satisfied with my detective work, I headed for the town square and that ice-cold beer I'd promised myself. My heart was still racing though, and perspiration trickled down my neck.

Fortunately, my favourite table was available in my favourite bar, hidden away under one of the many arches. The waiter served me – it didn't even embarrass me with my useless French – and shortly afterwards I took a long, slow gulp of the golden nectar. It tasted amazing, the best beer I'd had since I'd arrived. I couldn't help the smile that spread across my face. Everything would be okay.

As I tried to get the attention of the waiter to order another beer, something caught my eye at the opposite end of the square. Just as before, the day I'd seen Emily darting between the archways, somebody else seemed to look my way.

I brushed it aside, convinced my mind was playing tricks on me.

It wasn't until the waiter had left with my order that I saw the same person again. This time a little closer, and I could just make out it was a female although her faced was obscured by a large-brimmed straw hat. The square was crowded, and the figure frequently disappeared in and out of view. She walked along the row of shops at the far end of the square, yet, every so often, she would turn and look, either at me or in my general direction. Whoever it was, she appeared unperturbed by me staring back. Was my imagination working overtime? I convinced myself to stop being irrational. Soon she turned the corner and disappeared out of sight.

The very last thing I saw was her shoes.

White Converse training shoes.

REVIEWS

Enjoy this book? You can make a big difference

Honest reviews of my books help bring them to the attention of other readers.

If you've enjoyed this novel I would be very grateful if you could spend just a few minutes leaving a review (it can be as short as you like).

Thank you very much.

YOU'RE FAMILY NOW

OUT NOW!

The Brand New Psychological Thriller

from Jack Stainton

"A decidedly creepy but very compelling story. I doubt readers will be able to put this down."

Available in both eBook and Print versions

ACKNOWLEDGEMENTS

A huge thank you, to you, the reader. Without whom, this is just me writing for the sake of writing. I'd love as many people as possible to read my words; and now I can say that I've achieved something I've always dreamt of doing.

After thirty years working as a professional consultant, I have eventually put pen to paper and realised a lifetime ambition. I've loved the entire process, from first draft, to final edit and all the way to cover design. I genuinely hope that you've enjoyed my first foray into the world of books – it certainly won't be the last!

Talking of cover design, another huge dollop of gratitude to Vikki. She must have changed my book sleeve a hundred times, all without complaint.

I'd also like to give a massive thank you to my editor, Melanie Underwood. Her meticulous care throughout my manuscript must have driven her crazy, especially with my misuse of commas and apostrophes (should I have used them there?).

And finally, immense gratitude to my family and friends, who have driven me on when the going got tough. Late nights, early mornings and even weekends swallowed up by words; I know it couldn't have been easy.

All the best.

Jack

www.jackstainton.com

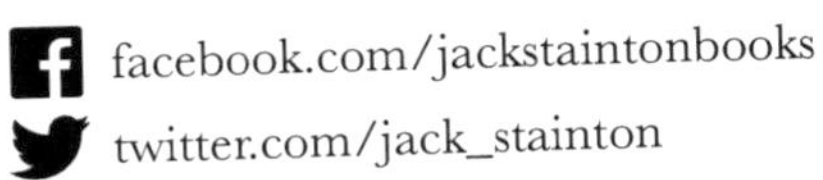

facebook.com/jackstaintonbooks

twitter.com/jack_stainton

instagram.com/jackstaintonbooks

Printed in Great Britain
by Amazon